Skeletons
OF
SOCIETY

MARIE MARAVILLA

Published by Marie Maravilla Books
1266 PO Box
Waterford, CA 95386
https://marie-maravilla.square.site
Copyright © 2022 Marie Maravilla

Cover by AS Designs
Editing & Proofreading by VB Edits
Formatting by AJ Wolf Graphics
ISBN: 9798817225709

To all of you whose "comfort" shows are about murder…
This is for you.

TRIGGER/CONTENT WARNING
skeletons of society

If you do not need these warnings and are concerned, they will give spoilers, then jump on into the book and have fun! But, if you are worried about what will be in a book, check out below. If you have a specific trigger or content warning you are looking for, please email or DM me.

This book revolves around a cartel, and due to that, this story is on the darker side of romance. And it is for those 18+ as it contains explicit sex/language, violence, and death.
Trigger warnings: Torture, mentions of sexual assault, emotional manipulation, mentions of sex trafficking, and abuse No details given. It does not happen to the Main Female Character).

SPANISH/PHRASES WORDS
you may want to know

Los Muertos: The dead
El Diablo: The Devil
Dios mío: My God
Dile hola al Diablo para mí:
Say hello to the Devil for me
Muñeca: Meaning doll
Brujita: Meaning witch, but it is
used as a term of endearment
Cabeza: Head, like the body part
Mí Guerito: My white boy
Pendejo: Spanish slang word
for idiot,stupid or dumass
Santa Muerte: Our Lady of the Holy
Death a cult image, female deity, and folk
saint. She is the personification of death

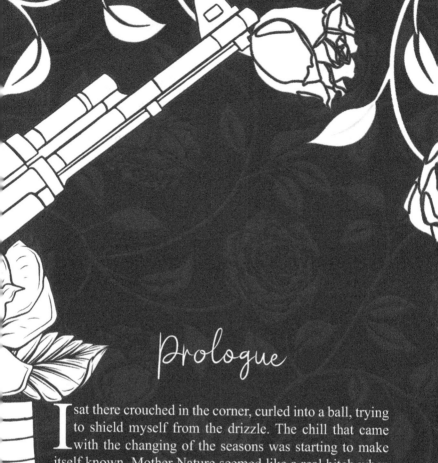

Prologue

I sat there crouched in the corner, curled into a ball, trying to shield myself from the drizzle. The chill that came with the changing of the seasons was starting to make itself known. Mother Nature seemed like a real bitch when you didn't have an actual bed to tuck into at night. The hood of my too-big sweatshirt was drawn over my head, hiding my face. All I could see was the trash-littered ground of the alley.

That was really all I needed to see.

All I needed to view was his boots—I would recognize those instantly.

Those boots were stained with the blood and tears of his victims. They would be the first things I burned. That kind of taint couldn't stay around in the world. I would set the souls of those victims free—he wouldn't be allowed to keep any part of them.

The hair on the back of my neck stood up, pulling me

from my inner thoughts and back to reality. Apparently, I didn't need to see his boots to sense when he was near. His malicious intent was palpable in the air, sticking to him like flies on a carcass. The whole city seemed to go silent, waiting on bated breath for what was about to unfold. My muscles twitched, my subconscious begging my body to move.

"Have you finally decided to let me into this shit hole you call your camp?"

The cocky tone of his voice caused my grip to tighten on the blade I had hidden in my front pocket, the steel biting into my palm. I peered up at him from my crouched position, assessing how close I was willing to let him come. A snarl escaped from my lips, like I was a wild animal.

Jimmy tutted his tongue, completely unfazed by my show of aggression.

"Look at you, waiting outside like a good girl. Are you ready to stop fighting me?" His eyes held a gleam of anticipation, and his tongue poked out, swiping along his chapped lips. I didn't dare break eye contact, afraid to see the bulge I knew he would have.

"Although, I do love it when they fight," he added.

He's disgusting.

My chest heaved, and hatred dripped from my tone as I spat out my response. "Fuck you, Jimmy."

The smile that appeared on his pocked face made me want to throw up what little food I had in my stomach. It was likely I would only spit up bile since food had been in short supply the past few weeks. All the money I made panhandling, or straight stole, went into buying the blade I was clutching—the blade cutting into my palm with how tightly I was gripping it.

Jimmy started to move toward me, dirty hands reaching down to unclasp his belt. He thought he had me cornered. That the weeks of pursuing me—hunting me—had paid off. Wasn't it ironic, the supposed hunter failed to see the trap he was stumbling into? Today he was going to be the prey.

2

"That's the plan, bitch, to fu—"

I didn't let him finish his sentence, launching myself up from the crouch I'd been waiting in and ramming the six-inch blade up between his ribs to where his heart was housed.

A startled cry rang out through the alley, sounding like music to my ears.

Poetic justice, fucker.

As soon as my knife was in, I jumped back like I'd been burned, realizing too late I was weaponless. But Jimmy was in shock and too high to try to retaliate. My back and palms pressed against the cold brick wall of the alley, and I watched in rapt fascination as blood began to pool around where my blade was protruding.

Jimmy collapsed on the floor. The color had drained from his face, and his hands were reaching up toward the wound as if attempting to put his blood back into his body. Huffing a humorless laugh, he looked at me from where he lay on the ground, the life already starting to leech from his eyes. El Diablo was coming to collect.

His voice came out a harsh rasp, but the words were clear.

"And so the streets taint another soul. Welcome to the club of killers, kid."

A physical chill from the truth of those words racked my body—they sounded like a curse spoken out into the universe. I ran, trying to escape the reality of what he had said. But I was stopped short by the sound of clapping coming from the mouth of the alley.

"That wasn't bad work. Sloppy…but oh so passionate. But I do wonder, how are you planning on hiding your kill? Or did you never get that far, *Muñeca*?"

In front of me stood a boy who appeared to be my age, seventeen. Eighteen at most. I'd seen him around, but he wasn't a street kid. His shoes were clean and new, and all his clothes fit him, showing off his athletic build and hints of tanned skin that matched mine. His black hair was cut close on the sides and long on top, perfectly styled. By all accounts, he was handsome, but the look in his brown eyes seemed unhinged. Making warning bells go off in my head. Warning bells I should have heeded.

He apparently didn't want an answer from me because he kept speaking.

"You know. I think I'll keep you. I mean, your life can only improve. Look at you." He gestured up and down my body with his hands. The look on his face told me he thought there was a lot to be desired. "When was your last hot meal? Or shower? I'll provide for you, Muñeca. All you have to do is come with me."

My hesitation must have been evident in my eyes because he dropped the sugary sweet tone, exchanging it for a threatening one.

"It would be a shame if the police received a tip about a teenage girl stabbing a man."

I bristled at his words. There it was, the cruelty whispered about when people brought up the young cartel heir. The reality of my situation sank in. Everyone in Tucson's underbelly knew Mario Jimenez, son of Sergio Jimenez, cartel kingpin of *Los Muertos*. And here he stood in front of me, putting me in a position that left me no choice but to exchange a life debt for a hot meal, a shower, and his silence.

Mario held out his hand for me, a look of triumph plastered on his face as I moved toward him. The moment our fingertips touched, I remembered my promise.

"Hold on. I need to grab his boots and my knife."

Ryan

10 YEARS LATER

There wasn't enough iced coffee in the world to fix my foul fucking mood this morning. What would fix it would be if ungrateful assholes could do their jobs correctly instead of thinking they could pull one over on me.

"*Dios mío*, Anthony, it's three in the morning. I'd prefer not to take a shower this late due to your blood spatter getting all over me." I released the bridge of my nose, looking across the room to where he was strapped to a chair. The color drained from his face at the statement, the reality of his fuck-up setting in.

"Ryan, I…I didn't know they would show at the drop." His panicked voice grated on my nerves; I wanted to shoot him just for annoying me.

My eyebrow quirked at his response, but I continued to stare him down. Interrogation *participants* hated when their excuses were met with silence. It made them squirm and spout out more shit. Sometimes they gave me helpful information. Other times, like with Anthony, they sputtered out more bullshit.

Unfortunately for him, my patience had hit its limit.

Nothing useful had come out of his ugly mug in the last fifteen minutes. Clearly, he either didn't have any more information or wouldn't give it up. My money was on the first. Men like Anthony had no loyalty. It's why he'd taken the lousy five hundred dollars to spill our gun drop location in the first place.

"Please, Ryan." His voice reached an octave I didn't realize was possible. "I can get you information. I'll give you my contact. You…you can find out who's trying to pay off people to rat." His head nodded so aggressively I thought he might give himself a concussion.

An irritated sigh left my lips. He was too dumb to realize I knew the truth.

He still thought some street thugs showed up and took the load before it made it to the intended destination— my club. In Anthony's defense, that's what he'd been told would happen. But the man should check his source before squealing because it was never thugs paying. It was me, flushing out the rats before they carried the plague of betrayal into my portion of this operation.

I pushed off the tiled wall, cold indifference settled over me like a second skin, a tangible change in my demeanor. Panicked, Anthony looked over toward the door at Sergio. As if Sergio would help him.

Doesn't Anthony realize who's in charge here?

Apparently not, or he wouldn't have tried to double-cross me and then proceed to waste my fucking time spitting excuses.

I strode across the blood-stained concrete, pausing in front of the drain his chair sat above. "Anthony, Anthony, Anthony…" My patronizing tone sounded cold to my ears.

He recoiled the moment we made eye contact, as if I'd

physically slapped him. The reaction pulled a cruel smile from my lips. I'd been told more than once that my stare was unnerving; my guess was it was because people could see my stained soul through my coffee-colored eyes, witnessing the curse given to me by a dying man's final words.

Eyes are the windows to the soul and all that shit.

Jimmy may have been my first kill, but he certainly was not my last. And my next kill was staring down the one who'd take his life. Dumb motherfucker stole from the wrong person.

"*Mira*, Anthony, everyone knows I live by the fuck-around-and-find-out policy. You fucked around on me, and now you're about to find out the consequences of your actions." A smirk crept up my face at the sight of the wild pulse in his throat.

His eyes widened at my words, his body shaking while sweat dripped from his face. When I peeked down, another sigh left my lips.

They always pissed themselves.

Thank *Santa Muerte* I didn't handle the cleanup. I had men for that. But this was not what I wanted to be dealing with at the end of my night, so he was about to receive a small blessing.

"Ryan, I can help you find the load. I swear, just—just let me go, and I'll contact my guy," he cried.

Fat tears rolled down his dirty face. The desperation in his voice might have broken others, but it didn't do a damn thing to make me reconsider.

"Ah, Ah." I wagged my finger. "You had your chance to make smart decisions, Anthony. Now it's my turn to make decisions."

We locked eyes for another second before I looked over my shoulder at Sergio, who gave me the slightest of nods. I didn't need Sergio's approval, not really, but he *was* the kingpin of Los Muertos, and old habits died hard. I respected him too much not to seek his approval when he was in the room for cartel business. Even if his showing up

9

tonight had been unexpected. Another reason I was ready to wrap this meeting with Anthony up. I wanted to know why the fuck Sergio was here.

Anthony must have seen the finality in my eyes when I faced him again. As I stood up, he started sputtering more nonsense in a final attempt to avoid his fate.

"Por favor, Ryan. I did nothing wrong," he pleaded. "In fact, I can get you information. There's been some guy asking questions about Mario and what he's involved with," he rushed out.

I scoffed at the audacity of this man to continue to treat me as if I was an idiot. Like I would trust the claims of someone desperate to stay alive after being caught as a rat. I reached to pull out my Sig from where I kept it at the small of my back.

"Too little, too late, Anthony. You knew my reputation and still thought you would be able to outsmart *La Brujita de Los Muertos*. You made your bed. Now you get to die in it. *Dile hola al Diablo para mí*," I said.

He opened his mouth, but a shot rang out in the room before he could waste more of my time. Anthony's head snapped back from the impact. He was lucky I didn't have steam I wanted to blow off, or his death would have been longer. A warm feeling caused me to look down at my once white shirt, now splattered with red.

"The one fucking time I don't wear black," I barked out in annoyance.

Sergio huffed a laugh while opening the door leading into the hallway.

"I don't know why you own anything other than dark colors for your particular line of work. Maybe you should start wearing painting coveralls, Brujita. Or at least stand back before you blow someone's *cabeza* off."

Of course he'd mastered the whole patronizing father tone.

I rolled my eyes. Sergio always made me feel like a teenage girl explaining why she needed another shade of pink lip gloss instead of a ruthless killer.

"Listen, Sergio," I poked him in the chest before pushing past him and heading toward the office, "I'm a female who was raised by the streets, and now I work for a criminal organization. Sometimes I want to remind myself and others that I like dick; I don't have one. Why do you think I keep this dark hair so long and luscious?" I paused to look over my shoulder at the large man who had a twinkle of amusement in his eye. Letting out an exasperated huff, I continued my speech, which felt pointless.

"And I didn't 'blow his head off.'" My fingers mimicked quotation marks. "I shot him between the eyes," I reasoned.

"At close range, Brujita."

He'd heard many versions of my "I don't have a dick; I just like it" speech since his son Mario had brought me home like a stray puppy at seventeen. That was when Sergio became a pseudo dad, stuck taking in and semi-raising a teenage girl. And since he was the leader of the largest cartel in Mexico, it was a bit of a fucked-up raising.

I knew how many grams went into a block of cocaine, the going rate to pay off a Mexican politician, and my favorite subject—how to extract information from an uncooperative participant. Not to mention I could fully disassemble and reassemble nearly any firearm I came in contact with. I didn't think Sergio knew what to do with a teenage girl, so he'd treated me like he did Mario. Now I wondered why he hadn't just sent me away, but Sergio and I had an unspoken agreement not to discuss certain subjects. So I never asked.

But I didn't end up too bad—killing and questionable moral compass aside. It could be argued that those traits had lived inside me well before I came to Los Muertos. Seeing as how my first kill had come before I joined the cartel. Vigilante justice made my soul sing, and being in Los Muertos allowed me to let my monster out to play. But I never killed anyone who didn't deserve it. Not that it made me a good person, but only killing those who were guilty kept my conscience feeling clean. Luckily, fucked-up personalities were basically a job requirement in this world, so Los Muertos had accepted me with open arms.

"Well, it's a good thing my dry cleaning bill gets paid with Los Muertos's money," I sassed.

An amused huff sounded from behind me, bringing a smile to my lips before my mind wandered again to my past. If I ever went to a therapist, I was sure they would tell me I had major mommy and daddy issues stemming from the fact they had been murdered when I was a kid. They fell victim to a random street mugging. The cops investigated, but there wasn't much to go on, so the case went cold.

I managed to get a hold of the case notes. My father had been stabbed. But my mother…I was sure she wished a stabbing was all she had to endure. The need for justice had burned in my veins like a disease, consuming me from the inside out. Until I couldn't stand it anymore. I ran from my foster family and moved into the slums of Tucson.

Hunting.

Waiting for the moment when I could take my vengeance—deliver my form of justice to the man who'd killed my father before assaulting my mother and sliding a six-inch blade between her ribs into her heart.

Jimmy, my first kill. The sin I would spend my life atoning for.

I pushed open the door to the office, trying to regain focus on the present. Velvet brushed my arms as I plopped down in the chair facing the desk, leaving my regular chair open for Sergio to take.

Sergio studied my face for a moment before speaking softly.

"Brujita, you know you could go do anything you wanted with your beauty and brains. You do not owe Los Muertos, or Mario, anything. You will be family regardless of whether you choose to do something outside the cartel."

He's mentioned before that I could leave, but where would a tainted soul like mine go? What would I do when the call for blood got too loud? And I very much doubted

Mario would take me leaving well. He barely tolerated me being here in Arizona when he had to travel back and forth to Sinaloa, Mexico.

Sergio must not have expected an answer from me, or maybe he knew the answer already, because he continued speaking.

"I'm here because there is an MC that wants to move into the territory. And they want to partner with us to run our guns." He paused to take in my reaction.

My head nodded in understanding as I tried to keep up with the subject change he'd just hit me with.

"We would be their supplier for their deals, taking a cut, obviously. And in exchange for exclusively supplying their MC, they will do our local drops. Taking that task off your plate," he finished.

It dawned on me which MC he was talking about.

A few months ago, the Skeletons of Society started to expand their territory, moving into Tucson. The cartel didn't worry too much about other criminal organizations in our territories as long as they realized who was in control. And when they didn't respect that, someone was sent to remind the offending party of who they were fucking with.

In Tucson, that person was me.

But I welcomed the Skeletons MC expanding because the Reapers MC was the alternative. And I had been fighting them off from trying to move into my area for years.

The Reapers dealt in skin, and nothing made me want to go on a murder spree more than men who thought they could sell women for their sick pleasure. That MC treated women as fucking livestock and not people with hearts and souls. Souls they ripped to shreds when they trafficked them. I would know. I saved those women, employed them, and scooped them off the bathroom floor when they OD'd because the pain was too much to handle.

My booted feet hit the desk, causing Sergio to glare at me as if the desk I was putting them on wasn't mine. I made sure to keep my emotions about the Reapers out of my voice before speaking. "Sergio, I'm the one who told you about the Skeletons of Society wanting to expand this way. But why are you telling me about them partnering with us? Is it because they'll be in and out of *Lotería*? They're welcome as long as they don't think they can touch my girls."

Sergio frowned in confusion, probably racking his brain to see if what I said was true.

I couldn't keep the smirk off my face as I reminded him of how he knew this information. To Sergio's credit, he ran the whole damn cartel. There were so many moving pieces of information to keep track of in an organization this big. And unlike The Families in New York, Sergio's only blood helping run Los Muertos was Mario. It was why I did my damnedest to keep my operation here in Arizona running smoothly. I didn't want to create headaches for Sergio or make Mario think I was incapable of being on my own.

I worked my ass off to prove my worth and how invaluable I was here running Lotería for Los Muertos. Both the legal side and the not-so-legal aspects of the club. Mario couldn't demand I go to Mexico like he wanted if Sergio assigned me a job here in Tucson. He may be the heir, but Sergio was still in charge. Sometimes I felt Sergio tried to distance me from Mario even more than I did. I always figured I imagined it, or maybe he wanted someone better for his son and didn't want to risk us getting too close. Regardless, it worked in my favor at the moment.

Sergio may care for me, but as Mario pointed out, he cared because I was the perfect tool for Los Muertos. You didn't last long in the toxic paradise of the criminal underworld if you didn't make sure you were valuable and hard to kill. And I was an ace up the Jimenez men's sleeve. No one expected a kill to come from a woman. Not in the Mexican cartel, anyway. Misogyny was alive and well in the criminal world.

"Well, this is perfect then, Brujita. Because I want you to take over the arms dealing here in Tucson officially. You're going to be the point of contact for this new alliance between Los Muertos and Los Esqueletos."

I rolled my eyes at Sergio's decision to give the Skeletons of Society a Spanish version of their name. All while trying to tamp down my excitement at being given the opportunity. I would need to stay here in Arizona with this new position. A shudder racked through me when I thought about Mario's reaction to the news. He had been pushing the subject of moving me to Mexico lately.

"Of course. You know I would be happy to, Sergio. Anything for Los Muertos." Despite my worries with Mario, I gave Sergio a genuine grin.

He smiled at my response, running a hand over his bald head. It was comical how closely Sergio fit Hollywood's depiction of a cholo gangbanger. Complete with the thick black mustache hiding his upper lip, although nowadays, the black had taken on some white and gray strands as well. Sergio had worked his way up in the cartel, starting on the streets of Santa Anna, California. I never asked the details of how he'd made it up to kingpin, but my bet was it had to do with the man's work ethic and loyalty. His commitment to loyalty was actually why my question slipped out before I thought about if I wanted to hear the answer.

"Why isn't Mario brokering the deal? He's the one in charge of Los Muertos's arms dealing. Or is he moving here to Tucson?"

I resisted the urge to fidget with the rings on my fingers. Being an interrogator made me hyperaware of people's tells. And fidgeting with the silver bands adorning my fingers was one of mine, but I didn't want to let on to the fact that him moving here made me anxious.

Mario had been given the position of arms dealer for Los Muertos when he turned twenty. Of course, I handled all the shipments moving through Lotería on his behalf. It only took one order for him to make Tucson my responsibility. But I didn't know if Mario had told Sergio he put me in charge.

Sergio arched his thick eyebrow at my question while

he leaned back and steepled his fingers.

"Ryan, the role of arms dealer may have been given to *mí hijo*, but you and I both know you are the real person who handles things here. No? What, you don't think I hear the whispers about our reputation here in Tucson?"

So he did know.

"I mean, I try to handle things while Mario is away... working."

Sergio huffed a laugh at my carefully worded response. We both knew Mario preferred flaunting his wealth to helping run the cartel. This was one of those subjects Sergio agreed not to discuss.

"I may be Los Muertos's kingpin, but you are La Brujita of Tucson's underbelly."

The comment brought a genuine smile to my face. Sergio wasn't wrong. Nothing happened in Tucson I didn't know about. It was why Anthony had been strapped to a chair this morning and the reason for Lotería's success. I made it my business to know everything. To hunt all those who thought they could hunt me.

A clap rang out in the room.

"So it's settled. You and I will meet with the Skeletons of Society's sergeant at arms and enforcer. Hash out the details of this arrangement, and move forward. I'll let you know when this meeting is. Now, get out of here and get some sleep. And take a fucking shower. You look like someone who works at one of those fuckin' horror houses."

16

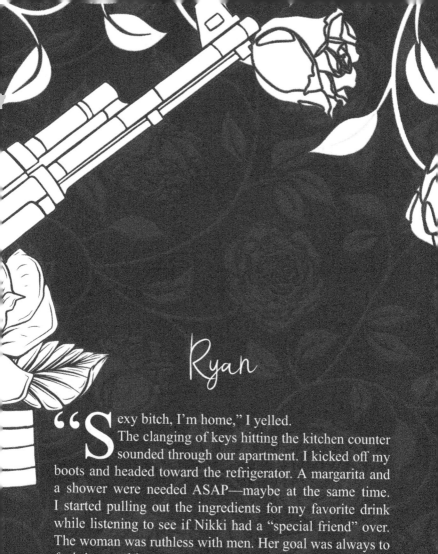

Ryan

"Sexy bitch, I'm home," I yelled.

The clanging of keys hitting the kitchen counter sounded through our apartment. I kicked off my boots and headed toward the refrigerator. A margarita and a shower were needed ASAP—maybe at the same time. I started pulling out the ingredients for my favorite drink while listening to see if Nikki had a "special friend" over. The woman was ruthless with men. Her goal was always to *fuck 'em and leave 'em*. And she told them up front, so it had to be a fetish for some of these guys because that line had them eating out of her hand. Or maybe some of them thought they would be the one to change her mind.

The door to her room opened, and out walked some finance-looking bro followed by Nikki. Over his shoulder, I caught her attention and raised an eyebrow at her choice of tonight's prey. She shrugged before answering my unspoken question.

"You know I don't discriminate. Have dick? Will sit on it."

I snorted a laugh. Not at her words but at the look on the guy's face when he heard what she said. I didn't want to be part of this kicking to the curb, so I turned back to my task of making a margarita on the rocks. I could hear the beginning of Nikki's "it's not me, it's you" speech from behind me.

"Listen, Chad…"

"It's Kyle."

"Of course it is. Now Chad, you're a bit vanilla in bed. Which I honestly should have seen coming because you're wearing a navy North Face vest... Anyway, the point being there won't be a repeat fucking. But get home safe."

Nikki seemed to think the sugary sweet voice would make her verbal castration more pleasant. She always used it, and usually, it ended in the same way I predicted this one would.

"You fucking whore!" he spewed.

Yup, he's not taking this well. You would think he'd be in a better mood, having just gotten off.

Unfortunately for him, any patience I had to deal with a man's attitude had been used up by Anthony. Before he could escalate the situation, I decided to intervene. Turning around, I pointed my Sig at Chad/Kyle.

"Listen, man, before you decide to insult my sister more, know it will earn you a bullet between the eyes. And ironically, you wouldn't be the first man I shot today either," I said, probably more casually than someone should when threatening to shoot a person.

All the color drained from his face when he realized a real-life gun was pointed at him. The blood spatter still coating my body helped back up my threat. Faster than I thought possible for the preppy dude, he ran out of our apartment, booking it down the stairwell.

Nikki skipped over to shut the door he hadn't bothered closing.

"Breaking up with them is so much easier when you're home," she commented, completely ignoring my eye roll. "I mean, like, don't they know Tinder is supposed to be for hookups? I don't get why they all get so upset when I tell them we had fun, but there won't be a repeat."

I needed the tequila in me, stat, for relationship conversations of any kind. Nikki never wanted to address why she wouldn't let a man close to her emotionally. And I wasn't exactly the poster child for healthy relationships. If I hooked up with someone, it needed to be someone Mario would never find out about. I learned the hard way that Mario didn't like men touching me, even though we weren't a couple.

I didn't have the emotional strength to think about all the baggage that came with the situation between Mario and me, so I decided to focus on Nikki's pouting.

"Maybe," I said, taking a gulp of my margarita, "it's because you went for that man's pride by telling him he was boring in bed. But seriously…a dude with loafers is who you went for?"

"He was helping me invest in stocks," she replied. I let her snatch my glass and take a sip. After witnessing the fuck buddy of the night, I could tell she needed the alcohol more than I did.

I shook my head at her reasoning. Of course, that's why she chose him. "Well, that's on you for thinking you would get something more than thirty seconds of missionary. Let me guess; he couldn't find your clit?" I asked.

"The man wouldn't have been able to find my clit if I shoved it in his face…which I did." Nikki gave me a sly smile, revealing one of her cute dimples before we both broke out in a fit of laughter.

Cute was the perfect word to describe Nikki. We were polar opposites. Her cornflower-blue eyes and blond hair complemented her light skin splattered with freckles. Where I had tan skin and long dark hair that usually fell in soft waves down my back. Nikki called me her Latin beauty of a sister.

Where she was soft and sweet, I was all sass and tended to stab when mad. The only things we had in common were our love for each other and our souls that had been shattered and healed with the splinters still inside. We showed our brokenness in different ways, but we both chose to embrace our inner demons.

Better the devil you know and all that.

"Well, I hope you got all you wanted out of him on the stocks front because Chad is likely never coming back to help you." I stood and made my way to my door. "And try to keep the sounds of your self-care down tonight."

I blew a kiss over my shoulder before making my way to the shower.

Shower margaritas were Santa Muerte's gift to earth, and I needed mine tonight.

Because Anthony managed not only to ruin my shirt, but leave blood and brain matter in my hair, making me go through my whole hair washing routine. And I would rather do a million other things than washing and drying my hair.

A light appeared from my phone plugged in on the nightstand, and a groan slipped from my lips. Lotería may close at one a.m. like other clubs, but I was on call twenty-four seven. My hand wrapped around the device, picking it up to check what pressing matter needed my attention now.

The hair on my neck stood on end when I saw the sender of the unread messages.

Mario: Muñeca. Why is it I'm being told by my father that you are staying in Arizona?

Mario: Answer me, Muñeca. You better have a good reason for not texting me back.

Mario was a complication in my life that I rarely had

enough energy to process how to handle. Nikki loved to point out that I refused to acknowledge Mario's obsession with me, and the longer I put off cutting him off, the more trouble I would be in. But how do you cut off the person who acted as your security blanket?

It was a twisted relationship between Mario and me. At seventeen, I'd been on my own for so long that I latched on to the first sense of security and affection given. But Mario's affection came with strings. Strings I didn't know how, or if, I wanted to cut at the time. And then, when I started becoming close with Sergio, the thought of losing another father figure terrified me, and Mario held the threat over my head. I tried to put distance between us, hoping his obsession would wane. But despite all his girlfriends and fuck buddies, I stayed the object of his attention.

Pulled back to my phone, I typed out a response. A coppery tang filled my mouth, where I broke the skin, gnawing on my lip and waiting for a response.

Me: Sorry. I was in the shower.

Me: And Sergio just told me tonight that I'm going to be running the arms deal with the new MC. Didn't know anything about it until a few hours ago.

Me: Your father employs me. You know I have to do as he says.

I hoped the last text would get me off the hook from any backlash, needing Mario to realize I hadn't planned this. I'd worked toward this goal the last few years, but he didn't need to know that. I may be a killer and have a whole slew of moral and psychological issues, but Mario...Mario was a completely different monster.

The three dots indicating typing appeared on the screen but then disappeared, sending nervous energy coursing through my body.

Mario: Yes. For now, you do.

A chill ran down my spine at those words. What the fuck did that mean, and why did it feel like a very thinly veiled threat?

    Mario: Sleep well, my Muñeca.

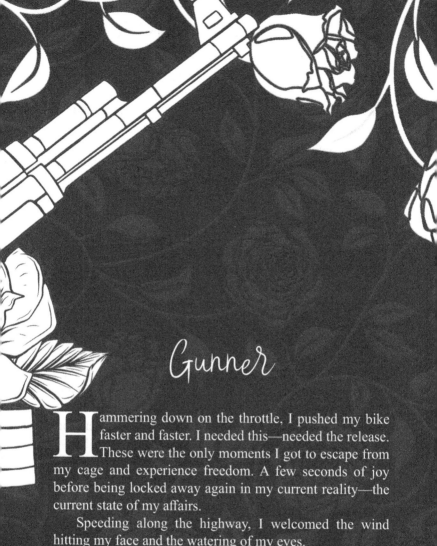

Gunner

Hammering down on the throttle, I pushed my bike faster and faster. I needed this—needed the release. These were the only moments I got to escape from my cage and experience freedom. A few seconds of joy before being locked away again in my current reality—the current state of my affairs.

Speeding along the highway, I welcomed the wind hitting my face and the watering of my eyes.

The clearing of my mind.

My job required me to stay focused and alert. See the signs of change in Tucson's underbelly and know what went on and who the top players were. Metal fencing popped up to my right, the walls of my cage coming into view. I pulled into the compound and parked in my usual spot next to Dex's ride. It seemed I arrived last at tonight's church. Throwing my leg over my bike, I made my way into the clubhouse.

From the outside, there wasn't much to see. It looked more like a warehouse than a place a bunch of bikers would live in, but that was by design. Skeletons of Society wasn't exactly a boy scout troop, so lots of effort went into shielding the club from wandering eyes—both from the law and from other "upstanding citizen groups" like ourselves.

A prospect whose name I hadn't bothered to remember ran up, pulling the door open for me. I nodded my head in thanks, showing him a bit of kindness. Something prospects weren't used to around here.

They were here to prove their loyalty to the Skeletons of Society in hopes of getting patched in. The initiation process was ruthless as fuck. And since every member went through it, complaining fell on deaf ears. In fact, if you said shit about getting hazed, you would never get back on club property again. Until prospects had been around for longer than a few months, I didn't bother getting to know their names.

The inside of the club looked nothing like the outside. There were two levels. The top housed all the patched brothers' rooms for anyone who wanted or needed one. Members with old ladies usually lived somewhere off compound, but for the rest of us, we stayed in rooms here.

The main level looked like a bachelor's MTV *Cribs* fantasy. The smell of sex and weed permeated the space. Big-screen TVs lined the walls, while a bar with every beer imaginable on tap took up the whole right side of the clubhouse. And, of course, stripper poles for all the club bunnies and hang-arounds to *perform* on were spread throughout the space. Not to mention the dozens of seating areas strategically placed to accommodate extracurricular activities that didn't make it to a member's bed. Or for members like me, who didn't want a girl to get any ideas that she'd be getting anything other than a fuck and maybe a high-five after.

"Gunner, get your fucking pretty-boy ass in here," Pres yelled, his head hanging out the door where we met for church. The irritation in his tone brought a cocky grin to my face.

Yup, definitely the last one to church.

My smirk only grew when I walked in and saw that Dex had saved my usual seat for me.

"What? Were you fuckers waiting for me?" I called out, getting me a middle finger from Pres and a snicker from Dex.

The enforcer was a giant of a man; it was why he'd gotten the job. That and his ability to get anyone to speak when needed. I'd never met anyone as proficient at breaking men. Then again, he didn't have anyone restricting which tactics he could use to do the job. Easier to get someone to talk when you could cut off appendages and there was no one above you to reprimand you. Pres gave Dex full rein as long as his methods worked. We were both a bit deranged at this point.

Seeing as much shit as we had over the years kept our moral compasses from working quite the same way as others still out in society. Sometimes I wondered if I should fall farther down the proverbial rabbit hole.

The boom of Pres's voice pulled me back to the present. "Assholes. It's time to get to business now that his royal highness has arrived," he called out.

Pres started calling me that when I first arrived. Said it was because I came with a lot of extra work.

He wasn't wrong.

Thank fuck, though, it didn't become my road name. Instead, the club went with Gunner after they all got to see me shoot. My affinity for guns made me the perfect fit for sergeant at arms.

Pres cleared his throat to get our attention. "All right, so as you assholes know, we have been trying to expand our business into Tucson for years now. But without a partnership with the cartel and their express permission, we would be asking for a turf war. One, we would lose to Los Muertos. But they want to keep the Reapers out as much as we do, so Sergio has agreed to a trial partnership where we run their guns."

The room began to cheer, and Pres's eyes found mine. We had worked for this partnership for a long fucking time. Two goddamned years, to be exact. There were a fuck ton of reasons to pair up with the largest of the Mexican cartels. For the club, getting involved with Los Muertos meant gaining a powerful ally. Plus, the alliance would hopefully keep the Reapers in check.

The Skeletons of Society might be a one-percenter club, but the club didn't fuck with hard drugs or the skin trade. Didn't want to be a part of fucking up communities with that shit.

Gunrunning was this club's poison of choice.

"This will be a good way to keep those slimy fuckers over at the Reapers MC out of our territory," Pres declared, slamming his fist on the table. Stirring up another round of cheers. "Money makes weak men into monsters real quick," he said, looking everyone at the table in the eye. His words were a warning. Anyone caught associating with the Reapers would be dealt with.

The Reapers worked for pieces of shit willing to buy women. Type of people who made everyone nervous—people with deep pockets and a long reach.

It was why Sergio didn't want the Reapers in his territory. He wasn't scared of the club; he was suspicious of who they dealt with. Besides, Los Muertos made plenty of money with their gunrunning and drug smuggling, and the cartel had staying one step ahead of the law down to a science. Skin trading would fuck that up.

I leaned forward in my chair, resting my arms on the table we all sat around. This was my area of expertise for the club, and I'd worked toward this partnership since getting here.

"Who are we going to be working with? Sergio? Mario?" I pried.

The word on the street was Mario was in charge of all

gunrunning for Los Muertos. I hoped that meant he would be our point of contact. That way, I could work directly with the man himself.

That would make my job so much easier.

Pres ran a hand through his salt-and-pepper beard. "Last I spoke with Sergio, that was the plan. You and Dex will meet at their strip club in Tucson and go over our arrangement. Check out what their current operation is like. Suggest tweaks if you feel they need to make them. Get whatever information you need to get your jobs done." Pres let the implications hang in the air.

An irritated grunt left my lips as I leaned back in my chair, my brain racing through all the things this meeting meant and the preparations I would need to make.

"Oh, I'm sure I'll need to fucking make changes. How can you successfully run guns out of a fucking strip club?" I closed my eyes. *Fuck.* I knew this shit wouldn't be as easy as I'd hoped. "I bet they've never even run guns out of Tucson. We're going to be their goddamned guinea pigs," I growled out.

The sound of my hand smacking the table echoed through the room. I was pissed my job now included reworking their system. I wanted to meet with Los Muertos and start the actual work. Not make revisions to a shitty arms-dealing operation.

Dex chimed in beside me, sounding way too cheery.

"I've heard they're booming with business. The dude seems to know what he's doing. All my contacts say they're happy with their shipments," he pointed out.

My brows furrowed. Of course that's what Dex heard.

"No shit. Who's dumb enough to leave the Mexican cartel a lousy review? That's how heads end up in boxes shipped to loved ones," I grumbled.

Dex shrugged, not at all concerned about the pile of shit that was dumped at our feet. Typical.

Los Muertos was way up there in the criminal world. No one dared cross them. In fact, the Four Families over in New York kept a tentative truce with the cartel. Neither organization was too sure who would win that bloodbath—if anyone. Unlike small street gangs, who fought over turf and disrespect, the big players only cared about the bottom line and avoiding jail time or deportation.

"Hey, children," Pres barked, done with my shit. "Let's remember, we might be in a partnership, but we can't trust them. And it's temporary—until we prove ourselves. Watch out for our own and use this deal in whatever way we can." Pres eyed me again, his tone carrying a threatening edge to it. "Stay alert, learn what you can, and don't give away any club business." He held my gaze until I relented and gave a curt nod.

"All right, church is dismissed. Gunner, I'll let you know the details of that meeting."

I needed a beer. Or three.

All the patched members might have been my club brothers, but Dex and I were true brothers. Not by blood, but by trial by fire. He was always the one I called on to have my six. Plus, he wasn't annoying as shit like some of the guys.

Soft leather gave as I plopped onto the stool next to him. Within seconds of my ass hitting the seat, red nails latched onto my arm, tracing the tattoos and making my hair stand on end.

Lolli's nasally voice sounded in my ear, making my eye want to twitch in irritation. "Gunner, baby. I've missed you," she purred, attempting to sound sexy.

I asked her once why she picked such a dumbass name. She claimed it was because she could suck a dick like a lollipop. For anyone else, that might have been a selling point. I glanced at the hand lingering on my bicep before taking the rest of her in. Her boobs were spilling out of her shirt, and her bleach-blond hair was piled on top of her head in what I heard the club bunnies refer to as a messy bun.

The woman was relentless. She wanted to be an old lady so badly she tried to get her claws into anyone she could. I

32

wouldn't touch her with a ten-foot pole, but she refused to take the hint. I guess she felt eventually she would wear me down.

The opening of the beer bottle hit my lips, and I chugged down the liquid patience. Most referred to alcohol as liquid courage. I didn't need courage. I needed patience so I didn't decide to start shooting shit.

Lolli continued to pet me like I was a damn dog. "Heard you have a new alliance, babe. Must be stressful. Need to let off some steam?"

My eyebrows raised at her statement. That was not information she should know. She mistook my reaction as interest in her offer and snaked her hands down to the zipper on my jeans. My rough hand clasped hers before they made it to their intended destination.

"Who the fuck told you that, Lolli? Club bunnies aren't supposed to know club business, so how the hell do you know about it?" I growled out.

Liquid patience was not kicking in fast enough.

Her face paled at my statement.

"I...I just overheard somewhere," she stammered.

"You better run off, Lolli. Gunner here has that ragey look he gets before he starts shooting people," Dex said, looking completely at ease while I was approaching attempted-murderer status. "Unless you want another hole in your body," he added.

Before I could question her further, she made herself scarce. Dex cleared his throat. "So, we're goin' to a seedy strip club run by a cartel. Think they make their dancers wear sombreros? Or maybe those luchador masks..." He paused to take a sip of his beer. "That last one might be kinda hot."

I looked over at Dex, worried about how serious he sounded. There was no indication he was joking, and I couldn't hold in my question any longer.

"You want a lap dance from a chick wearing a Mexican wrestling mask?" I asked incredulously.

Dex's face scrunched up as he considered it. "I'd be down." His response made me laugh aloud, causing some brothers to turn to look at us.

"You're a strange fucker, Dex."

He smirked at my comment before making one of his own.

"Oh, don't even talk about my sexual appetite, Gunner. I see how the women leave wrecked after being with you. Bitches can't wait to get another opportunity to be shoved up against a wall and fucked. Maybe we can get a good lay while we're there. I need a little variety from the club bunnies."

I nodded in agreement, but I had no plans on getting distracted by Los Muertos's pussy.

I had a job to do.

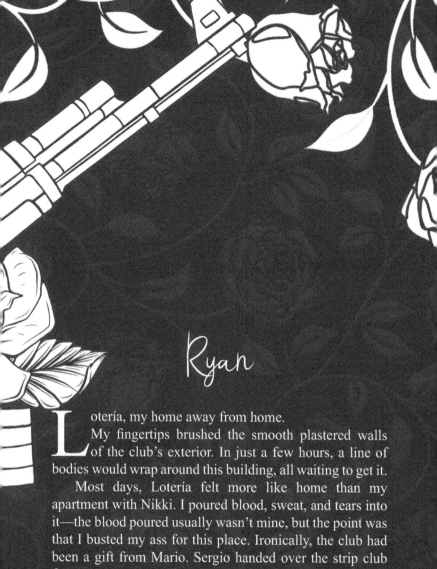

Ryan

Lotería, my home away from home.

My fingertips brushed the smooth plastered walls of the club's exterior. In just a few hours, a line of bodies would wrap around this building, all waiting to get it.

Most days, Lotería felt more like home than my apartment with Nikki. I poured blood, sweat, and tears into it—the blood poured usually wasn't mine, but the point was that I busted my ass for this place. Ironically, the club had been a gift from Mario. Sergio handed over the strip club for me to manage at his request. I'd begged for a role in Los Muertos, and Mario wouldn't allow me to strip. Not that I wanted to, but I was annoyed he'd kept me up on a shelf like a doll.

My gaze caught on the main stage, reminding me of what a shit hole this place used to be.

The moment my happy ass walked in all those years ago, I knew the reason Mario had insisted on this particular club. He didn't think I could actually do anything with it and would run back to him. When I'd taken over, it was a dilapidated strip club in the ghetto of Tucson. The girls were turning tricks and selling drugs. None of them felt an ounce of loyalty to Los Muertos. I didn't think they even knew the cartel owned the club.

So I cleaned house. Anyone not willing to fall in line found their ass out on the curb. My big dreams for the place, and the need to be noticed for what I could bring to Los Muertos, kept me motivated.

Now we were the fucking Studio 54 of Tucson, and I cleaned a shit ton of dirty money for Los Muertos because of that popularity.

The sight of my office door pulled me out of my nostalgic state. I strode through, only to find Nikki sitting in one of the chairs facing my desk rather than downstairs working like she should be.

My voice cut through the silence of the room. "Honestly, do you do any work while you're here?"

She didn't bother looking away from the screen of her phone when she flipped me off.

I rolled my eyes. We both knew I wouldn't kick her out. "Also, I'm pretty sure I'm a nocturnal creature at this point. I probably should be taking some vitamin D supplement for the lack of sun I get." I didn't know if Nikki was listening or if I was saying shit to the universe at this point.

My ass hit the chair, pulling a groan from my lips. I'd slept like shit thanks to Mario's texts replaying in my brain all night—they had me acting like my day job was as a cryptographer.

"That's not the only vitamin D you need in your life."

Her breathy tone had me raising my eyebrow in annoyance. Of course Nikki couldn't hold a conversation without bringing sex into it. She started cracking up at her joke, and I tried to hide my smile while I rolled my eyes.

"Besides, I'm the only *Sunshine* you need in your life," she said.

My arms crossed over my chest as I flicked my gaze to Nikki.

"*Ay Dios mío*...Nikki, just because you chose *Sunshine* as your stage name does not mean I'll call you that. It's almost as bad as if you would have chosen *Cookie* or, God forbid...*Candy*." I faked a shudder at the mention of that last one, knowing she would pick up on the reference.

She drew in a gasp of horror, her manicured hand over her heart like she was some southern bell. I knew damn well she wasn't. I didn't actually know where she was from, but the accent she tried to hide from time to time wasn't southern. And the swear words she would say under her breath weren't Spanish.

"Do not insult me by putting my stage name in the same sentence as hers."

Laughter spilled from my lips at how offended Nikki was pretending to be.

Candy was the name of the skanky bitch I'd kicked out from Lotería a month ago. Nikki let out an irritated huff, pushing a stray lock of hair out of her face.

"That whore thought because Mario was the one who hired her she could do whatever the hell she wanted," she seethed.

Including showing up high and doing lines in the dancers' dressing room. All that might fly at other clubs, but not mine. The girls knew they were required to be clean, or they could pack their shit and go.

"Now. We never got to talk about why the fuck you showed up at home last night with blood spatter all over your damn self..."

She was letting me decide how much I would tell her. Nikki started as just my employee and turned into my soul sister along the way. When we decided to get a place together, I figured I'd let her in on my extracurricular activities. She knew I ran Lotería for Los Muertos, but not that I was *hands on* with some of the nastier parts of being in a cartel. But it would have been hard to hide the small armory I kept in my room, so I told Nikki.

My head hit the back of the chair, and I welcomed the weight of my arm over my eyes.

Maybe I could hide in my office forever.

"I had an...*interview* to conduct. But Sergio showed up and crashed it." I paused for a second, peeking at Nikki from under my arm. "Something has been off lately in Tucson. The normal players I keep an eye on are waiting for something. But I don't fucking know what."

I chewed on my bottom lip while thinking about all the ways this could play out.

"Ugh." Nikki pinched the bridge of her nose like *she* was the one who had to sort out this shit when it inevitably hit the fan. "You and your goddamned vibes, Ryan. You're always right when it comes to bad shit."

Her blue eyes met mine, which were still just barely peeking out from under my forearm. An accusing finger pointed my way.

"La Brujita is such a fitting fuckin' name for you. Witch—you're actually a witch."

Without missing a beat, Nikki and I yelled out simultaneously.

"You're gonna look at me, and you're gonna tell me I'm wrong?" We fell into a fit of laughter before finally settling down. My hands rubbed my face. The exhaustion and stress were catching up to me. And my night was barely getting started.

Nikki was right. My vague feelings usually came with bad shit. Needing a change in subject, I moved on to why Sergio had been at the club.

"Anyway, Sergio wanted to meet to tell me I'm leading the new arms deal he brokered with the Skeletons of Society MC. He wants me to run it since I know the inner workings of Tucson's underbelly," I explained.

"No," Nikki drew out the one-syllable word. "Sergio wants you to run it because his narcissist asshat of a son is busy running around banging whores and leaving you to handle all his shit here." A scoff of disgust left Nikki's mouth. "At least now you get to be the boss bitch you are and force people to acknowledge it."

I played with a loose string on my shirt, frowning at Nikki's words. She wasn't going to like the texts I received last night from Mario.

"What the fuck did he do now, Ryan?"

Damn, she was good.

"Nothing," I muttered.

Lights and movement pulled my attention toward the glass wall, looking over the club below. Hopefully, Nikki would have a harder time reading the worry in my face from the profile view. Most of all, I was hoping it would keep her from calling me on the bullshit I was sputtering.

"You know how he is. He thought I would give up on Lotería and move to Sinaloa with him. So anything new that comes up for me to do, he doesn't like." I didn't mention that his text messages felt weirdly threatening.

It was late. You're reading into it.

Another mediocre attempt to convince myself the lack of sleep was what was making me suspicious. I looked over when I heard Nikki sigh. The fact that she looked like she'd sucked on a sour lemon was a red flag. I wasn't going to like what she was about to say.

"Listen, this will be the last thing I say on the subject because we both know I'm just as much of a fuck-up when it comes to feelings and shit." She flashed me a smile meant to disarm me before she added on. "But it's easier to comment on other people's shit than fix our own. Ryan, you are a badass who fucking unalives bitch-ass men. You took a shitty strip club and made it a haven for women who have been abused but feel they have no other line of work they can or want to do. You give girls like me a chance to survive. You stay strong enough for everyone down there on that floor. They get paid good money that you don't ever take a cut from, and you protect them from ever being abused again—" The way her words dropped off suddenly made my stomach lurch. "But you don't seem to recognize how you're trapped too."

I bristled at her words. Damn, Nikki knew how to go straight for the jugular.

All the things she said hit too close to home, but I was terrified of opening up that proverbial door to analyze if what she said was true. For years I'd been shoving emotions and memories I didn't want to face into the back closet of my mind. In moments of pure honesty, I could admit I didn't worry about the damage denial was causing because I thought I wouldn't be around long enough to see it.

There was a reason there weren't many women running around with criminal organizations. In fact, Scar was the only other one I knew. And she had her own fucked-up situation she was dealing with over in New York.

The cold indifference I didn't usually show Nikki slipped into place. I had work to do, and I wasn't willing to dive into this subject with her—with anyone.

"I'm not trapped, Nikki. My relationship with Mario is complicated. Okay?" The icy tone made it abundantly clear there was no room for discussion.

Nikki could read a room, and people, almost as well as I could. So she switched the subject without skipping a beat. But I didn't miss the slight widening of her eyes. This was the first time it dawned on her the predator I was.

Movie nights with Chinese food and every version of *Bring It On* imaginable had a way of hiding my deadlier side from her. But this moment gave her a peek at me without the rose-colored glasses. A prickle of worry she would find me unworthy of affection ran through my body. But her cheery tone helped ease the feeling.

Maybe she'll stick around a bit longer.

"So, you get to meet a bunch of old bikers. An age gap can be very sexy, you know. Get an older man to take care of all your needs." Nikki added an exaggerated wink, as if I didn't already know almost everything she ever said was an innuendo.

"I will not be hooking up with any of the Skeletons of Society MC members, Nikki," I said dryly, earning me an eye roll. "I'll be running the deal with them, so I need them to take me seriously."

A pout appeared on Nikki's face for a moment before she moved on, pulling out her phone and typing like a madwoman.

"In that case, you'll need to wear your bad bitch outfit, Chica." She looked up at me with a smirk, and it suddenly felt like I was the prey and Nikki was the predator.

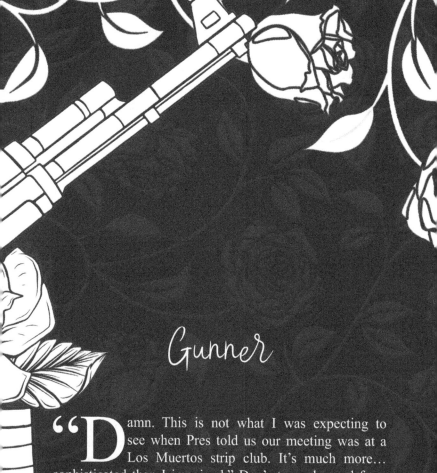

Gunner

"**D**amn. This is not what I was expecting to see when Pres told us our meeting was at a Los Muertos strip club. It's much more... sophisticated than I imagined." Dex's tone changed from awe to disappointment. "This doesn't look like the kind of place I can fulfill my luchador mask fantasy."

I looked over and raised my eyebrow at the genuine sadness in his voice.

"I worry about you, man." Shaking my head, I focused back on what I was seeing. My brother wasn't wrong. In front of us stood a modern Spanish-style building with sleek white plaster walls, a tile roof, and a metal sign with graffiti lettering. The strip club's name was illuminated in red.

Loteria.

My jaw clenched at the turn of events. "How the fuck did we not know what this looked like? I hate shit intel. Do we know anything going into this?" I paused for a second, trying to rein in my temper. "Let's go. We have a meeting to get to," I said tightly, throwing my leg over my bike and storming off toward the club. I was pissed off that we were starting in the dark.

The original deal was that we would be working with Mario. But Pres got a call from Sergio earlier today changing our point of contact. Now, all of a sudden, we were being given the run-around and getting someone we knew nothing about. Plus, the short notice meant I couldn't get any intel on them before we met.

I called out over my shoulder to Dex. "I bet this Ryan person doesn't even know how to fucking oversee an arms deal properly. Sergio is playing with us."

Dex could hear the frustration in my voice and wisely chose not to comment. My eyebrows shot up as we approached the entrance to the club. I hadn't expected the cartel to own a strip club with a giant archway covered in bougainvillea. The only thing that seemed normal about this place was that the entrance was manned by a hulk of a human.

What the fuck did his parents feed him?

My gaze moved to the line of people curved around the building, and I was shocked to find it wasn't made up of horned-out men waiting to get in. I didn't see anyone typically associated with a seedy strip club. What the hell was going on? Dex was thinking along the same lines because he called out to the security.

"Hey, ése, something happening tonight?" he asked in a faux Spanish accent that made him sound like an asshole.

The doorman cocked a brow.

My elbow rammed into Dex's ribs, causing him to let out a strained grunt. "Really, Dex? Ése? Don't piss off the giant man who could eat you. And your Spanish is shit," I hissed.

Dex waved his hand in dismissal and kept on talking. Thank God he dropped the accent. "For a strip club, there are a lot of chicks and non-pervy-looking dudes waiting to get in."

The doorman huffed a laugh while opening the velvet rope to usher us in.

"Don't let Ryan catch you calling this place a strip club in front of customers. It's a Latin *Burlesque* club around them." He indicated toward the line with his head. "A bigger client pool, if we call it that. And *gringos*, let me tell you. That fancy pussy is nice," he stated.

It pissed me off that I was impressed. Smart move to not call it a strip club to appeal to more people. A legally successful business meant not as many eyes were looking for not-so-legal activity.

"You get to fuck the strippers?" Dex's tone was one of astonishment. "That seems messy for business." Of course he was stuck on the subject of pussy.

"No, *cabrón*, the women who come in here get all worked up watching the show, and then they need a man to fuck 'em up against a wall. You know?"

Then the big man's voice took on an almost fearful tone. "The boss would cut our balls off if we went near the dancers, but the patrons are fair game. By the way, good luck with Ryan." He snickered.

Interestingly, the doorman was more concerned about us dealing with Ryan than Mario, but before I could put too much weight into his comment, the club's interior distracted me.

"Holy Shit," Dex whispered as we made our way through the exterior archway into the heart of the club.

I blinked at our surroundings.

Damn. Money wasn't an issue, I guess.

The bar was made entirely of marble, with back glass shelves filled with top-shelf liquors. Red light bounced off the bottles, adding to the sensual feeling of the space. The walls and ceiling were painted a charcoal gray, and giant framed photographs portraying the different elements of the Lotería card game hung on the walls.

My head shook in disbelief. No wonder we hadn't found any creepy-looking assholes outside.

Stairs led to a recessed area housing the main stage. Smaller elevated stages with poles dotted the space between tables. My eye caught on a couple in a sensual embrace performing some Latin dance up on the main platform. At the same time, women in deep red lingerie and sugar skull masks mimicked the routine on their poles.

An elbow from Dex drew my attention. "Dude, think they would hire me? I'm into their uniforms. I could be shirtless with tight mariachi pants. Fuck yeah."

"What the fuck are you talking about, Dex?" I asked before spotting one of the male waiters.

"We would hire you. The ladies like something to look at." A woman with short blond hair approached Dex and me. "And they would like to look at you two. On Thursday nights, we have male dancers up on the poles. It's one of our most popular nights." A smirk appeared on her face.

Clearing my voice, I tried to get us back on track. "It looks like the place does well...business-wise."

I could admit when I was wrong, and it seemed like this Ryan person may know how to run an operation. Or at least a damn good strip club.

The woman gave a curt nod but stayed tight-lipped on the subject. "Gunner and Dex, I presume." Blondie was practically eye fucking Dex, but as quickly as she started, she stopped. Turning on her heel, she walked toward a partially hidden staircase by the bar. Calling out to us over her shoulder, she said, "Please follow me. I'll show you where you'll have your meeting."

Dex watched her ass all the way up the stairs. The man was a manwhore, and every woman was fair game to drool over in his book.

I whispered to him, "I think she'd put on the luchador mask for you."

A sly grin crept up his face, and he wagged his eyebrows in response. I stifled a laugh, attempting to hide it with a cough.

"Gentlemen." Blondie stopped in front of the first room at the top of the stairs, waiting for us to catch up before pushing the door open. For the second time that night, the place's interior caused my eyebrows to hit my hairline. The whole left wall was one-way glass—overlooking the club below. Directly in front were two velvet chairs facing a large wooden desk. The office's mood matched the club, but nothing particularly personal gave me insight into the owner.

Blondie's feminine voice sounded from behind me. "Please have a seat. They'll be in shortly."

I waved a hand over my shoulder in acknowledgment, too busy trying to assess the room to turn around.

"What my asshole friend means is thank you for showing us to the office." Dex's flirtatious tone had me rolling my eyes. As his ass hit the chair, I heard the telltale click of a door shutting.

Dex broke the silence first, speaking quietly in case anyone—or anything—was listening.

"I think this Ryan guy might be useful. Seems like Sergio and Mario give him a lot of leeway. We might've found an in with the Los Muertos," he whispered.

"What would be better would be to work with Mario directly," I said bluntly, letting out a disappointed sigh. "But you're right, we've gotta work with what we've got, and he might be our best bet."

Before we could comment further, the door opened. I blinked, and in the next moment, the weight of my Glock was in my hand, pointed at a man in the doorway. I relaxed slightly when my brain caught up to the fact that it was Sergio walking in. His thick black eyebrow rose in response to having two guns pointed at his chest.

Well, three. Dex liked to carry two. Said it made him feel like a cowboy or some shit. But Sergio was freakishly calm.

"Buenas noches, gentlemen. Antsy, are we?" There was a hint of amusement in the kingpin's voice.

"Used to having a gun pointed at you?" I threw back at him.

I didn't personally know the guy, and seeing him in person reminded me that Sergio was a scary-looking motherfucker. So while the alliance meant we should be safe at this meeting, I wasn't stupid enough to let my guard down. It would take more than a spit-shake agreement between criminals for that.

Especially since there were rumblings—the heir to Los Muertos didn't have the same commitment to loyalty the cartel was known for. It would be stupid to assume he didn't get that trait from his daddy. So until proven otherwise, I wasn't trusting any member of Los Muertos not to turn on me.

"Drawn on me? Nah, gringo, I'm used to being shot. Are you going to be the next one to do that? Because if not, put your fucking guns away," he said.

I plastered on a grin before speaking, keeping my tone light. "Naw, I just wanted to impress you with my quick reflexes." There was a thin line between asserting yourself and pissing on someone else, and I needed to be careful not to fuck that up.

"In that case," Sergio walked behind the desk and took a seat. His gaze roamed over Dex and me, "thanks for the demonstration, and welcome to Los Muertos territory."

I didn't fail to notice the warning in Sergio's tone when he mentioned being in Los Muertos's territory. Message was clear. Regardless of our alliance, he wouldn't tolerate disrespect. I admired that, but Sergio would learn that I was in charge here, and it was my brother and I who shouldn't be disrespected.

"We heard you have a new protégé handing our arms dealing. We're meeting him as well, correct?" I tried to hide my edge of irritation that the dude wasn't already in here.

Who shows up late to a first meeting?

Sergio scowled slightly, but a smile quickly replaced it—looking like the cat that ate the fucking canary. It wasn't meant to look threatening, but it put me on edge.

"Some business came up last minute, so *Ryan* will be joining us after that's handled. In the meantime, can I get you boys a drink? I can text Nikki our order to bring up from the bar." He finished by pulling out his phone and looking at us expectantly.

Dex and I rattled off our orders, and I sat back in my chair, preparing for the small talk I would have to endure while we waited for Nikki. But moments after the text was sent, the door was flung open.

"That was fas…" Dex's comment cut off, and his mouth hung open at whatever he saw at the door behind us. Before I could turn around, I caught sight of a woman's backside from my peripheral and nearly snapped my neck to get a better view. Her black hair was pulled into a slick ponytail that hit her lower back. The swing of it was a cock tease on its own, begging me to wrap one hand around it while the other held her throat. A groan tried to escape when I saw what she was wearing, a fitted white suit that looked like she'd been sewn into it.

Coffee-colored eyes met mine the moment she turned around. They were hard and challenging—this was a woman with confidence. I nearly choked on my tongue when my eyes trailed down her body. Her suit jacket was buttoned a few inches above her navel, but she wasn't wearing a shirt underneath.

Instead, I was graced with the sight of her tan skin and cleavage. Blood instantly rushed to my cock, and my brain felt foggy with lust. I had no clue a suit could be so sexy on a woman, but she looked like a fucking exotic goddess. All I wanted was to rip that suit off her, bend her over Sergio's desk, and drive my throbbing cock into her warm pussy. A wave of possessiveness came over me when I caught Dex adjusting himself out of the corner of my eye. The urge to yell at Dex to close his eyes or I would rip them out was almost unbearable.

But my veins instantly turned to ice when I caught the mischievous smile Sergio was giving her. My lip curled in disgust at both my reaction and her.

Obviously, this Nikki woman was meant to be a distraction. Women were often used like this in the criminal world, and most of these women got off sleeping with men in power, never caring who they stabbed in the back on their way to the top.

I was sure this woman was no different.

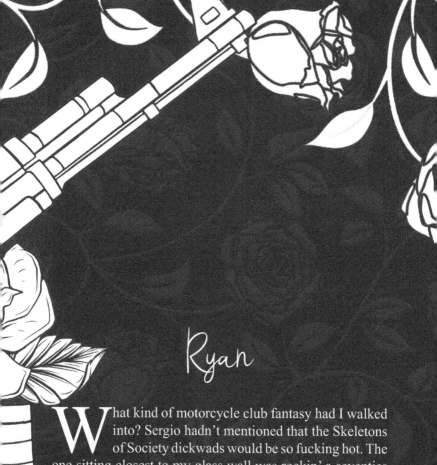

Ryan

What kind of motorcycle club fantasy had I walked into? Sergio hadn't mentioned that the Skeletons of Society dickwads would be so fucking hot. The one sitting closest to my glass wall was rockin' a seventies porn 'stache that was literally what my wet dreams were made of.

I'd always told Nikki my sexual awakening happened with Tom Selleck.

My eyes roved down his body; he looked like he could throw me around. I noticed that purely for tactical reasons… because I was a professional.

His dark hair had that effortlessly messy look going on, and he was covered throat to fingertips in tattoos.

God, this man was beautiful.

My tongue swiped along my bottom lip, checking to make sure I wasn't drooling, especially since he was taking in my every detail. He narrowed in on the movement, his fists tightening. I nearly choked when his assessing green eyes met mine. I couldn't tell if the heated look he gave me was because he hated me or wanted to fuck me.

Then again, could be both.

His body language was meant to look at ease. But he couldn't hide from me that he was positioned so he could see the door and desk, keeping his gun easily accessible. The man had training. And he trusted the giant sitting next to him since he allowed his back to be exposed to the wall of glass. Sure, we were on the second floor, but in our line of work, you didn't make it very long if you started assuming you were safe.

Apparently, real-life Jax Teller was in a pissy mood. The scowl he was rockin' probably made grown men shit their pants.

His voice was smooth like well-aged tequila, making my thighs clench. "This is a private meeting. I believe Sergio sent you our order. Why don't you get that?" He looked away, effectively dismissing me.

I scoffed and looked at Sergio with an *ex-fucking-scuse me. Did he just do that?* look.

Am I on criminal Punk'd?

Asshole's eyes swiveled back to me, looking me up and down with a sneer. "Oh and Nikki, knock next time instead of barging in, and bring Ryan whatever he normally drinks. I'm sure you're well acquainted with his likes." The last part was said with a little extra venom.

My eyebrows hit my hairline. Apparently, homeboy was pissed *Nikki* might be well acquainted with *Ryan*. His irritation brought out a slight New York accent, making him sound even more like a jackass.

Fuck, how can his voice turn me on and piss me off?

Before I could even attempt to respond to the bullshit out of this prick's mouth, there was a knock at the door.

"Enter." I stared the lead asshole down while giving the command. I didn't think I'd ever seen Sergio smile as wide as he did when the real Nikki walked in the door. He was taking great joy in this whole situation.

"Okay, I have everyone's drink. Sergio, I don't understand how you can choose a Modelo when we have top-tier tequilas in this place. And Ryan, I assumed you wanted a margarita on the rocks." Nikki looked up from her tray, utterly unaware of the bomb she just dropped on the boys.

"Thanks, Nikki. You're so well acquainted with what I like." I used the same sickly sweet tone she used when verbally chopping off men's balls.

She wrinkled her nose in confusion but didn't comment, leaving as soon as the drinks were on the desk. Sergio burst out in laughter the moment the door shut. I swore tears were forming at the corners of his eyes. Meanwhile, I could feel the death glare I was receiving.

We were off to a great start to this partnership.

"Oh shit." A whisper yell left the lips of the large man with lead asshole. He looked like he was watching a telenovela. His eyes were as big as saucers while taking a giant swig of his drink, and he snuck glances over at his club brother. I had a feeling alcohol was going to be needed for this meeting.

Finally settling down, Sergio decided it might be a good idea not to be a dick and sort out the shit storm he'd created. My fingers pinched the bridge of my nose. It would have been nice if he'd bothered to clear up the confusion before I showed up. Curse my mother for wanting to be trendy and "more American" by giving me a white man's name.

Dios mío.

"Gentlemen, this is Ryan. *She's* my lead man for this arms deal partnership." Sergio looked up to where I was standing at his side, his hand gesturing to homeboy with the man bun. "Ryan, this is Dex. The Skeletons' enforcer. *Y este cabrón* is who you will be working the closest with. Their sergeant at arms, Gunner."

I didn't know if I wanted to ride his face or punch it. Maybe I would just suffocate him with my pussy.

Psh, he would be lucky to die between my thighs.

I chuckled at my inner ramblings, causing Gunner to cut me a glare and then leaned forward to rest his forearms on the desk.

"We didn't come here to be fucked around with Sergio," he sneered. "If you don't want to take this partnership seriously, we'll leave the Reapers MC to be your fucking problem."

I shot him a dirty look.

Nope. He doesn't get to die happy between my thighs.

Dex's face turned serious, reaffirming what his brother was saying. Both men glanced my way. I was sure it was to see me react to their insult. All they got was a cocked eyebrow.

Years ago, I would have shown how pissed I was at Gunner's words. Probably by stabbing him in the thigh. But being a woman in the cartel was a bitch, so I'd grown a thick skin. Their words didn't affect me.

However, these two dumbasses hadn't considered Sergio might not take their insult well. He didn't become the kingpin because he said please and thank you. And he definitely didn't accept someone insulting him and his ability to run his operation. I took many men's fingers as payment for their disrespect to Sergio.

Sergio leaned forward in his chair, resting his forearms on the desk. When he responded, his tone was so icy it felt like the temperature in the room dropped five degrees.

"I will let your comment slide, Gunner, out of respect for your president and the fact that you don't know Los Muertos or me well. But this will be the only time I grant you that blessing. Be sure to never question my word again." Sergio paused for Gunner's reaction and only continued speaking when the sergeant at arms gave a cut nod. "I agreed to this partnership with your club, so don't insult me by assuming I would have you working with anyone other than the best person for the job. Her not having a dick doesn't make her less capable. Ryan's been running our gun smuggling operation for the last three years out of Lotería."

Gunner's eyebrows pinched in confusion, which didn't surprise me. Mario was the name attached to Los Muertos's arms dealing—even if he wasn't the one doing any of the work. At least not here in Tucson. That was all me. I got to sort through all the shit, and Mario got to claim the credit. But I didn't care. This moment alone was worth the secret.

"Understood. In that case, let's move forward with this meeting." Gunner sat back in his seat and draped an arm over the back of the chair in an attempt to look relaxed. But I could see the tension in his muscular back and the popping of his jaw. The man was pissed to be working with me. Too bad for him—I didn't give a fuck.

Locking eyes with me, he continued, "I want to see the way you run this operation. See what tweaks we need to make. You can tell me what you know, and I'm sure Sergio or Mario can fill in the rest," he said.

I crossed my arms over my chest and watched as Gunner's eyes dipped to my cleavage, causing me to smirk.

Men. So easily distracted.

"You can ask Sergio or Mario whatever the fuck you want. The answer you're going to get is to reach out to me." My hands hit the desk and I leaned toward the infuriating man, pissed that I had this urge to get closer to him. "You may not like it, *mi güerito*, but I run this area. So the rumors I know you've heard about Los Muertos's operation…it was someone with a pussy pushing all those guns," I asserted.

The smile he gave me while rubbing a hand across his jaw made me squirm. Now I got what Nikki meant when she said a man's hand could be the biggest turn-on. Images of those tattoo-covered hands wandering my body kept popping into my brain. The fucker was an asshole—and annoyingly sexy.

"All right, *Brujita*. You show me yours, and I'll show you mine."

Fuck. A white boy speaking Spanish was hot when his pronunciation was on point.

Gunner licked his bottom lip, trying his hardest to keep his eyes on mine. I was now painfully aware of how much cleavage was showing. Fuckin' Nikki and her bright ideas. But two could play the eye-fucking game.

I looked down to where his bulge was clearly straining against his zipper, taking my time bringing my eyes back to his.

"Try to keep up, big boy."

With that, I pushed off the desk and made my way out the office door, knowing they would follow. I was still within range when Dex finally spoke.

"Fuck. The sexual tension between you two is like fuckin' foreplay."

My soaked thong seemed to agree with his observation.

Gunner

This whole damn meeting was not going how I thought it would. How the fuck did we not know Ryan, the goddamn cartel's arms dealer for Tucson, was a woman? And not just any woman, a fucking sex goddess of a woman. My dick had been hard from the moment I saw the sway of her hips and the perfect curve of her ass. But then she spoke, and I about came in my pants like a teenager. I didn't think I was a masochist. But the verbal lashing she gave me when I questioned her ability to do her job was such a turn-on.

"Get your eyes off her ass, Dex." I growled at my brother when I caught his eyes dipping down.

He let out a snicker beside me while holding his hands up in surrender.

I didn't like the possessive feelings I was having for this woman. I was here to do a job, and I couldn't afford a distraction. I was hoping her operation would be shit, which would piss me off enough to get me to move on. Plus, it would mean I'd be too busy fixing her fuck-ups to pay attention to her. I was willing to bet she handed over the reins to some other person in Los Muertos. Sure, Mario might have left her in charge, but she probably just delegated to someone else. I watched her long, lean body stride down the hallway to another set of stairs.

Yeah, that body wasn't doing manual labor. I bet her hands were as soft as her curves—they'd never seen hard work. Ryan must have been a figurehead. She sat up in that pretty office, looking down at the club while drinking margaritas on the rocks. Paid to look pretty, and when shit hit the fan, I was sure all she did was find people to fix it. Or went crying to Mario.

I bristled at that last thought. What was her relationship with Mario? Sergio seemed to be close to Ryan, but it felt familial. I knew Sergio didn't have any living relatives besides his son, so they weren't family by blood. Did Mario view her as a little sister? And why the fuck did the thought of him not seeing her as a sister piss me off?

At the bottom of the stairwell, Ryan came to a stop at a thick door with a keypad. "Okay, boys, try not to fuck anything up, please." With that, she opened the door and walked into what could only be described as a warehouse of sorts. Shelves of liquor lined the walls. Crates were neatly stacked in one portion, and there was a large bay door for trucks to back up to. Coming to a halt in the middle of the room, she turned to face us.

"This is where we accept shipments." She nodded over to the stacked crates. "Lotería is a legitimate business, and we move large numbers when it comes to alcohol. So no one bats an eye at all the deliveries we receive weekly."

Walking over to a crate, she pried off the top and pulled out a bottle of Anejo tequila. "To our club-goers, we are known for our specialty tequilas from Mexico. And to the criminal underground…" She reached her hand back into the crate, pulling something else out. "We are known for our excellent handguns."

Her grin made me want to bend her over and smack her ass for being cocky.

Dex let out a whistle. "Well, damn. You do know what you're doing."

Ryan gave a blinding smile at the compliment before continuing with her explanation of their operation.

"You probably know that Los Muertos is the largest cartel in Mexico. We run out of Sinaloa specifically, and that's where these crates come from. When I took over Lotería, I changed it from fully nude to partial so we could serve liquor."

She looked at me before continuing. Probably to make sure I was paying attention. She didn't realize I couldn't give my attention to anything other than her, even if I wanted to. And it was beginning to piss me off.

"Liquor sales and half-naked people bring in a lot of cash, so after we started becoming more popular, I began laundering money out of Lotería for Los Muertos."

I moved closer. The moment I was beside her, she flipped the firearm, handing me the grip. My calloused fingertips brushed her soft skin, and I saw her slight shudder.

Good to know I'm not the only one being affected here.

"You guys weren't laundering money out of here before? Usually, strip clubs have plenty of cash to clean the dirty money with." Dex's question got Ryan's attention, giving me a moment to look over the gun and mentally try to pull myself out of wanting to fuck her on these crates.

"They were, but I don't take a cut of the girls' money. They keep everything they make on the stages and tips." Her tone left no room for discussion on the matter. This subject had clearly created arguments in the past. "They put in the work, so they deserve to keep the cash. I knew selling Mexican tequila would provide the perfect cover for receiving regular shipments. So I started moving firearms out of here."

That statement made me look up at her.

"You decided to run guns?" I asked incredulously.

She gave one quick nod in response. "Up until you guys, men I trusted moved the guns from here to other markets. Being popular in arms-dealing circles is a blessing and a curse. I have the clientele, but not enough people I trust to move the weapons. I have a connection as far as New York. She handles the East Coast and international side. I just have to get it to her. But the fucking Reapers decided they wanted in on it. So far, I have been able to keep their fucking noses out of my business. And hopefully, with you now running the guns, they'll back off." There was clear disdain in her voice when she spoke about the Reapers MC.

None of us commented on the elephant in the room, which was that the Reapers were likely to take this partnership as a slap in the face and retaliate. Dex once again broke the silence. Quiet made the fucker nervous. Said it was because that was when the demons took over—in the silence.

"How have you managed to keep them out of your business?"

My cock twitched at the bloodthirsty smile that touched her lips.

"I beat anyone who needs a reminder with a bat. Fucked-up faces make good messengers," she replied.

My mouth fell open at the nonchalant shrug she gave after her answer. And before I could touch on her response, the door we entered was pushed open, and another hulk of a man walking in.

"Damn. Do you only employ giants here?" I hadn't meant to ask the question aloud. Ryan looked over at me and rolled her eyes.

"So says the six-fucking-two man who looks like he could take out a house."

I stepped closer to her, our bodies barely touching, and whispered in her ear, "So...you were eye fucking me upstairs."

Her head whipped around, making it so our faces were inches apart, a determined look on her face. She wasn't going to stand for my bullshit.

"How's your cock feeling against your zipper right now? I imagine that isn't going to feel great on the ride home." She tilted her head to the side and gave a condescending smile.

Damn, was she ballsy.

My tongue ran along my bottom lip before I responded. "You know. You have quite the mouth on you."

Ryan moved even closer, cutting the distance between our faces in half. She peeked at my lips before moving back to my eyes.

"I can do a lot of things with my mouth, Gunner," she replied, her warm breath caressing my lips.

My heart nearly jumped out of my chest. The tension between us was so thick, it felt like I was suffocating. There was bound to be half-moon-shaped marks on my palms from how tightly I clenched my fists to keep my hands from tangling in her hair and slamming those pouty lips on mine.

She pulled back; the distance between our bodies made me frown, and my scowl only deepened when I thought about the reaction I was having to her. I needed to find a way to banish this woman from my thoughts.

"Too bad you'll never get a chance to experience those other things."

She flipped me off before walking over to where her employee had entered the warehouse.

Dex's large body appeared beside me. "Dude. You're fucked. You're going to have blue balls for a long fucking time working alongside her." When I turned to look at him, he was adjusting himself again. My elbow landed in his ribs, which just caused him to laugh.

"Quit looking at her ass so I don't have to watch you fondle your junk," I hissed.

Another chuckle fell from Dex's lips. "Oh, it's not just her ass that has me *fondling* my dick. I told you. Watching you two is like foreplay. I'll have to rub one out before the ride back." Nodding my way, he added on. "Looks like you will, too."

Ryan walked back over. "Boys, you're going to have to see yourselves out. Some shit's come up that I need to take care of. Sergio already set up things with your president. I'm supposed to stop by the clubhouse on Friday. So I'll see you then. Adios." She turned on her heel to walk away.

"Wait. Why are you coming to the clubhouse?" I called out.

This was news to me. And while the thought of her on my territory was appealing, that feeling quickly diminished when images of her being eye-fucked by a bunch of assholes there popped into my head. I knew that would happen because the weekends were always parties at the clubhouse. So that meant club bunnies, strippers, hang-arounds, and a bunch of other fuckers would all be there.

She didn't bother stopping her exit, opting to throw her answer over her shoulder. "*No sé.* Ask your president. He's the one who told Sergio he wanted me to come. Probably to make sure your winning personality didn't fuck up the partnership. Robert will show you guys out."

"Hey," I called after her once more. "Don't wear anything like you're wearing tonight on Friday."

That comment made her pause. She turned around with a look of confusion and peered down at her outfit before meeting my eyes. With a mischievous smirk, she blew me a kiss and flipped me off before walking out of sight. Robert, as Ryan called him, cracked up.

"Hey ése, word of advice on Brujita there. Her bite is just as bad as her bark. Worse, actually. That's a woman who doesn't need a man to stand in front of her. She needs one who knows when to stand beside her, behind her, or kneel in front of her. *¿Entiendes?* You do those things for her, and she'll gift you her submission and loyalty. And that woman is loyal…to a fault." I looked over at Robert, taken aback by his statement. The last part was said under his breath, but I still caught it. And the implication that someone was taking advantage of her made my jaw tick. But before I could form a response, Dex jumped in.

"What kind of jedi love shit was that, Robert? Damn. That had me all up in me feels." He thrust his phone out toward the guy. "Imma need you to write down some brilliant shit like that so I can use it when I'm sexting chicks."

I rolled my eyes at Dex. But Robert's words played on repeat in my head.

I used the whole ride to the compound to try to sort out what the fuck I was feeling. There was a lot to think about after that meeting with Los Muertos. Not including the Mexican beauty. It dawned on me why Ryan would be required to come to the clubhouse Friday night, and I was not happy about it.

The moment my bike was parked, I was off and striding into the clubhouse. Dex hadn't even fully come to a stop, but he called after me.

"Gunner. It's club rules, and Sergio would have known when he switched from Mario to Ryan. You can't do anything about it, so don't do anything stupid. You know what's at stake."

I clenched my teeth at his words, knowing he was right, but I was still pissed off. I reined in my anger before walking up to talk to Pres over at the bar. Disrespecting him would get me a bloody lip and black eye at best, and a shallow grave out back at worst.

Taking a slow sip of his whiskey, Pres looked me up and down, taking in my demeanor.

"Watch yourself, Gunner. I may give you more rope than most, but that just means there's more available for you to hang yourself with."

I waved a hand, dismissing his concern. "Yeah, yeah, I know." I plopped my ass down on the stool and signaled for a beer. "But did you know Sergio's new man is a woman?"

Pres cocked an eyebrow at my statement.

So he hadn't known.

I took a beer out of a prospect's hands. I needed alcohol in me as quickly as possible, and I didn't care if I was being a dick about it.

"I heard rumblings there was a woman Sergio and Mario kept rather close. I thought it was Mario's bitch or something." My grip tightened around the bottle at hearing Ryan be referred to as a bitch. But I didn't say anything. A reaction from me would raise questions about why was pissed. Questions I didn't have an answer to.

"I didn't realize she was actually involved in the cartel side of shit," he added.

Nodding my head, I took a swig of my beer before launching into the specifics of the meeting.

"Made complete asses of ourselves, Pres. Sergio seemed to enjoy that, though. We thought *Ryan* was going to be someone with a dick. So when a woman barged in"—I took another swig while shaking my head at the memory—"I told her she could take her sweet ass out to get our drinks and remember her place before coming back in." My rough hand raked over my face, recalling her fierce look when I was giving orders thinking she was Nikki. I heard a burst of laughter from my left and looked over at Pres, who seemed to be just as amused as Sergio'd been. *Fucking old pricks.*

After a moment, he settled down enough to continue the conversation. "So, does she know how to run an operation, or are we going to have to do a fuck ton of work before we can even attempt running the first shipment?"

I sighed and pinched the bridge of my nose because I wasn't entirely sure what that answer was. "Well, I don't know how much she actually does or if she just delegates and sits her cute ass up in her office. But Los Muertos's setup was impressive. They hide the guns in tequila crates, and because they run a popular Latin club known for its selection of Mexican tequilas...no one bats an eye at the truckloads from Mexico they receive."

I looked over to see Pres nodding his head in approval. "Well, I guess we'll see what this Ryan chick is made of come Friday night."

I groaned at his response. "Pres, you're not really going to make her participate on Friday, are you? I mean, you didn't see her. She's not cut from the same cloth as us. She was wearing a white suit to the meeting, God dammit. I don't even know how she got involved with Los Muertos, but I bet she's basically their interior designer and club manager. It probably just gets her pussy wet to play arms dealer."

Cutting me a glare, a hint of a threat in his tone, he said, "Gunner, every fuckin' person involved is required to participate. It's in our bylaws, and I told Sergio about them before making the deal. Made sure he knew exactly what would be required of them if we partnered. The loyalty and toughness they would have to show. So, if she's as prissy as you say, then Sergio is sending her to the wolves on purpose."

He tapped his fingertips on the bar top, clearly in the middle of a thought.

"In fact, stay close to her on Friday. I want to figure out why she's being led to slaughter and why we're being used for that." He paused, looking me in the eye. "Maybe Friday was just a convenient opportunity because Sergio knew about it before pulling Mario." Pres pushed to stand up. "Fuck, maybe his son is just a pussy."

Ryan

I peered out my windshield at the chain-link fence in front of me. I'd done my research, unlike knuckleheads one and two. The Skeletons had a ten-foot-tall chain-link fence surrounding the entire compound with razor wire along the top. A rolling fence that was constantly manned was the only way in or out. And if you did get in, you had to contend with a clubhouse built to withstand a goddamned war filled with armed bikers.

I pulled up to the gate and rolled down my window.

"Damn, sexy, this thing yours? How many blow jobs did you have to give to get this?"

I raised an eyebrow at the child who stood in front of me. He couldn't be older than eighteen, and I knew I had to shave more upper lip hair off than he did.

"First of all, don't call me sexy. Don't call any woman you just randomly met sexy. Learn our fucking names first.

It's not a turn-on like you think it is. And second off, 'this thing' is a fully restored '67 Impala. Be respectful."

Babyface stood there with a shocked look before recovering. His tone was no longer flirty.

"Well, who the fuck are you? This is a closed event, bitch."

The audacity of some men.

"Oh, so I was only going to be let in if I sucked your dick? Or were you going to get a blow job and then turn me away? Fuck you, kid. I hope you catch the clap. And *I am* the fucking event," I seethed at him. "Name's Ryan. I'm with Los Muertos."

His face went through a multitude of expressions and colors. He was bright red and pissed when I told him off, but the color drained from his face when I dropped my name and what organization I was a part of.

"Don't bother saying shit. Just open the gate." I rolled up my window and turned up Slush Puppy's "Eat Spit!" When the gate opened, I pulled forward and drove toward where a grouping of other cars was parked.

After handling another rat problem the day I'd met with Gunner and Dex, I'd spoken to Sergio about how we felt about our new partners. I thought Gunner had a fucking attitude problem and was a total misogynist, but…he would be good for the job. When Sergio decided that Los Muertos should go through with the partnership, he filled me in on what my Friday night activities were going to be.

He had me worried at first when he said I would have to prove my loyalty and there was no way out of participating. I thought maybe he would tell me I had to join in on an orgy or something. Which, whatever floats people's boat, but I wasn't the orgy type of girl. So I was both relieved and stoked when Sergio said I had to participate in their fight night. The Skeletons had a bylaw that stated new members and club partners were required to fight in their ring. They felt that agreeing to potentially get your shit rocked proved commitment. They weren't wrong. Weak men like Anthony would have never agreed to those stakes.

Sergio said he knew I lived for this shit, so he never bothered mentioning it before the meeting.

He was right. When you live on the streets, you quickly learn that you better know how to fight if you want to survive. And as a scrawny kid, I had to know how to fight people bigger than me. My thirst for blood made me vicious, and I used my speed to my advantage. Not to mention that getting the shit beat out of me a few times gave me durability. When Sergio took me in, he encouraged me to embrace my desire for violence, so I learned to fight properly.

I made Los Muertos good money in our underground fight circuit. Sergio took a lot of pleasure in shocking people with a female fighter who could take men down. And while on paper it might have looked like Sergio used me as a shiny toy to show off, I never felt that way. It always felt like a proud father-figure type shit. If your father wanted a bloodthirsty daughter, that was.

But I was excited for tonight. One, because a good fight kept the demons contained. But more importantly, I couldn't wait to see the look on Gunner's face when I stepped out of the ring. Based on how his misogynistic ass treated me at the meeting, I figured he didn't think I would go through with this. He probably thought I didn't even know what I was in for tonight.

Let's have a little fun with that. Play "helpless damsel," then kick someone's ass.

I stepped out, taking a moment to check my surroundings. Sergio said fight nights were held once a month for the club. It was how members worked out shit between one another. All patched members attended, and they opened up the compound to any hang-arounds who wanted to come.

Fighting, fucking, and booze. What more could anyone want?

The smokey scent of bonfires hung in the air, and I could see people gathered around, their laughter hitting my ears. I made my way over to the crowds, trying to spot where the cage was. I didn't know if we would be fighting outside in the dirt or if they had a more official setup. Not that it mattered to me; I'd fought in all sorts of locations. But asphalt hurt like a bitch to grapple on.

Glances started coming my way as I approached. The men looked at me like I was a new toy, and the women looked at me like I was a new threat. My hands curled into fists to avoid flipping them off.

"Don't piss off the rowdy crowd of bikers, Ryan. Shooting your new allies is frowned upon," I mumbled under my breath, sighing in relief when I spotted a familiar face.

It was easy to spot Dex in the mass of people. The dude was a fucking brick shit house. Gunner and Dex thought Robert was big, but apparently, neither of them ever looked in the mirror.

"Dexy boy. Good to see you again," I called out.

His head whipped around, a murderous look on his face. Apparently, he thought someone was disrespecting his road name, but the look was replaced with a goofy smile when he saw me approach. The guy was a puzzle. Every warning bell inside me told me he was dangerous, and not only because of his size. But he gave off some serious golden retriever energy. Robert said Dex had made him type out texts to a long list of girls.

Men. Although Nikki wasn't much better.

"How do I get myself alcohol around here? Preferably some that hasn't been spiked with anti-freeze from these bitches giving me death glares." I gave him my interpretation of a sweet smile. Which probably didn't look anything like how I imagined.

He let out a genuine laugh, causing heads to turn. Ignoring the glances, he handed me the unopened beer in his hand.

"Ryan, where the hell ya been, loca?" he asked.

Now it was my turn to laugh. "Dexy, did you just quote *Twilight*?"

74

The goof wiggled his eyebrows. "What? You think that because I'm in a biker gang, I'm uncultured? Of course I quoted that cinematic masterpiece," he scoffed.

I opened my mouth to answer when the hair on the back of my neck stood on end and my nipples hardened underneath my sports bra. My body knew who had shown up behind me, and it was a goddamned traitor since it thought we should be excited to see Gunner again. His hot breath hit the shell of my ear, sending chills down my spine. I clamped my mouth shut, trying to keep my moan in.

"I see you followed my instructions and wore something more practical," he whispered. I swore I felt his nose brush along the column of my neck, but I whipped around before my brain could register whether that was wishful thinking or reality. "You seemed to like my outfit just fine, if I remember correctly, Gunner. By the way, how was your ride home? Comfortable?" I hadn't bothered to step back, and now I was close enough to feel the rumble of his chest as he chuckled.

"Do you always let someone else fix the problems you cause?" He gave me a haughty smile.

I bristled at his question. It felt like there was more to it than just flirtatious innuendos. Gunner didn't think I knew what I was doing. He still thought Sergio was fucking with the Skeletons and not taking this partnership seriously.

"Well, I figured you would be the best person for the job, because with that winning personality of yours, I'm sure the only action your dick sees is from your hand," I threw back, a rush of heat pooling between my legs at the flash of challenge in his eyes.

My eyes trailed down his fit body, taking in the way his shirt was stretching over his biceps as he folded his arms over his chest. The minute my eyes hit his muscular thighs, I looked away.

Why the hell am I excited about his response?

But before he could answer, skanky red nails appeared on Gunner's chest.

"Gunner…"

The whiny voice made me scrunch up my nose in distaste. Who fucking talked like that? And his name didn't end with twenty *r*'s.

A bleach-blond head popped out from behind Gunner. Her tits were barely contained in her crop top, and I wasn't sure why she bothered wearing shorts. I worked with half-naked women for a living, but somehow this chick made them all look like church nuns. Something about her instantly put me on guard.

Gunner plucked her hand off his chest, dropping it back to her side like it had burned him. It was apparent he didn't want anything to do with her. Or at least he didn't want anything to do with her right now.

"What do you need, Lolli?" He didn't bother looking at her when he asked the question. His eyes hadn't left mine, and we were still only inches from one another. I raised my eyebrows at her when she pressed herself to Gunner's side and looked at me with a nasty glare before answering him.

"The girls and I are concerned about the new girl here." The whiny tone of her voice could have made my ears bleed. She turned her gaze to Gunner before talking about me as if I wasn't right fucking there. "Kandy said that when she was giving Roy a blow job, he mentioned that this whore here came with a Los Muertos member. She said she's with some guy named Ryan. And now she's trying to get at our men!" Lolli looked back at me with a victorious smirk. I had to work seriously hard at not bursting out in laughter at the fool she was making of herself.

But Dex didn't have as much luck, and he let out a roar of laughter. "This is great. Ryan, you should come every weekend!"

Lolli's eyes became the size of saucers when she heard Dex use my name. And since I wasn't above being a petty bitch, I shoved my hand in her direction and decided to introduce myself.

"Hi, I'm Ryan. Los Muertos's arms dealer. Roy probably

said all that because he was pissed that I told him I hoped he caught the clap. And I can't take a man who was never yours." I used the same sickly sweet voice Nikki used when she was destroying men's egos. It seemed to work well on bitchy whores too.

Gunner untangled himself from her second attempt at latching on to him and walked over to my side. He placed his arm around my waist and pulled me into the crook of his side. My eyebrows wanted to shoot up into my hairline, but I kept my face neutral. Not wanting bottle blonde to see my reaction.

"Fuck off, Lolli. And if I catch you calling Ryan a whore again, I'll be sure you get banned from all club functions."

I bit my bottom lip at Gunner's words and the butterflies they caused. He probably only said those things to protect the alliance between Los Muertos and The Skeletons of Society, but my hormones didn't get that memo. Gunner pulled me away from Lolli and Dex, keeping his arm around me.

"Sorry about that. Lolli is like a goddamned leech. She wants to be an old lady so badly that she will try anything. She probably thought bringing gossip about you to me would be an in," he said. I nodded my head in response, surprised he had even bothered explaining what had just gone down.

"Come on. We have to meet Pres. He'll explain why you have to be here tonight." The irritation in his voice spoke volumes, and I was almost touched that he was worried about me. But then he opened his mouth and inserted his foot again.

"Just so you know, I tried to get you out of this. I don't think you're cut out for it." Dropping his arm, he continued walking—leaving me to follow behind him.

Fucking misogynist.

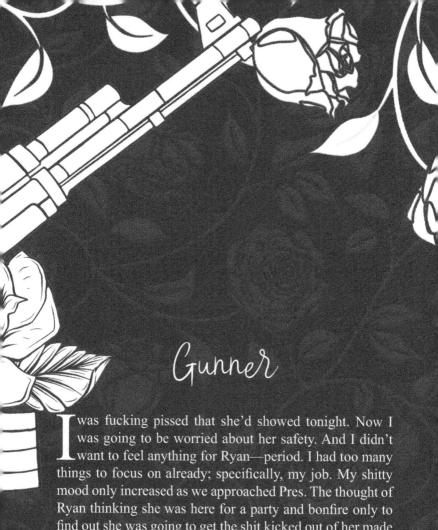

Gunner

I was fucking pissed that she'd showed tonight. Now I was going to be worried about her safety. And I didn't want to feel anything for Ryan—period. I had too many things to focus on already; specifically, my job. My shitty mood only increased as we approached Pres. The thought of Ryan thinking she was here for a party and bonfire only to find out she was going to get the shit kicked out of her made my skin itch with anger. I'd watched her with Dex. Her demeanor was calm and casual, which told me she had no clue that she would be forced to fight tonight. But I couldn't do a damn thing to stop it from happening.

After Pres filled her in on what was going to happen, I was going to try to give her a crash course on how to throw a punch. Which would do fuck all for her, but I could at least show her how to block her face and turtle up. I even bought her a bottle of the expensive as fuck tequila I saw in her office. She would need it for her nerves before the fight and definitely for her injuries after. Dex wouldn't stop giving me shit for it, but I could tell he was worried about her too. As much as I thought the princess had no business being in this world, I couldn't help but have some type of feelings for her. I didn't know what those feelings were, but the woman had been on my mind since I'd met her.

"So you're the woman who has Gunner all out of sorts," Pres called out, pulling me to the present.

Without hesitation, Ryan strode forward and reached out to shake his hand.

"I don't know anything about Gunner's issues, but I'm the woman who will be running Los Muertos's end of our partnership."

Pres smirked and nodded his head in appreciation of her answer before his tone turned serious. "Speaking of the partnership, our MC has a set of bylaws we follow to the letter. One of those bylaws states that any newcomers, those patching in or not, have to prove their loyalty and commitment." He made eye contact with me over Ryan's shoulder before continuing. He wanted me to take in her response when he told her she would be fighting. I moved to Pres's side to watch her beautiful face. I wasn't looking forward to seeing the look of horror flash across it when Pres dropped the bomb on her.

Ryan nodded in understanding. "And what will I be required to do to prove myself?" She was still calm. I had this nagging feeling that maybe she was too calm. But I didn't know her well enough to know if that was because she was clueless or acting.

"Well, it's proven with blood. You either spill yours or your opponent's. Unfortunately, when this was all set up, we were under the impression that you were a man, so…you're going to be fighting Torque," Pres said.

My head whipped to the side to look at Pres. I knew she would have to fight, but I never imagined Pres would put her up against a patched member. We had plenty of club bunnies who fought on fight nights. But I couldn't say anything to protest this now. That would appear that I was disrespecting my president. Dex chimed up from behind Ryan.

"Pres…"

Pres raised his hand to silence Dex from continuing. "Rules are rules, boys."

My fists tightened, and my jaw hurt from how tightly I was clenching my teeth. This was worse than I thought it was going to be. Ryan was going to be a bloody mess on the floor after this. That image made me feel like I was teetering on going into a murderous rage. I didn't know how I would keep myself from jumping into that ring once Torque started throwing punches. For his sake, he better pull his fucking hits and wrap the fight up quickly once he saw he was fighting a woman. One who clearly shouldn't be in the ring.

I looked over at Ryan's face, expecting to see horror or tears. But all I was met with was the sight of her biting her bottom lip. The woman was so out of her element that she didn't even realize how scared she should be right now. Maybe that was a good thing.

"It's okay, Dexy. This should be fun," she commented.

I let out a scoff at her flippant response to the pile of shit just dropped at her feet. I couldn't help but voice my opinion about how naive she was.

"You think getting your ass handed to you will be fun? You're not going to like what it feels like to do actual work, Brujita." I crossed my arms over my chest, the fabric of my shirt straining against my arms.

I expected angry words, or maybe she would finally realize how bad this was and cry, but instead, Ryan just winked at me.

"Gunner, you and Dex go bring her to the cage. Get her set up. Wrap her hands," Pres ordered. I grunted before I walked forward and gripped the upper part of Ryan's arm, pulling her toward the ring.

"Hey, Neanderthal, quick dragging me around. I'm capable of following you on my own just fine."

I ignored her protests and continued to pull her over

toward her corner of the outdoor arena. When we got there, I pushed her down onto the folding chair and grabbed her hand to start wrapping it.

"Listen, I knew you would have to fight, but I had no clue it would be against Torque. I'll teach you how to protect yourself as best you can. Your goal is to take the least amount of damage as possible. Do you know how to throw a punch?" When she didn't answer right away, I looked up from my task. Her head had a slight tilt, and she looked at me with an expression I couldn't quite place. I softened my tone, thinking the reality might be setting in.

"Ryan, I need answers, babe. Can you throw a punch? I don't need you breaking your hand in there too." My thumb rubbed across the top of her knuckles. She wouldn't even get the opportunity to land a punch on Torque, but I didn't want to tell her that.

"Gunner, I think I'll be okay."

Her voice was soft, and it felt like she was trying to console *me*. God, she had no clue how bad this was about to be. Shaking my head, I pulled out the tequila I'd bought for her from under the chair and pushed it into her hands.

"Take a swig. It will help with the nerves. And watch what I do with my hands when Dex tries to punch me. Okay?"

Dex and I demonstrated some basic blocking. We both knew that it was more for moral support than anything else. The girl was fucking screwed, and my stomach was in knots over it. Before I was ready, I heard Pres get into the ring and begin announcing the main event.

"Are you ready for fight fucking night? We have a very special fight for you tonight. A Los Muertos member thinks that she is worthy of riding alongside a Skeleton!"

The roar from the crowd was deafening, causing me to wince. Just what she needed, more intimidation.

"So…do I get a walk-out song or some shit?" she asked.

"Ryan, fucking focus," I barked. "You need to be thinking about staying alive, not what T-Swift song you'll

82

play."

She smirked at my answer, not even remotely fazed. "T-Swift, Gunner? Someone is a fan if that's what you call her."

I threw my arms up in exasperation.

This girl is fucking clueless, and this is going to be a bloodbath.

My attention was drawn to the cage. Torque walked in, hyping the crowd up for the fight. He was our newest patched member, but he had been around the club since he was a kid. He wasn't as big as Dex and me, but at six feet and two hundred pounds, he was massive compared to Ryan. The woman looked like she wasn't much bigger than five-two and a buck thirty.

"Ryan, I want you to…" I turned to find the chair empty. Maybe she had gotten smart and decided to run. That would solve so many of my problems. She should go home and tell Sergio to fuck himself for setting her up. But Dex caught my eye and pointed to the entrance of the cage. There she was, standing at the opening with a look of determination that took me by surprise.

"Do you think she's crazy? Like certifiably? Because that chick is way too calm for someone walking in to get their ass beat."

I didn't have an answer for Dex. I watched as Ryan gave Torque a cocky smile before stripping off the oversized sweatshirt she had been wearing, and my eyes widened in surprise.

"Holy fuck. She's jacked," I whispered to no one in particular, but I saw Dex nodding his head in agreement. The woman was built like an athlete, something I had managed to miss since both times I had seen her, most of her body had been covered. Standing there at the entrance, she looked like a fighter.

Ryan glanced over to me and blew a kiss before walking toward Torque at the center of the cage. I couldn't hear what they were saying to each other, but it was evident that they were talking shit. The ref gave them the ring rules—there were essentially none. The only things not allowed were eye gouges and nut shots. Otherwise, it was all fair game. Torque and Ryan bumped fists, signally the start of the fight, and my fingers gripped the edge of the cage so tight that my knuckles were white. It felt like my heart would burst out of my chest. I didn't give a fuck what the rules were. If I thought I needed to go in there for her, I would.

Everything be damned.

The two began circling each other, waiting for the other to give an opening. I was so absorbed in seeing if I needed to intervene that it didn't even dawn on me how that move alone meant she knew what she was doing in the ring.

Ryan faked a punch before moving to Torque's inside and landing two quick jabs to his jaw before dancing back out of his reach. The crowd lost their shit. Torque shook his head and gave Ryan a bloody smile before attempting to land some punches of his own. Every time he threw something, she managed to block or turn out of reach. Frustrated, Torque rushed her.

"Fuck, if he gets her on her back, it's over."

I moved to get into the cage, but Dex put a hand on my shoulder and nodded for me to keep watching. Ryan sprawled and stopped the takedown. Torque wasn't expecting that from this tiny girl, and she didn't waste the opportunity to land a knee to his face before moving back out. Neither Dex nor I could keep our eyes off the two in the cage. No one in the crowd could; the fight wasn't expected to go like this.

"Fuck, Dex. I was all wrong about this chick."

My brother let out a grunt in agreement. "I'd fucking say so."

Torque caught Ryan with a right hook she couldn't completely block. My blood ran cold when I saw it connect. She looked up and smiled, licking the blood off. I couldn't recall the last time I had been as turned on as I was while I watched her pink tongue poke out and swipe across that pouty lip—a bloodthirsty look in her eyes. The crowd roared, and money was being exchanged now that this fight was turning out to be interesting.

Torque landed a leg kick that forced Ryan to change her stance, making it evident that he'd injured her. He followed up with a kick to her other leg, but Ryan blocked it with a knee and rushed forward. The move looked reckless and caused me to cry out.

"Babe, what the fuck are you doing?"

"Oh, it's babe now?" Dex asked.

I didn't bother answering his verbal jab, flipping him off while watching the scramble that broke out. But faster than my eyes could track, Ryan somehow ended up latched onto Torque's back. Her legs were wrapped around his waist while her arms were around his throat. I heard Dex take a sharp inhale.

"What the fuck is it, Dex?" I asked, not willing to take my eyes off her and risk missing anything.

"She's got him in a goddamned standing rear-naked choke. Holy fuck, Gunner. Your girl is the real deal. That shit doesn't happen by chance. That's fucking high-level grappling she's doing."

My chest filled with pride over this woman I barely knew—this violent goddess. How did I ever think she was a princess playing cartel member? Dex continued with his cage-side commentary.

"The cocky fucker isn't going to tap." He huffed a laugh. "He thinks he can outlast her strength, but she's got that bitch in deep. She's going to put him to sleep."

On cue, Torque dropped unconscious.

I didn't know how I got there, but I was inside the cage in the next instant, lifting Ryan into my arms and carrying her out.

"Look at me, babe." I demanded.

Ryan's eyes found mine, her pupils blown from the adrenaline coursing through her. Blood still coated her split lip. My tongue ran across it without thinking the action through, lapping up the blood. A moan slipped from her mouth, causing my cock to get even harder than it already was. I wanted to know what other noises I could pull from her. Needing distance between us, I sat her down on the chair I had used when wrapping her hands—when she let me believe she was about to be pulverized in that cage, knowing full well she could fucking fight.

"You lied to me, Ryan," I growled out. "You didn't tell me you could fight." I grabbed her chin and made sure she was paying attention to what I had to say. "All actions have consequences, babe."

She gave a sly smile at my comments. "I didn't lie, Gunner. I just let you continue with your misogynistic bullshit."

My face dropped a bit at her response. I hadn't meant to come across that way. But if I was being truthful, the feeling of Ryan not being cut out for this life had stemmed from her being a woman.

"Hmm. I'll work on that. It's obvious you're more than capable. And that I need to get to know my new partner better," I mumbled, kneeling between her thighs and pulling out the tequila.

She started to argue until my words registered in her head. She gave me a strange look, like a man had never admitted being wrong to her before.

"Now, open your mouth, Ryan." I reached up and grabbed her jaw. My dick twitched at the heat in her eyes as I held her mouth open.

Fuck. The things I could do to this woman.

I brought the tequila bottle up to her lips and poured a shot in. Never breaking eye contact as I slid my hand down to her throat.

"Swallow, Ryan." My voice was thick with lust, and I caught the squirm she did in her chair.

I felt her throat contract, and the desire for her to swallow something else hit me with full force. For the second time that night, I leaned forward and licked her lips

before pulling back and standing up.
This woman was going to wreck me.

Ryan

I was definitely tipsy.

It was hard not to want to join in on the festivities of fight night, and everyone kept bringing me drinks in congratulations of the win. I didn't bother telling them that the fight was a cakewalk compared to some of the ones I had been in for Los Muertos. Torque was a good sport about the ass beating I had given him, and to his credit, he did land a good punch to my face. My tongue prodded the busted lip he'd left me, and I would have gnarly bruises from his leg kicks. He asked me if I could teach him some grappling. But my handler growled *no* at him before I could respond. That landed Gunner an elbow to the ribs.

My mind wandered to the sexy as sin biker lording over me. He had the fucking audacity to pour me a shot of my favorite tequila while looking like a wet dream. I thought I would die of horniness when he gave it to me while kneeling between my legs with his hand on my throat.

His moods were giving me whiplash. When I arrived at the party, Gunner had looked like he wanted to throw me back into my car and demand I leave. I thought it was because he didn't like me or want to work with me on the arms deal. But with the way the man was fussing over me, it almost felt like he was concerned. I was still trying to wrap my head around that being the case. Sure, I knew he thought I was hot and would probably fuck me if I asked him to, but he was acting like he genuinely cared.

This kind of thinking needed to be drowned out with more alcohol.

My hand wrapped around the drink on the table.

"There's no way I'm letting you have another drink, Ryan." Gunner's voice cut through the turmoil of my thoughts.

I frowned at the large tattooed hand that appeared on the neck of my beer bottle. Looking up, I was met with Gunner's grumpy face as he pulled the drink out of my hand. My eyes rolled so hard I was sure they would get stuck. This man thought he was my keeper, and that shit would need to stop right away.

"*Escucha güerito,* I run a strip club and work for the cartel. I can have a drink or two if I want. Fuck, I can have a whole case by myself," I snapped.

At some point during my rant, Gunner had moved in closer, his body now caging me in. One arm on the back of my chair, and the other on the tabletop. The hair of his mustache brushed against my ear as he spoke, so only I could hear him. He was making my teeth grind at the sensation. I didn't want the feeling to turn me on, but I was powerless to stop wondering how his mustache would feel between my thighs.

"Ryan, unless you plan on sleeping in my bed tonight, I suggest you work on sobering up so I can take you back home." His words snapped me out of my daydream, and I turned in my seat to look at him. Gunner's sober gaze met mine.

"Why would I be sleeping in your bed, Gunner? I'm sure I could sleep on a couch or floor...or someone else's room." His nostrils flared with anger at the last part of my statement. Our faces were still so close together that I could smell the mintiness of his gum on his breath when he spoke.

"Brujita, if you are ever staying over at the clubhouse, you won't be sleeping anywhere other than my bed," he growled out at me, sending heat pooling between my thighs.

No. Nope, calm down, chica.

Before I could compose myself enough to respond, Gunner shoved a water into my hand and walked away.

"Close your mouth, Ryan. Gunner may take that as an invitation to put something in it." Dex taunted.

I snapped my mouth close before flipping him off. Of course Dex had been watching that whole conversation go down. I should have known since those two were like two peas in a pod.

"Are you sure it's not your mouth that he likes to shove things into?" I hissed. "You two are always together."

Dex just snickered while wagging his eyebrows and walked away, not bothering to respond. It wasn't really fair of me to lash out at Dex, but Gunner seemed to disarm me in a way I didn't understand, and that pissed me off.

Usually, when men gave me orders or spoke to me the way Gunner did, I stabbed them. But with Gunner, it never felt disrespectful. I didn't know why he could give me directions, and it didn't make the hair on the back of my neck stand up like a cornered animal or send me into a murderous rage. The rage Gunner stirred up in me made me want to be thrown onto a bed and fucked—by Gunner.

Before I could psychoanalyze any more, my phone chirped with a text. The hair on the back of my neck did stand on end the moment I read the messages.

Mario: Are you having fun tonight, Muñeca?

Mario: I heard you fought well for me. Make sure you represent me well.

Mario: And remember who you belong to...

91

The messages came in one after another before I could even comprehend how he knew where I was or what I was doing. Mario hated to be kept waiting and would expect a text back, but I didn't even know how to respond to what I was reading.

My head snapped up from the screen to scan the area. Did Mario have someone watching me, or had he heard from Sergio that I would be fighting at the Skeletons' clubhouse tonight? It didn't look like anyone was sober enough to pay close attention to me. The only people whose attention I seemed to have were Gunner's and Bimbo Barbie from earlier—along with her legion of hoes. I considered Gunner for a moment, wondering if he was the one reporting to Mario, but decided he didn't feel like the type of man Mario could control. I would be willing to bet that the two would hate each other if they ever met. That was probably part of why Sergio had appointed me to run this whole partnership.

Mario: Muñeca.

Me: Of course, Mario.

Mario: Good answer, Muñeca. Now go home.

Mario didn't ever want to hear your opinion. He just wanted to hear your agreement. I found it was easier to give the man what he wanted. Unfortunately, it looked like he still wanted me to play the part of his little doll.

"Ryan." Gunner's deep voice pulled me out of the mental trap Mario's words had placed me in. His brows were furrowed when I looked up, and I had the strangest urge to take my thumb and smooth out the wrinkles.

"Are you okay?" His voice was soft and filled with concern.

The man was so damn observant. This would be a great trait in any other instance, but I didn't want Gunner to look at my emotions too closely.

"Yeah. Mario is checking in on things."

Standing up, I plastered on a smile that probably looked like I was in pain instead of happy. Even if Mario hadn't demanded it, it was probably time for me to go. And if Mario did have eyes and ears at the party, I would be getting text messages about Gunner standing too close or touching me. Even if it was only a few innocent brushes against my skin. My cheeks heated thinking about the few times tonight that Gunner and I hadn't had such innocent touches. Without thinking, my fingertips touched where he had leaned forward and licked the blood off my lip.

My thighs clenched at the memory. And, of course, Gunner caught the movement. He raised an eyebrow at me, and a smirk emerged on his stupidly handsome face. The prick would assume I was thinking about him.

I was. But he didn't need to know that.

His large hands wrapped around my upper arm as I went to move past him, halting me in my tracks.

"Where are you going, babe?"

"I'm going home, Gunner. It's been fun, but I'm tired, and some of us still have shit to do this weekend instead of fucking off and getting drunk with club bunnies."

He laughed at my response. I didn't know why I decided to share my irritation at the thought of leaving Gunner for the weekend with Bimbo Barbie. It wasn't like Gunner was mine to stake a claim on. I didn't even know the man. Hell, I didn't even think I liked him, yet the thought of him partying all weekend and probably having sex with club bunnies irked me.

"Naw, babe. You're not going to drive yourself home. You've been drinking, and I won't have this partnership end before it even begins. Come on."

His hand slid from my upper bicep to my hand, interlinking our fingers while he pulled me past the groups of patched brothers still drinking and partying.

"Fine, I'll let you take me home, but we're going to stop by my car first so I can grab my shit."

I thought about pulling away, especially since someone might be here to narc on me, but his calloused hand felt too good against mine. I decided to give myself this moment to enjoy it. The flimsy excuse that Gunner and I needed to get comfortable with one another since we were partners ran on a loop in my head.

You're literally gaslighting yourself so you can touch this man.

After grabbing my shit, I let Gunner lead me to his ride. He walked me up to the most beautiful Indian Scout Bobber I had ever seen. Without realizing it, I walked over to the bike and ran my hand along its sexy matte black curves.

"Good fucking Lord, this bike will get a girl wet," I mumbled.

A choking noise came from behind me. I said that louder than I had intended to. Gunner's body was at my back a few moments later, and the urge to lean into him and let his heat envelop me was overwhelming. Hot breath caressed me, making my eyelids flutter. Thank Santa Muerte it was dark and no one was around. I realized he had a thing for whispering in my ear. And it made me feel like his words weren't for everyone's benefit—they were for me. Secrets he was trusting me with.

"Maybe my girl will get you off on your way home," he purred.

It was my turn to choke on his words as tingles shot up my thighs. He wasn't wrong. I'd felt like a goddamned live wire all night. The adrenaline dump of the fight combined with tonight's interactions with Gunner had me horny and itching for relief. But I would be damned if I orgasmed on the back of Gunner's bike. I barely knew the guy. Under normal circumstances, that was what I wanted in my hookups. But I was going to have to work with him, and how the fuck would I do that if every time I looked at him, I thought about me using his bike like a giant vibrator?

His body was hovering over me, with only centimeters between us. He thought I would be intimidated or back down, but he didn't know me well. I turned to face him, not bothering to put any distance between us. My breast brushed his chest, causing his breath to hitch and my nipples to pebble.

94

Fuck, this might backfire.

"Well, at least you know you need someone, or something, else to get a woman off," I snarked as my hand patronizingly patted his chest.

What the hell does this man bench?

The growl that left his lips sent delicious chills down my spine and moisture pooling between my thighs.

"Babe, I would have no problem giving you the best orgasm of your life, right here, right now." His hand came up and threaded in my hair, pulling a small gasp from my lips. "I'll make you come so hard you won't have any doubts about my ability to get a woman off." His green eyes were full of lust before turning cold.

Gunner was thrusting a helmet into my hands in the next instant, and his voice was filled with irritation.

"Here, put this on."

I was experiencing whiplash with his sudden change in demeanor. I didn't know if I was pissed off or thankful that Gunner had enough self-control to keep us from fucking in the dirt. I was seconds away from getting on my knees and saying please—maybe Torque hit me harder than I thought. Throwing a leg over his bike, he looked back at me expectantly.

"Put the damn helmet on, Ryan, and get on the bike," he bit out.

Why the fuck did his domineering personality do something for me? This was not normal.

My answer was terse. I was irritated that I was experiencing this emotional rollercoaster for Gunner.

"This one time, Gunner. This one time, I'll let you tell me what to do. But don't get used to it."

I was fucking glad that Gunner couldn't see my face as I slid onto his bike behind him because I was sure that even my tan cheeks were showing hints of pink. A Scout Bobber wasn't the biggest of bikes, so of course, Gunner was sitting right between my legs. I was sure he could feel the heat radiating from my pussy and hoped to God I wouldn't leave a wet spot on the back of his jeans.

The fucking prick knew what this was doing to me, too, because he gave his ass a little shake. Creating friction against my clit that almost had me moaning out loud.

Want to play this game, fucker? After you were just a clit-tease? Let's play.

The leather of his cut was cold against my chest, causing my nipples to harden even more than they already were. I felt the rumble of his chest as he let out a groan when my hands trailed down his fit body, making their way to rest low down on his waist. I had to bite my lip to hold in a moan when my fingertips brushed the hard-on in his jeans.

Holy shit. This man would reach my cervix for sure.

The need to wrap my fist around it was almost unbearable. But I smirked when Gunner cleared his throat and tried to wriggle his thigh to put space between his dick and my hand before starting up his beauty.

The rumble of his Indian was so intense it did almost make me orgasm. This piece of machinery was a beauty, and I wasn't sure if one ride would be enough. Maybe if I could get on Gunner's good side, he would let me on this—alone. I wasn't sure that would ever happen, though. MC brothers were protective of their bikes. The order of important things in their life went: the club, club brothers, their bikes. Everything else may not even ever make the list. Occasionally an old lady would, but I couldn't tell you where she would fall on it. It would depend on the brother.

Gunner pulled up to the gate and gave that head nod thing all men seem to fucking do to the douche canoe from earlier. His eyes met mine and narrowed, a snarl appearing on his face. So I made sure I flipped him off with both hands. Gunner stiffened against me. I could tell he was going to get off.

There's no way he's getting off to beat douche canoe's ass for me...

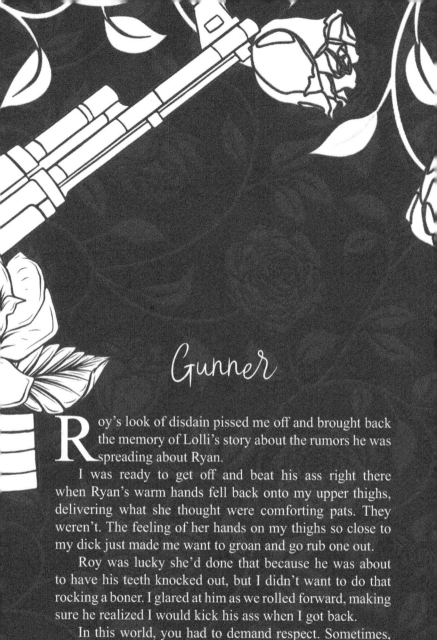

Gunner

Roy's look of disdain pissed me off and brought back the memory of Lolli's story about the rumors he was spreading about Ryan.

I was ready to get off and beat his ass right there when Ryan's warm hands fell back onto my upper thighs, delivering what she thought were comforting pats. They weren't. The feeling of her hands on my thighs so close to my dick just made me want to groan and go rub one out.

Roy was lucky she'd done that because he was about to have his teeth knocked out, but I didn't want to do that rocking a boner. I glared at him as we rolled forward, making sure he realized I would kick his ass when I got back.

In this world, you had to demand respect. Sometimes, that meant beating the shit out of someone to show that they were too much of a pussy to do anything but grovel at your feet. The woman whose arms were currently wrapped around me was more than capable of doing that on her own.

But for some reason, I wanted to be the one to enforce the respect that she should be given.

My attention was pulled back to Ryan when I felt her squirm behind me, bringing a smirk to my face. The heat from her pussy against my back was driving me crazy. It took all my willpower not to reach back there and feel how wet she was.

A bucket of ice water had already been dumped on me once tonight. Ryan had gotten me to rise to her bait when she told me I wasn't able to get a woman off—to get her off. But as I took in her beautiful brown eyes, lit with lust and told her how I could make her come, I realized I was playing with fire.

I wanted to fuck her. Right there in the makeshift parking lot with people just yards away. I knew I had to put distance between us. We had jobs to do, and I couldn't afford to be distracted. I told myself that I'd been hovering over her all night because Pres had told me to. But Pres hadn't asked me to keep every motherfucker who breathed her way at bay. My back stiffened at the memory of Torque asking Ryan to teach him to grapple; I'd gone into caveman mode and dragged her to an empty table, snarling at anyone who wanted to get close to her.

An irritated sigh left my lips as I recalled that taking her home was supposed to be my solution to getting space between us and not worrying about some asshole trying to hit on her. But now, I was stuck on a bike, going over eighty, with her lithe body pressed up against mine, her hands gripping my lower waist.

So much for space.

My dick was aching with how close her hands were to where I wanted them. Needing something to distract me from how close she was, I hammered down on the throttle, taking us faster down the road. Ryan's laugh fluttered behind me, bringing an unwelcome smile to my face. She was just as much of a daredevil as I was. It was clear she had been on a bike before because she kept her thighs pressed against mine and leaned with each turn we hit. I didn't want to overthink if she was used to her own bike or being on the back of another man's bike.

I pulled up to the address Ryan had given me back at the clubhouse, instantly missing the heat of her body and wishing I had a reason to keep her on my bike longer.

"Well, partner, now that I have proven my loyalty to your club, can we finally get to business?" she asked. "Because we have shit to get ready before the next shipment arrives."

Our fingers brushed against each other as she handed the helmet back, her eyes zeroing in on the point of contact. The corners of my lips tipped upward; she was just as affected as I was, but I gave myself a mental shake and focused on keeping things professional. She had asked a partnership question, after all.

"Yeah, we can get started now. I need you to walk me through the shipment process at Lotería, as well as the shipment schedule. I'm guessing you want to move that product within twenty-four hours of delivery."

Ryan may have been involved in the illegal side of shit for Los Muertos, but I'd seen Lotería. She took pride in that club, and while she may never say anything to Sergio or Mario, she didn't want to risk her legal business getting busted. Keeping illegal firearms from Mexico stored too long was an excellent way to do that.

"That would be ideal. But Mario couldn't always make that happen, so if we need to store them longer, we can make it work."

Something in the tone of her voice and the way her body tensed when she spoke of Mario put me on edge. I noticed it at the party earlier when she mentioned him texting her. Pres said they were close, but her reactions didn't paint that same picture.

"I can move them out of there as fast as you want, babe," I answered, eyeing the way she was biting her bottom lip.

"Let's meet at Lotería on Monday. I'll give you a more

in-depth tour, and we can go over the deliveries scheduled and who they're going to and all that."

A chirping noise came from her hand. Her brows furrowed, and her beautifully plump lips turned down. She was displeased with whatever she was reading on her screen. She suddenly seemed completely sober. If I hadn't watched her all night, I wouldn't have known she'd had a single drink tonight. It was none of my fucking business. In fact, the break in the conversation was the perfect opportunity to get my ass back to the clubhouse. Yet instead of doing that, I found myself pulled to help fix whatever was bothering her.

"What is it, Ryan?"

She looked up at me like she was surprised I was still here, or maybe she was surprised I was asking about what was wrong.

"Just some shit going down at Lotería. I have to go change and then get down there," she answered distractedly. Ryan hadn't even finished her sentence before turning around and heading toward her building. I leapt off my bike, reaching for her arm before she got too far away.

"Whoa, babe. I don't know how hard you got hit tonight, but you got here on the back of my bike. How are you planning on getting to the club? And it's one in the morning. There isn't anyone else to handle this tonight?" I asked, tugging her arm to get her to face me.

If looks could kill, I would have been dead on the spot. The woman was pissed. I wasn't sure if it was at me or whatever was happening at her club. My guess was it was probably a combination.

Her words came out cold and clipped. "Uber, Gunner. I was able to survive in the world before meeting you. I can figure out how to get to my damn club. I'm buzzed, not stupid."

I stiffened. Damn, the woman was feisty, but it pissed me off that she felt like she needed to defend her intelligence and ability to handle herself. That was not what I meant to insinuate, but obviously, she got that enough to go on the defensive. I did something I should not have done for the millionth time that night.

Cupping her dainty face, I tipped her head back so she would be able to see the sincerity in my eyes when I spoke to her. She furrowed her eyebrows, confused by my actions.

"Ryan. I don't, in any way, think you're stupid or incapable. I only asked you so it would help me see how I can help. You were in a fucking fight tonight and kicked ass, but still, you need your rest." My thumb rubbed along her cheekbone, and I watched as her defenses lowered. "That's why I asked if there was someone else to handle whatever it is that's going on. But if you feel it needs to be you, let's get you changed and over to the club."

Surprise filled her eyes when she realized I was proposing to go with her.

"You want to go with me?" she asked hesitantly.

I gave her a curt nod, her face still in my hands. You would have thought I asked her to marry me with the way she was looking at me.

Has no one ever looked out for this girl before? Or does she just think no one outside of Los Muertos would look out for her?

Ryan

There are reapers here.

That was what Nikki's text had read. What the fuck were those good-for-nothing bastards doing at my club? That MC was filled with the scum of the earth, and I had banned them from Lotería years ago. They knew the rules, but apparently, they needed a reminder of what happens when I'm crossed.

I barely registered the thumping base, dead set on my goal of finding the assholes with death wishes. Pushing past the sweaty bodies tightly packed into any free space, I made my way behind the bar and looked for Nikki's blond locks. Gunner and I had made it to Lotería fifteen minutes after her text came in.

Fuck, Gunner.

My head whipped around. Had he followed me? I hadn't bothered to look after we pulled up to the club and I leapt off his bike. The bloodlust was pulsing through my veins, demanding I take what I was owed.

He hadn't followed me in. This wasn't his problem.

Despite my inner dialogue, some part of me hoped he had. That he would stand next to me while I doled out punishments. I was questioning my sanity with that thought. Did I want to let Gunner witness my darkness? Sure, he'd watched me fight, but that was socially acceptable violence.

He hadn't seen me be outright violent yet. What would he think of me then?

I shook my head. When the fuck had I cared what a man would think about my violent tendencies? Right as I was about to turn away, green eyes caught mine. My mouth went dry as I watched him move smoothly through the crowd, hands tucked into the front pockets of his black jeans. He looked relaxed and at ease, but I could see how he was scanning the club—looking for the threat I had yet to fill him in on—hand close to his Glock, ready to put a bullet in someone at a moment's notice. He reached my side right as Nikki rushed up, her cheeks flushed, and beads of sweat dotting her forehead.

"There are three reapers here," she said in a harsh whisper, looking like a deer in headlights.

I felt Gunner stiffen beside me at the mention of the rival MC. I was sure he was trying to figure out if they had been invited or were trespassing. The wrong answer would make Los Muertos and The Skeletons enemies rather than partners.

My hands came to rest on Nikki's shoulders. I rubbed small circles on her skin with my thumbs, trying to help her control her erratic breathing.

"Nikki, where are they?" I asked, making sure to keep my voice calm.

"They're sitting at a table in the back corner and are demanding to speak to Mario. I told them he wasn't here and didn't even run the club. But they didn't like that answer. They want whoever is in charge." Nikki's words came out rushed, and there was a slight quake in her voice. She hung her head and absently rubbed her wrist. The movement drew my attention. I reached to gently grab her hand, wanting to confirm what I was suspecting.

"Ryan…" she stammered, concern laced in her tone.

The look I gave her silenced her.

"Ice it, Nikki," I answered coldly, "and tell Robert to prepare my office before meeting me at the table. I'll be working tonight." I turned and headed toward where Nikki said the MC members would be. I didn't have to check to know Gunner was following. His presence was like a solid wall of support at my back. It wasn't lost on me that he hadn't pushed me for answers or rushed forward to meet the MC members—he'd let me lead.

I spotted the three men sitting in a partially hidden corner on the main floor. The fuckers even dared to wear their cuts in my club. Sure, MC members lived and died in those damn things, but the Reapers had been expressly banned from Lotería. And here they sat, not even trying to be discreet. Well, if they wanted attention, they'd gotten it. Nikki joked that I should get *fuck around and find out* tattooed on my body because I said it so often, but it wasn't my fault that I constantly had to put weak men in their places.

The moment I reached the table, my fingers wrapped into the greasy blond hair of the man whose back was to me, and I slammed his head forward into the table with enough force to break his nose and knock him out. The fact that the asshole didn't think he needed to watch his back in my club pissed me off. Thank God for Pitbull because Mr. Worldwide made sure none of my *welcome* patrons heard the crunching sound of cartilage and bones breaking or the startled yelps from his club brothers.

"Gentlemen. I have been informed that you want a meeting with the person in charge," I said coolly. My body shielded the regular club-goers from seeing the pistol held to the unconscious man's head. "Unfortunately for you, you're getting one."

The Reapers may be scum, but they seemed to have at least a tiny amount of loyalty to their fellow club brothers. So they wouldn't attack while I held a gun to dumbass's head, especially since they weren't on their turf. The man across from me was snarling like a rabid dog. A smile split across my face; he was the one in charge.

"Who the fuck do you think you are?" His voice rose with each word. "We want a meeting with Mario."

The asshole beside him made the mistake of opening his mouth too. "Run away, little girl, and we won't bend you over and fuck you right here for your disrespect," he mocked.

Faster than my eyes could track, Gunner had the man's face pressed to the table, hand splayed out on top.

"Which finger should I take first? Huh? Because I'll cut them off and then shove them up your ass until you learn some respect." Gunner's voice was cold and menacing, and there was no way it should have turned me on the way it did.

The head reaper went to move on Gunner, but Robert, who had just appeared at the table, shook his head, making him reconsider.

"Fuck yo—"

A scream rang out and Gunner slapped a hand over the man's mouth to muffle it. A bloody middle finger lay on the table.

"Look, now you can fuck yourself," Gunner said, deadpan. The guy struggled to get away.

Excitement skipped through my veins, which was the opposite reaction someone should have when watching a finger be hacked off. Yet here I was, biting my bottom lip and resisting the urge to take Gunner to my upstairs office and fuck on the desk. A groan from the man whose hair I was still gripping brought me back to the present problem I was dealing with.

"Get your sorry ass up and follow Robert," I said sharply.

The one I was betting was the leader gave me a scathing

look before moving to get up. I wasn't intimidated. None of these *pendejos* had a weapon on them. My doormen knew well enough not to let anything in the club, and they would have triple-checked a reaper. That line of thinking had me wondering how they'd even gotten in.

"Robert, how did these fuckers even get into my club?" I asked.

Robert raised his hands. "*No fui yo, jefa.* Geraldo said they told him they had a meeting with Mario," he answered before quickly adding, "we've been swamped tonight, and Mario called earlier. I guess Geraldo just assumed what they were saying was legit."

I nodded my head, taking in the new information and dismissing Robert to take the reaper to my office. It seemed they did want something—specifically from Mario. I finally untangled my hand from the third member's hair and signaled to one of Lotería's bouncers.

"Take these two to the back."

He hoisted blondie over his shoulder like a rag doll while barking at the man now missing a finger to move it.

"Where on earth do you find giants like that?" Gunner asked incredulously.

Despite the shit show I was currently dealing with, Gunner managed to pull a laugh from me. I looked over my shoulder to where he stood, reading on his face the burning questions he was trying hard to keep to himself. Questions I didn't owe him any answers to, but found myself wanting to tell him anyway.

"Amazon." I winked before turning to follow Robert.

Weaving through the tables, I walked slowly enough to make it clear that he could follow. I told myself I was letting him join me as a show of good faith in our new partnership, an opportunity for the Skeletons' sergeant at arms to question a reaper without starting a bloodbath in the streets. But that was bullshit. I wanted Gunner around because I was beginning to like the asshole.

I approached a discreet door on the far back wall. Most

patrons didn't even notice it, and if they did, they assumed it was a utility closet or something. A side panel housed a thumbprint scanner and pin pad. Any door in Lotería that led to Los Muertos's less than legal business required the fingerprint of a member with access and a specific pin that changed at random.

I thought it was a bit overkill on the security measures, but Scar insisted on it. Honestly, I should have expected it from her since she *was* a security expert—who also happened to be a professional thief as a side hustle. She and I had met because of an arms deal with the New York Italian mob.

"That's a lot of security measures to open a door," Gunner commented, glancing at the biometric scanner and keypad. "I don't remember Nikki having to do all this when we walked up the main stairs to your office."

"Ask the real question, Gunner. Don't be shy now. I just watched you cut off a finger for me." I turned to face him head-on. "So, ask me what you want to know." I placed my hands on my hips, watching his demeanor.

My eyes locked on where his tongue was poking out, wetting his bottom lip. He liked it when I challenged him.

"What fucking office are we going to, babe?" he asked, his tone deliciously demanding.

Even in the dim lighting, the man was a sight to see. I searched his handsome face, taking in all his features while deciding what to do. His green eyes were bright with curiosity, his hair looked like he had been raking his fingers through it, and the goddamn mustache I was so obsessed with was tempting me to lean in and bite at his bottom lip.

I was also looking for a sign of what I should do. If he had been pushy, demanding, or just a downright asshole tonight, I would have kicked him to the curb way before this point. Gunner and I were supposed to work together on the weapons deals between our two organizations. Nothing more. But here I stood, wrestling with the decision on whether I was going to let Gunner join me on something outside of that arrangement.

The pad of his thumb was rough against my bottom lip as he worked to release it from between my teeth.

"We are partners, Ryan, remember? I told you that tonight after your fight. If you want me to go with you, I will." His thumb continued to graze across my lip as he spoke gently. "Besides, the Reapers are an enemy to both the Skeletons and Los Muertos. We may gain some valuable information on how to keep them out of the Tucson territory."

I had to fight to focus on his words and not the idea of pulling the digit into my mouth and sucking on it. The thought of tasting any part of this man made my panties wet, which was so not the appropriate thing to be thinking about at a time like this.

I let out a heavy sigh. "Okay. But in here, I'm in charge. I run the show."

"That's fine. You can have this space to be in charge. I have others..." he replied.

The wicked glint in his eye made me think that his statement had a hidden meaning, but I didn't have time to think about that.

I had interviews to conduct.

Ryan

"How are your shoulders feeling?" My tone was emotionless.

The moment my feet crossed the threshold of my office, all humanity was turned off. I was a machine in here, methodical and cold. I proudly took on the role of judge, jury, and, if needed, executioner for the men who had yet to be served justice.

That was my rule.

This room only held guilty men; I didn't extract information from innocents. Sergio and Mario knew that if I didn't find proof of their guilt, I wouldn't be torturing them.

Spit hit the concrete floor near my feet. "You're going to pay for this, bitch," he seethed.

"Oh, I don't know about that. How is your club going to even know what happened to you?" I asked flippantly.

I walked over to the cabinet, opening it up and pulling out some of my favorite tools.

"What the fuck are you talking about?" His voice now held a tinge of panic to it.

Glancing over my shoulder, I found his eyes were glued to me. I tilted my head and smiled, ignoring his question—it always made them squirm when I did.

"How do you like my office? Designed it myself." I pointed to a spot below where he was sitting. "The drain makes it so much easier to rinse down the blood." I turned back to my cabinet, continuing to speak. "All I have to do is slather the room in bleach and hose it down."

When I faced him again, his face had turned white. He hadn't considered that I might kill him or torture him. The reality of his situation started setting in, and he attempted to thrash in his seat. A smile split across my face watching him struggle because I knew he wouldn't be able to free himself. I'd watched too many hostages break their chairs and escape, so I'd developed my method.

Seated, with their ankles shackled to the metal chair and arms strung up above their head. I was sure someone, at some point, could find a way out of this, but I didn't make a habit of leaving them alone long enough to figure one out. Most of the men who found themselves here were pussies who didn't even try to escape. They would prey on the weak and then whimper when I held them accountable.

"Where the fuck is Mario? I asked for the person in charge, not some bitch playing badass," he yelled out, but the shake in his voice revealed his fear.

Gunner landed a right hook before gripping the man's wiry beard and wrenching his head back around.

"Watch your fucking tone." Gunner shook his head in disgust. "You asked for the person in charge, and here she is, gracing you with her presence, and your fucking sorry soul is going to be disrespectful?" he asked incredulously.

The man's eyes widened when he took in Gunner's cut. None of the reapers had noticed he was a member of Skeletons of Society, but this one sure as shit noticed now. I moved up beside Gunner and placed a hand on his arm in an

114

attempt to calm his rage and the rapid beating of my heart at his response. I couldn't afford to get distracted.

"What is it you wanted to discuss…" I looked down at his cut where it had his club name and position stitched—he was also a sergeant at arms, interesting. "Spinner?"

Blood was freely flowing down from his nose, and his eye was already beginning to swell. Instead of an answer, bloody spit landed at my feet. He had learned his lesson about calling me a bitch in front of Gunner. I rolled my eyes at his childish antics. Men always wanted to test me and see if the fact that I was a woman was some game the cartel was playing.

It had been in the beginning.

Part of me had always thought that Mario included me in those first torture sessions to see if I would break. If the emotional splinters I possessed could be wedged down even deeper. Maybe he thought he could fix me if I fell apart, or maybe he knew that this vigilante justice would make me feel like I was atoning.

But the problem with atoning for sins with sins is you can never break the cycle.

"I asked a question, Spinner. Since you don't seem to know anything about me, I'll give you some helpful hints on how I work." I circled him as I spoke, watching him squirm under my cold gaze. Years ago, I learned that people got nervous when they couldn't keep you in their line of sight.

"I ask a question, you answer. And I only ask once," I whispered in his ear.

The stench of his fear now overpowered the faint scent of cleaner. I smiled, knowing Spinner realized that I was the predator and he was the prey. After a few more seconds of silence, he decided his best chance at getting out of Los Muertos's territory alive was to cooperate.

His voice was rushed and pleading. "I was just here to talk to Mario. I thought he would be here, and I just needed to sort some things out. I swear. "

My brows furrowed at his words. Moving back around

to the front, I watched his face for any tells.

"Did Mario know you were coming?" I asked, pissed that confusion was evident in my voice because Spinner picked up on it and immediately shut down.

Sneering, he leaned as far forward as possible with his wrists attached to the ceiling.

"Who the fuck are you to ask questions like that? I wanna talk to someone who makes decisions." Spinner angled himself to point toward Gunner with his chin before continuing.

"For all I fucking know, this is just the cock you hop that pretty pussy on. In fact, this scum probably pays you for that pussy. How many other brothers do you fuck?" His voice was laced with venom now. "No, bitch, you don't have a fucking say at Los Muertos. You're just here fucking with me." His eyes cut to the two-way mirror, and he yelled at it as if someone was watching. "Mario, I want to talk to you."

Gunner was practically vibrating with rage next to me. I had to hold him back with a hand on his chest while this asshole was spewing his conspiracy theories about what was going on. A woman in this world got used to being accused of whoring herself out.

Hey, more power to the beautiful bitches who brought men to their knees and then made the assholes pay to worship them. I ran a fucking strip club; obviously, I was very pro-sex worker. But unfortunately for Spinner, that wasn't the type of work I did for Los Muertos.

Before he knew what was happening, I closed the distance and put a bullet through his kneecap—shattering it and blowing out half his calf. Spinner's yells of agony reverberated off the tile walls.

My voice came out calm and unfazed. "Hear it's tough to ride with a shattered knee. Sometimes, the doctors can't ever restore mobility. Too much to try to reconstruct, even for skilled surgeons. In the worst cases, they have to amputate." I tilted my head in a way I knew made me look deranged. "Do the Reapers take their men to hospitals now?

Or do you guys still use a club doctor?" The malice was evident in my tone.

Spinner whipped his head back and forth in torment, on the edge of unconsciousness. I knew he wasn't registering anything I was saying. But I wasn't saying it for his benefit. I was saying it for his two club brothers who were watching a feed of what was happening from their interrogation rooms.

My fingers dug into his jaw.

"Escúchame pendejo, consider this your official warning that Tucson is Los Muertos's and Skeletons of Society's territory, and you are not welcome. And tell your president to do some research next time because La Brujita de Los Muertos doesn't appreciate the disrespect, and I'll start dropping off bodies at his doorstep if he pisses me off further. ¿Entendes?"

His eyes widened at the mention of my street name, confirming that these assholes must all be new.

As soon as Spinner passed out, I turned toward Gunner. Catching his gaze, I tried to assess his reaction to what had just gone down. Innocent men were never brought back to these offices. So I rarely felt guilt when conducting this type of business. But the moment I pulled the trigger, my heart sank to my stomach at the thought of what I would see on Gunner's face. Would he even be able to look at me?

He looked me up and down, assessing. But he didn't seem to be repulsed by the type of violence I was capable of. That only slightly soothed my worry. I knew I would forever be viewed in a different light after what he just saw. I was having major regrets about letting Gunner witness this, but I didn't know how to put the proverbial genie back in the bottle.

My palms met the rough texture of my jeans as I tried to wipe off the sweat. I was nervous about what he was going to say to me. In two steps, he had closed the distance between us. Bringing his large hand up, he rubbed on the wrinkle between my brows.

"Stop looking so worried. Do you think I haven't seen a

gunshot wound before?"

His hand slipped down to my shoulder, working on getting me to release the tension I was holding there.

A soft moan slipped out before I answered, "I just shot a man, Gunner. And not in self-defense or any other legally acceptable reason to shoot someone. Of course I'm worried about what your reaction would be," I sassed back.

Gunner raised a brow at me. "Legally acceptable? You think I'm a cop or something?" he teased, more than likely in an effort to get me to relax.

I turned to make my way over to the door.

"No, asshole. I don't think you're a cop. You fucking cut off someone's finger and threatened to shove it up his ass." Gunner let out a snicker at the memory, making me roll my eyes. Men. "I was trying to point out that it's a normal reaction for me to be worried about how someone is going to take witnessing me shooting someone's kneecap."

"Ryan."

I paused, turning around to face him, catching him running his hand through his hair and staring at Spinner's unconscious body.

"If you're wondering if I think there's something wrong with you, I don't. Right and wrong are not as black and white as people want to pretend. The gray area is where people who do the most good for others live. We are willing to bear the burden so others can stay solely in the light."

I opened my mouth to speak but found I had no words. I had no idea how to untangle the web of emotions his words and actions brought.

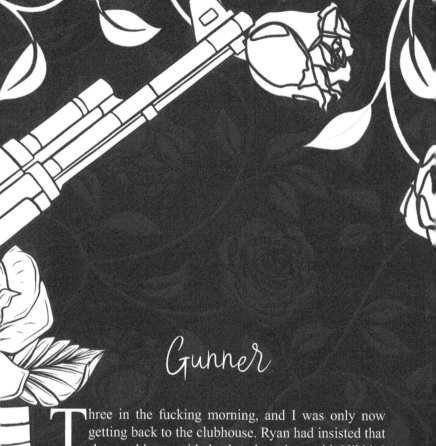

Gunner

T hree in the fucking morning, and I was only now getting back to the clubhouse. Ryan had insisted that she would get a ride back to her place with Nikki. I wanted to argue with her about that, but there was no good reason why I had to be the one to bring her home. Other than I wanted to stay with her longer. Which was absurd. I barely knew the woman. But being around her was like experiencing life again, stepping outside the drag of my current routine.

Fuck.

Of course, the fight night rager was still going on when all I wanted to do was lie in fucking peace and quiet and think about what I'd learned tonight. But that wasn't what you got when you lived at an MC clubhouse. You got constant booze, bitches, and noise. Lots of noise.

"Where the fuck have you been, asshole?" Dex was sitting on one of the leather couches, arms draped over the back and a club bunny busy between his legs. The sight made me pinch the bridge of my nose. These living arrangements were not always as fun as they looked on paper. Sometimes I just wanted to go back to a typical home where the mailman knew my name and only one person fucking lived there.

As soon as that thought entered my head, so did the image of a raven-haired beauty wearing only my shirt and cooking me dinner. I shook my head at the visual. One, because that wasn't in the cards for me. And two, Ryan would never cook my dinner like a submissive housewife. The knives in that kitchen would be for stabbing, not chopping onions.

"Dude…" Dex prodded, reminding me that he had asked a question.

"I was out taking Ryan home, but we had a change of plans when she got word that reapers were at her club…"

I let the implications of my statement hang in the air. I didn't know whether Dex was too drunk to talk about work right now, so I tested the waters. But the instant I mentioned the MC, his gaze narrowed, and he lifted the chin of the club bunny giving him head.

"That was fun, sweetheart, but Daddy needs to do some work now." The chick nodded her head enthusiastically, tucking Dex's dick back into his jeans before rushing away. Tits hanging out of the front of her top and all. I had no clue how he even got girls when he said shit like that. I had known the fucker too long, and the very sound of Dex referring to himself as *Daddy* made me want to throw up in my mouth.

The moment she was gone, his demeanor changed.

"What the fuck do you mean there were reapers at her club?" Dex growled. "I thought the cartel didn't work with the Reapers."

Dex was more coherent than I'd first thought. He asked the same questions I had when Ryan mentioned that reapers were at Lotería.

I rubbed a hand over my face. "They went there looking for Mario."

"Did she know?" he asked. His face was guarded.

I decided it was best to sit down for the rest of this conversation because I was sure Dex would have questions, especially when I told him about what happened in Ryan's secret office.

"No." I looked at him sharply. "The Reapers were not welcomed guests at Lotería, and Ryan didn't know why they were looking for Mario."

Dex opened his mouth to ask how I could be sure of this, but I carried on before he could.

"Ryan walked up behind one and shattered his nose on the table before holding a gun to his head and threatening the others. Then, in her *special office*, she shot their sergeant at arms in the knee, blowing out his calf," I said evenly, placing my arms along the top of the sofa and giving my words a minute to sink in. I left out that I had cut off a finger because I didn't like the way he'd spoken to her.

"*Fuck*," Dex said, dragging out the *u* sound in a way he knew I hated.

I rolled my eyes before continuing. "Pretty positive she knew it would need to be amputated since the Reapers would have to go to an actual hospital to have any hope of saving it. But with all the shit they're involved in, I doubt they would take that risk."

A thick silence sat between us as Dex digested what I had just dropped in his lap.

"You watched her fucking shoot a man in the kneecap…" Dex sounded like he had just fallen in love, and it fucking irked me. So I opted to nod my head in response. Of course that would be his reaction to this situation. I would be lying, though, if I didn't admit that the sight of her in that room, bloodlust running through her veins, wasn't a fucking turn-on.

Sometimes late at night, I would lie awake and wonder if the darkness that now surrounded my soul was always there or if I'd tarnished myself over the last few years. But tonight, when I saw Ryan in that room, exacting vengeance for what they did to Nikki and asserting her authority for trespassing on her territory. I realized that darkness didn't equal evil. Good intentions often needed to be accomplished with what someone had determined were sins.

"So why the fuck were they there? Why risk getting fucking shot?" he asked incredulously.

I shrugged my shoulders. I had wondered the same thing.

"I think they thought they would find Mario there tonight. They had no clue who Ryan was," I answered thoughtfully, running my hand through my hair. "But it's hard to know if that means anything because up until recently, we didn't know anything about Ryan either. Sergio and Mario may let her do the grunt work for them, but neither was talking about her to the rest of the underground circuits."

Across from me, Dex was rubbing his hands down his face. Like if he scrubbed hard enough, answers would appear. But we were missing too many pieces of the puzzle to finally finish it. He looked up, making eye contact. The seriousness of his gaze put me on edge.

"She's a good source for intel. You said yourself; she does a lot of grunt work for Mario and Sergio. She's in the inner circle, Gunner. Ryan will know shit, whether she's supposed to or not. She will have information."

I ground my teeth at the implications of what Dex was saying. He saw the resistance in my face and pushed on before I shut him down.

"Listen, man, I know you think she's hot and shit; hell, I like her too. But we have a job to do. She's the in we've needed to get a foot in the door. Make a connection with her, use her as a resource, and we'll be able to do what we need to do. Keep this partnership going and successful. But brother, to do that, you can't stick your dick in this. And you sure as shit can't stick your feelings in this."

Now I was scrubbing my face, hoping for another solution or a flaw in Dex's words. But he was right. I had to get close to Ryan to use her for information and insight.

This partnership wasn't a long-term promise. We were being given a trial run here, and if it got fucked up. If I fucked it up—bye-bye all that we had worked for.

I let out a defeated sigh when no other solution came to me.

"Fuck, you're right," I mumbled.

Dex nodded his head in approval, glad I agreed with him on this.

"In the meantime, we need to figure out why the Reapers needed to talk to Mario. They risked a lot showing up there tonight, and I want to know why. It was all real cloak and dagger shit. Spinner didn't think Ryan was in charge, so he played his cards real close to the vest. And Ryan was a bit trigger-happy after she saw that they'd hurt Nikki's wrist."

I barely got those last words out before Dex was sitting at attention. The killer in him coming to the forefront. It's how he'd gotten his road name. Dex, short for Dexter, because the man was fucking scary when he turned on this side of him. Cold and calculated; able to extract information and inflict pain without batting an eye. Our time in the MC had irrevocably changed both of us, or maybe it just allowed us to be our true selves.

"What the fuck did they do to Nikki?" he asked, his voice harsh.

That question got me to raise my eyebrow. I wasn't surprised that Dex knew Nikki's name; he knew a lot of women's names. I was surprised he knew which woman the name belonged to and gave a fuck that she'd been injured. Dex may have come across as fun-loving, but feelings and caring for people weren't his thing. He kept that shit locked up tight. It's why his "Dexter" side would come out so quickly when provoked. He kept his feelings off to begin with.

But pointing out his reaction would be like throwing rocks from a glass house, so I kept my mouth shut and just answered his question.

"When we showed up, Nikki ran up to Ryan to let her

know what was going down. She didn't account for how observant her boss was and made the mistake of rubbing her wrist. Ryan caught the movement. Pretty sure it's what got the men sent to her special office and not the one upstairs. I'm guessing one of them just got too handsy. I didn't exactly get the chance to ask Nikki about it."

Dex looked like he was about to hop out of his seat and take off, so I raised my hands to signal him to chill. "Before you go all psycho killer in ways you're not allowed to, Ryan took care of the punishment."

Dex relaxed his shoulders slightly, but I still wasn't positive he wouldn't try to go fuck up some reapers. I thought he and Nikki barely knew one another, but his reaction suggested otherwise.

"Dex." My voice came out commanding; it was the tone I used when he knew I meant business. "Remember what you just told me. We have a job to do. We can't go fucking up all we've worked for by starting a war with the Reapers. Besides, I have this gut feeling one is coming anyway."

That seemed to snap him out of whatever he was wrestling with.

"You're right. Just don't like to hear about women getting hurt, you know." He locked eyes with me, conveying the message that we weren't going to talk about the shit with Nikki anymore. "I'll reach out to some contacts and see if there has been any unusual movement. Do you think the Reapers will retaliate?" he asked.

I had been thinking about that the whole ride back to the clubhouse. Technically, they had gone into someone else's territory without an invitation. And not just anyone's; the goddamned cartel's territory. But the Reapers didn't abide by many unwritten rules criminals go by. They probably wouldn't give a damn that Ryan was within her rights to do what she did. What worried me was that they would retaliate because she was a woman. The Reapers probably felt that Los Muertos letting a woman fuck them up was more disrespectful than trespassing.

The look on my face must have conveyed my concern because Dex decided to stand and walk toward where we held church.

"We're gonna need to inform people that we think the Reapers may retaliate. We have to be ready for what this might dredge up. See where you can get with Ryan. Gunner, don't fuck this up." He stopped and looked at me. "You need pussy—there's plenty here to scratch the itch. But we have shit to accomplish with Los Muertos."

My head hit the back of the couch.

Fuck, he's right.

There was too much riding on this partnership. I couldn't fuck it up. I was sure that whatever connection I made with Ryan, I was going to watch it be shredded to pieces when this was all over. That thought caused my heart to ache, and I didn't know what to think of my reaction.

One thing I knew for sure was that while she may hate me when this was all over with, I would do everything in my power to make sure she came out of this as unscathed as possible. Use whatever resources I had to keep her from feeling the blowback of what was to come.

Because every instinct I had told me something was coming. The tides were shifting, and we were all about to be fucking hit. I didn't know what was going to happen, but I'd learned a long time ago to listen to my instincts.

They'd saved my life and the lives of others time and time again.

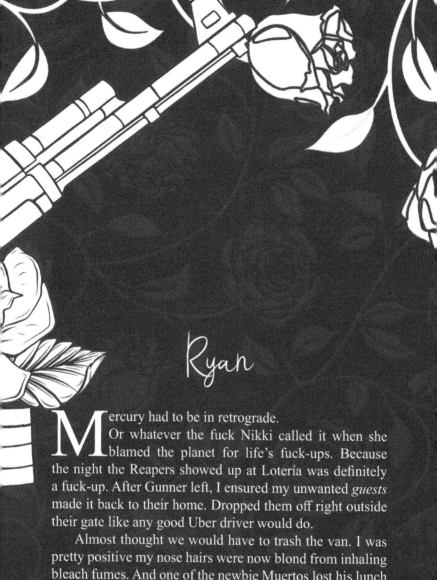

Ryan

Mercury had to be in retrograde.

Or whatever the fuck Nikki called it when she blamed the planet for life's fuck-ups. Because the night the Reapers showed up at Lotería was definitely a fuck-up. After Gunner left, I ensured my unwanted *guests* made it back to their home. Dropped them off right outside their gate like any good Uber driver would do.

Almost thought we would have to trash the van. I was pretty positive my nose hairs were now blond from inhaling bleach fumes. And one of the newbie Muertos lost his lunch watching the river of blood run out while hosing it down. Pussy.

A frustrated groan left my lips as I leaned back in my office chair, closing my eyes. I'd been racking my brain for answers to why the Reapers showed up here. Most of the crime world viewed me as an anomaly. *If* they knew about me. Some vaguely knew Mario kept a woman close, but he always had so many women circling him that they just lumped me in with those bitches and moved on.

OGs knew Sergio had taken in a teenage girl ten years ago, but once my gender was mentioned, they didn't feel the need to learn anything more about me. Most of the time, players, especially new ones, only knew "Ryan" ran shit for Sergio and Mario in the Tucson area. And like The Skeletons of Society had, they all thought I had a dick between my legs.

But the Reapers should have known who I was.

A few years ago, I personally delivered a message to their clubhouse that they were to stay out of Tucson and Los Muertos's territory. And they sure as fuck were not allowed in Lotería. The bat I took to the bike and the man who assaulted one of my girls should have made the message pretty damn clear.

When Sergio let me have Lotería, I knew I would protect my girls with every fiber of my being. It was why these giant-ass men worked here. Almost all the girls were survivors of something. I didn't ask any questions. Their pasts were theirs and theirs alone. They didn't have to share anything with me.

But I did have some strict rules.

They were all drug tested. Other than marijuana, I didn't want them on shit. They pissed hot, and they could work at Peepers. They got to keep every dollar they made on that stage and private dances, but no sex acts in the club. I wasn't going to get randomly searched because rumors leaked that you could get a margarita and a dick suck at Lotería. That would make it dangerous for the less than legal activities we ran out of here.

For the patrons, there was one hard and fast rule. They weren't ever to touch any of the girls. The reaper I beat to a pulp went way beyond that rule, and they had all been banned ever since.

So why the fuck did the Reapers think my rules had changed? I hadn't heard of any changes in power over at their MC, but I'd never seen any of the three that had showed up at the club. Spinner was not the same sergeant at arms I knew. And what the hell did he need to see Mario for?

"Muñeca, you look stressed. Is the something causing you problems?"

A chill ran down my spine at the sound of that voice. My eyes popped open, and I was met with the view of Mario leaning against the frame of my office door.

The wolf in sheep's clothing. Or Gucci, rather.

Where Sergio was the embodiment of cholo from the hood, Mario was a complete one-eighty. I'd never seen him out of a tailored suit and expensive loafers. There was no denying that Mario was handsome, but he never made me wet just by looking at him. Until recently, I didn't even know that could happen.

I took a moment to collect myself, not wanting to let him know how startled I was to see him.

"Mario, what are you doing here? I didn't realize you were going to be coming to Tucson. Usually, you let me know when you're coming to visit." A slight tremor was evident in my voice.

I felt like a rabbit captured in a trap when he looked at me, his cold gaze always calculated and assessing. It was one of the first things I noticed when we'd met in that alley all those years ago. At times I felt more like an object he possessed than someone he cared for, as he claimed. Yet despite all of that, I always stayed at his side. Afraid to lose the only affection I'd received since my parents were killed.

My eyes tracked his movement as he walked from the doorway to in front of my desk. I focused on slowing my breathing and gaining control of my reactions.

Of course he was going to make me wait for his answer. He hated when I questioned him. Didn't matter that it was a logical fucking question since, last I heard, he was in Mexico.

His hand wrapped around a frame that held a picture of Nikki and me when we received the keys to our apartment.

His eyes narrowed, and he pursed his lips in displeasure.

The two had never gotten along. Nikki was vocal about her distaste for Mario, so I made sure to keep them far away from one another. Mario tended to have a short fuse for disrespect, and even I wouldn't be able to save Nikki from Mario's wrath if she pissed him off. I told her that too.

When he spoke again, there was an edge to his tone, warning me that I was trying his patience with my questions. The need to roll my eyes at his theatrics was overwhelming.

"Muñeca, have you forgotten? I'm heir to this empire, and I'm the owner of this club that I *let* you run for me. I may show up whenever I please and with as much or as little notice as I wish to give." He held my gaze, daring me to object.

The emphasis on *let* grated on my nerves, but I held my tongue. Opting to dig my nails into my palms instead.

"Of course, Mario. I was surprised that you were here." I gave him what I hoped looked like a sweet smile, trying to smooth over the tension between us.

A wolfish grin appeared on his face. He always was pleased with my submission. For the first time in a long time, I wondered why I let Mario treat me like the nickname he'd given me—a doll.

"Now, back to my original question, Muñeca. What is it that is bringing you stress?" he prodded.

His insistence on getting me to answer this question piqued my interest. I zeroed in on his body language, looking for tells.

Mario didn't ever care what was happening at Lotería. At least, he never cared to know about the problems. All he wanted was to know what Lotería's successes were so he could claim them as his own. But the problems—he couldn't give two fucks about knowing those. In fact, it was my job to make sure those problems got fixed before they ever made it to Mario's ears. So why was he wondering what was happening now? Maybe he was concerned because he thought the problems causing me stress were personal.

Those were the problems he tended to be overly invested in.

I slipped into my interrogator persona, not wanting to give information away with my tone or body language.

"Some reapers showed up the other night. When they have been expressly banned from the club. But the fuckers still decided to come to Los Muertos territory. So I delivered a message about how I felt regarding their disrespect." I paused, leaning forward on my desk. Assessing him. "But what I want to know is why those pendejos thought they would be welcome to begin with."

I didn't mention that they asked to see him, trying to figure out if he already knew that tidbit. Mario looked down and picked at the nonexistent lint on his sleeve before speaking.

"Hmm, I see. Did you happen to ask them why they were in my establishment? Or did you let your thirst for blood take over?" he asked, his tone tight.

I bristled at his words but answered his question.

"I did ask. He said they wanted to speak to someone in charge. When I told him that was me, the conversations died."

Mario looked up at that, raising an eyebrow. His insinuation made me roll my eyes.

"No, Mario. The conversation didn't die because I killed him." I bit my lip, realizing my following words wouldn't sound like a less violent alternative.

"It died because I shot him in the kneecap."

That drew a genuine laugh from him. Something I hadn't heard in years.

"Muñeca, you never cease to amaze me."

The men gave me whiplash with their moods. First Gunner, now Mario. The icy tone he'd been using was gone. Replaced with the joking tone that pulled at my heart.

"That's why you stay around. You think he's redeemable. He's not, and you will get yourself killed waiting around for it."

Nikki's drunk words popped into my head, my mind creating a replica of the sorrowful tone in her voice. Like her warning was based on personal events.

"I'm so glad I kept you all those years ago. Now, put the Reapers out of your mind. I'll take care of anything that comes up on that end," he said, pulling me to the present.

That brought a scowl to my face. He never wanted to handle anything, but Mario didn't bother giving any further explanation. Instead, he moved on to the reason I was assuming he was here.

"But we do have some business to discuss. I need you to arrange a meeting with the sergeant at arms from the MC we partnered with. I want to make sure he's aware of what is expected of him."

Before I could even respond, he was making his way back out of my office.

"Make that for today, Muñeca," he demanded.

Fuck Mercury and her retrograde.

I pulled out my phone to text Gunner. I hadn't spoken to him since that night. I didn't know how to process what I felt when he was around. And rather than dive into that emotional pool, I'd chosen to disassociate from life with a romance book and my vibrator for the rest of the weekend.

My fingertip hovered over the send button like I was a fucking middle schooler working up the courage to talk to her crush. What was my issue? This was a business deal; I was used to these. I slammed down on the send like it had personally offended me. Thank Santa Muerte, this didn't need to be a FaceTime call. I would be here all fucking day.

"Oh, but you can shoot someone in the knee, no problem. That's real normal," I muttered to myself, rereading the groundbreaking message I'd sent.

Me: We need to meet today.

The three dots indicating he was typing appeared almost instantly. I was trying to ignore the butterflies bouncing around my uterus while waiting for his response.

Gunner: We meeting at your place or mine?

I was about to respond when another text came through.

Gunner: If we meet at yours, I need to know if you have XL condoms, bc if not, I'll have to bring them.

What. The. Fuck? Was he sexting me? I pulled my bottom lip between my teeth, gnawing at the skin, trying to work out how I felt about his message. Blowing out a breath, I decided I needed to keep it professional. My fingers flew across the screen, typing out a response before he sent more dumb shit, and my resolve cracked.

Me: We aren't meeting so we can fuck, Gunner.

Gunner: Gotcha, don't want to go for the home run yet. How do you feel about 69, then?

Gunner: I have been dying to taste that pussy of yours...

Gunner: You left a wet spot on my back the other night. What I would have given to get you off while on my bike. Do you wear underwear under those leggings of yours? I bet you don't. I could have just ripped a few seams and had access to that pretty pussy. I haven't seen it yet, but I bet it's pretty.

Gunner: Did I mention that it's sexy how bloodthirsty you are?

I didn't know what had gotten into him, but he wasn't giving me any time to wrap my brain around the fact that he was sexting me. I bet Dex dared him into this. The problem was the words on my screen were turning me on. My thighs were clenched, trying to move in just the right way so that the crotch of my jeans rubbed against my clit.

"What am I? A horny teenager?" I grumbled. "You text him back right now and tell him to cut this shit out..." My pep talk didn't do shit. The moment another message came through, I devoured the words on the screen.

Gunner: Send a picture.

My face contorted in confusion. "The man must be drunk or have a concussion or something," I said to myself.

Me: What? Why do you need a picture of my face?

Me: I'm not even going to bother responding to the rest of your messages.

Gunner: I don't want a picture of your face. I want a picture of your pussy. Weren't you paying attention? My dick is hard just thinking about seeing it. Fuck it, send a picture of your face too.

Gunner: Think you can take the picture while bent over your desk? Bc that's the image I jacked off to all weekend. Fuck, Ryan. You have me trying to hide my hard-on, and you haven't even sent the picture.

Gunner: If I bought you a butt plug, would you wear it? Bc fuck, that's the picture I want.

I was back to biting my lip, rereading his messages. Why did I not have a vibrator stashed in my desk? For two seconds, I considered playing along. But a bucket of ice water was poured on me when my office door opened, and Mario poked his head in.

"Have you set up that meeting yet?" he asked.

I could feel my cheeks flame like I'd just gotten caught doing something naughty. I hoped Mario couldn't see the color from where he stood.

"Doing that now, Mario," I called back, clearing my throat before answering.

The moment the door closed, I relaxed, but only slightly. That was a reminder that I needed to keep my shit together. Don't let the hot man distract you, Ryan.

Me: Not the time for sexting, Gunner. Go rub one out and get your ass to Lotería. Mario is here.

The dots appeared and then disappeared before his response finally came in.

Gunner: I'll be there soon.

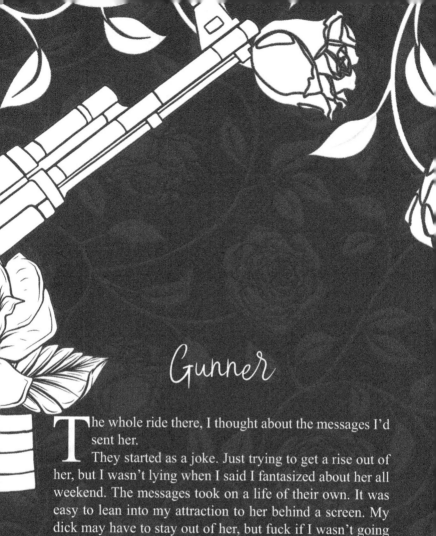

Gunner

The whole ride there, I thought about the messages I'd sent her.

They started as a joke. Just trying to get a rise out of her, but I wasn't lying when I said I fantasized about her all weekend. The messages took on a life of their own. It was easy to lean into my attraction to her behind a screen. My dick may have to stay out of her, but fuck if I wasn't going to flirt with her.

I told myself that flirting was part of getting her to fall for me. And she needed to fall for me so she'd share information. But I knew I was playing with fire with that approach.

Loteria's crimson sign came into view, and the corners of my mouth turned upward. Now that I knew Ryan, I felt a swell of pride looking at the building. Her blood, sweat, and tears had gone into this place. The moment my engine cut, tension prickled on my skin, causing me to pause.

Something was different here tonight.

Geraldo, the giant of a man who manned the door, wasn't at his post. Instead, there stood some asshole who looked to be pretending to be a mafia member in a low-budget movie. Who was going to tell him he was in a cartel? I let my sergeant at arms persona slip over me before walking up to the asshole.

"Club is closed tonight, gringo. Go somewhere else to pay for pussy," he spewed out.

I looked down at the hand pressed to my cut before dragging my eyes back to his ugly mug.

"The pedo 'stache isn't a good look," I said coolly, watching for his reaction. Swinging first wouldn't go over well, but swinging second…that I could get away with.

My dick twitched the moment I heard her voice. *Down, boy.*

"I'd move your hand from his cut before you get your shit rocked." Ryan walked out from behind the idiot. "And not everyone has to pay for pussy, Armando. Don't put your lack of pussy problems on other people. Now, let him in," she demanded, a cold look in her eyes.

God, she was hot when she was bossing people around. The weight of Armando's hand was suddenly gone, and I shouldered past him. But his mumbles about Ryan being a bitch reached my ears. Faster than he could anticipate, I slammed him against the wall. My forearm pressed against his throat.

"What the fuck did you call her?" I growled out, blocking out the sensation of his nails breaking skin as he tried to relieve the pressure on his windpipe. "Oh, I'm sorry. I can't hear you."

At this point, Armando was flailing around. His face turned ashen from lack of oxygen. I moved closer so he would clearly understand what I was about to say.

"When I let your worthless ass go, you will crawl over to her on your hands and knees and apologize for being a rude asswipe. Nod your head if you understand," I seethed.

140

Satisfied that he got the message, I removed the weight on his throat, letting him crumple to the floor. He lay in a heap at my feet, desperately trying to get air into his oxygen-starved lungs. My lip curled in disgust—piece of shit.

I looked over at Ryan, who'd been quiet during this whole exchange. Her heated eyes traveled up and down my body. Fuck, how was I going to stay away?

Her responses to my sexting didn't give away shit about how she felt.

Seemed she liked me violent. Noted. Bring her the heads of men who offend her.

Ryan didn't bother looking down at Armando, who was now in front of her, begging for forgiveness. Instead, she kept her eyes trained on me as I strode over.

"When I'm around. No one will disrespect you," I whispered in her ear, loving the shiver that racked her body. Before thinking better of it, I pulled her earlobe into my mouth and sucked. Her hands gripped my cut, and the breathy moan she let out instantly made me hard. Emboldened by her reaction, I ran the tip of my tongue along the shell of her ear for good measure. Dex may have said I couldn't fuck her, but he didn't say I couldn't push the boundaries.

"Great, now my cock will be uncomfortably hard during this entire meeting, babe," I whispered.

She pulled back slightly so she could look at my face.

"All actions have consequences, Gunner," she said, throwing my own words back at me. A playful look in her eyes. The little minx turned and walked toward the stairs. My eyes lingered on the curve of her ass, almost missing that none of the crew tonight looked familiar. I'd only been to the club twice, but it had been the same staff both times. And from what I could tell about Ryan, she would keep her staff circle small—only bringing in men she trusted. I would bet my left nut the asshole at the door was not one of hers.

Ryan stopped abruptly, causing me to reach out and grab her hips to prevent myself from running her over. A soft groan fell from my mouth at the feel of her body in my hands. Her curves were a perfect handhold.

But my blood ran cold when she faced me. Her furrowed brow told me she was worried about something, instantly putting me on edge. Ryan had never been anything but confident. Now, she wouldn't look me in the eye.

"Listen, I don't know why Mario wants to talk with you. He showed up this morning unannounced and demanded I schedule a meeting." She finally looked up. I could tell she was wrestling over something, but I didn't know what.

"Mario won't take any disrespect, Gunner. He's not like Sergio. He has no softness and no room for second chances. Gunner, you have to be cautious in this meeting. Tell him what he wants to hear," she rushed out.

That's when I saw it—the fear in her eyes.

My blood boiled at the thought of her being scared of Mario. But this didn't make any sense. They were supposed to be close. Mario found Ryan on the streets at seventeen. From everything I knew, they were like family.

Was she scared for me? Or what I was going to be told?

"Ryan, I have no problem being respectful," I answered, my thumb drawing circles on her hip.

I needed to let her go, but my hands wouldn't cooperate. I homed in on her shoulders, watching them lower from up by her ears.

She really was concerned about how this would go. But it was my job to prepare for this meeting, and I wasn't planning to ruin this opportunity because I couldn't keep my attitude in check.

With a single nod, she removed her body from my hands and jogged up the last few steps. Seated behind the large wooden desk was the infamous Mario Jimenez. I knew all about the heir to the Los Muertos Cartel. According to my sources, the man was a ruthless asshole.

I could already tell the rumors were true. He was reclined back, feet up on the desk—a smug look on his face. Now I saw where the moron outside got his outfit inspiration from.

Mario looked like he wanted to be a mafioso instead of a cartel member, with his slicked-back hair and designer suit. On his wrist, he wore the gaudiest gold watch. Prick didn't bother changing his position as I took a seat.

"Aww. Mr. Gunner, I'm glad you arrived when asked," he said, a fake smile plastered on his face.

He was baiting me. Trying to see if he would get a rise out of me by insinuating that I was under his thumb. But I saw through his manipulation. So instead, I gave a quick nod of my head in response, making sure to keep my face blank.

His eyes showed the slightest twitch of irritation before sliding over to where Ryan stood behind me. Whatever he saw behind me made him sit up.

"Muñeca, come stand over here, please," he demanded.

I bristled at how he watched Ryan. When she was within reaching distance, Mario pulled her down onto his lap and buried his nose in her hair. It took all my willpower to avoid slamming my fists into his face. A look of confusion flashed across her face, mirroring how I felt inside, but I refused to let it show.

What the fuck is their deal?

The man looked unhinged when he finally pulled his face out of the crook of Ryan's neck.

"Let's get down to business, shall we? I hear that The Skeletons of Society feel they are worthy of working for Los Muertos," he commented.

Let the dick-measuring contest begin, I guess.

I relaxed in my chair, pretending to be at ease, making sure to match the arrogance coming from Mario. In this meeting, I would have to tread carefully and walk the line between holding my own and not pissing him off.

"Yes. Your father felt we would be good partners, seemed Ryan here needed some extra support getting her product out to her clients," I replied.

Yeah, asshole. I know now that you aren't the one doing any of the work here in Tucson.

143

His nostril flare was the only tell that my words had hit their mark. Unfortunately, when you deal with slimy bastards, it's hard to predict what they'll do next. Mario snaked his hand up Ryan's ramrod straight back until it was nestled in the space where her neck and shoulders met. The movement was possessive but not in a romantic manner. More like a child with a favorite toy he wasn't willing to share—a plaything.

And I wasn't convinced Mario was careful with his playthings.

The scene before me reminded me of a puppeteer with his marionette. Ryan sat there, waiting for her strings to be pulled. This was not the woman who would verbally go to war with me or instantly make me hard with the intensity of her glare.

"Yes, my *fiancée* has done a wonderful job handling business for me here in Tucson. I'll have to be sure and reward her," his slimy voice rang out.

It felt like getting punched in the gut, his words pulling the rug from under me.

Ryan's head attempted to snap to look at Mario, but I watched as his fingers dug into her neck. A warning that she should behave. Or maybe my interpretations were all wishful thinking. Maybe Ryan had been Mario's girl this entire time. She figured flirtation would get her what she wanted.

I stiffened at that last thought. Was her reaction because she was shocked that Mario had spilled the secret so soon? My jaw clenched at the thought of her lying to me.

Which was hypocritical since I was lying to her.

This whole partnership was built on deceit. No one could really tell the truth from a lie. We thought Mario was in charge here—lie. We thought Ryan was a man—lie. We told Los Muertos we were entering this partnership to be at their beck and call—lie. Were any of us actually telling the truth?

I dropped the shutter down on my feeling, cutting off

the little bit of myself I had allowed to slip through when I met Ryan.

My eyes stayed with Mario, not sparing Ryan another look. But I could only hold out for so long. I glanced her way before continuing the conversation. It was eerie how cold and calculating her face was. Indifferent. Her feelings were effectively turned off. She'd shown more passion and emotion when interrogating Spinner. This version of her looked like her soul was dead.

A doll.

"Will it still be Miss Jimenez-to-be that we are working with, or have you come back to take your place?" Even to my ears, my voice sounded harsh.

Silence stretched between the three of us as Mario made his decision. This meeting seemed to be nothing more than a pissing match from a man who wanted to try to assert his authority. In typical narcissistic fashion, Mario needed his ego stroked. That was probably why he wore those loafers with the stacked heel. An attempt to combat his little-man syndrome. He was not particularly short, but my six-foot-two-tall ass would tower over him. God, was he going to hate Dex.

His voice finally cut through the silence. "Yes, you'll be seeing me around now. It seems that I'm needed here in Tucson to…keep an eye on the current activities."

My stomach soured at the thought of being around this man. But it was a necessary evil if I was to get my job done. I was trying not to think of how his staying in town meant I would have to watch him and Ryan be a couple.

"Was there anything else you needed from me? Or does that conclude this meeting? Because I have club business to attend to if we're finished," I asked, already pushing off the chair to stand.

I knew I was being short, but I couldn't give two fucks. I was itching to get out of this damn office, needing to distance myself from Ryan. I still had a job to do. So I needed to get my shit together regarding her—quickly. I couldn't figure out why I was worked up over this situation. I should be happy. Her being taken would make it easier to keep my dick in my pants. Yet my brain didn't seem to give a damn about the logic.

Mario nodded his head before speaking again. "You have a shipment and delivery happening in the next few days."

My eyebrows shot up. This was the first I'd heard about this, and a few days didn't leave much time to plan. Mario's comment seemed to rouse the Ryan I'd come to know from whatever spell she'd been under during this meeting.

"What shipment? I don't have anything scheduled for delivery," she pried, attitude spilling into her tone.

Blood pooled in my mouth with how hard I bit down on my cheek when I caught Mario throwing a murderous glance at Ryan. Apparently, she wasn't allowed to question his competence in front of people. I always thought the sign of a bitch-ass man was when he was scared to be called out publicly.

Mario looked her in the eyes and answered through gritted teeth.

"I just scheduled one, Muñeca, which is within my right to do as the owner of Lotería. Not to mention I'm in charge of Los Muertos's arms deals," he seethed.

I waited on bated breath for the sass I'd come to love. But it never came.

"Ryan will reach out to you with the details soon." The asshole didn't bother looking at me as he dismissed me from the pointless meeting he had called me to. I headed for the door without saying a word, wanting out of there. Fuck, I should be working on getting into Mario's good graces. Getting close to him.

But I couldn't bring myself to do it.

Not today, not with Ryan sitting on his lap. Wishing it was mine she was on. At the last moment, I looked over my shoulder in her direction. It was stupid, but I was powerless to resist seeing her face one last time. I fully anticipated that she would be avoiding eye contact, but she wasn't. She was staring directly at me. But her emotions were so locked down that I didn't know if she was trying to tell me something through those coffee-colored eyes or not.

Part of me felt that she was waiting for a sign from me. But what that was, I didn't know. We'd been doomed from the beginning, so why drag out the torture?

So I turned my back and strode out the door.

Ryan

The moment the office door closed, I launched myself out of Mario's lap.

"What the fuck was that, Mario?" I seethed.

He leaned back in the office chair, unfazed by my outburst, which pissed me off further. He steepled his fingers and took a moment to rove over my body. Assessing me like I was a museum piece. There was no heat in Mario's gaze the way there was in a certain surly biker's. His eyes finally met mine.

"What, Muñeca, is it that you're upset about? That you didn't know about a shipment happening earlier than you had scheduled?" His head cocked to the side in confusion. "I think that's hardly a reason to be so worked up. I do know how to run an arms deal. I have the details worked out."

There was no way to hide the shock on my face. The fucker couldn't actually think *that* was what I was pissed about. I pinched the bridge of my nose, figuring out the best way to approach this conversation with him. Because one thing I knew for sure was that Mario could not be dealt with in the same way I handled other men.

A quiet part in the back of my brain asked why I couldn't. But I attempted to push that aside. Like I'd done for years when Mario overstepped my boundaries.

It dawned on me at that moment. He didn't overstep them.

I moved them for the fucker.

"Yes, I'm pissed about that too. But that wasn't what I was referring to, Mario. I'm talking about that you announced me as your *fiancée*," I stated, disbelief clear in my voice.

Mario's face scrunched up in genuine confusion, making my jaw drop. How could it come as a surprise that I would be upset about that?

"Muñeca, is this because I haven't given you a ring? I do have to admit; I should've rectified that years ago. Probably would have saved me the trouble of meeting with that piece of shit. I can't believe my father thought the Skeletons of Society MC would be worthy of working for me." A sigh left his lips. "But oh well, it is done. For the time being."

Mario took my stunned silence as an opportunity to lean forward and grab my hand, pulling it to his mouth and placing a kiss on my ring finger. The sincerity in his words was visible in his eyes.

"I'll get you a ring now, Muñeca," he commented.

What kind of fucked-up dream was I having? Thirty minutes ago, I was hot and bothered watching a man choke someone for me. I was ready to let Gunner take me against a wall. Any wall. Fuck, all the walls.

Now, I stood, letting my mouth open and close like a fish—*idiota*.

Mario was serious about this whole fiancée business. All the conversations about moving me to Mexico with him came rushing back. Nikki was right. I should've put a stop to his obsession years ago. Because now here I stood, apparently fucking engaged.

The flash of betrayal that I witnessed on Gunner's face was the worst part of this whole situation. And I hadn't helped anything with my silence. How the fuck would I go about fixing a shit show like this?

"Oh, hey. Remember how Mario told you I was his fiancée, and I didn't say shit? Yeah, well, I'm not his fiancée, and I think we should have sex."

I took a deep breath, deciding to rip the Band-Aid off when it came to Mario. But I would be fucking lying if I said I wasn't nervous about how he would react. I'd seen a man die for sitting in a chair Mario decided was his. He said disrespect was a killable offense. How would he take me breaking off an engagement?

Santa Muerte, please let me not get shot before I make out with the biker. Amen.

"Mario, we aren't together, not romantically. Weren't you out with someone a few weeks ago? I care for you. Or, I mean, I owe you this whole world you brought me into. And I'm thankful you've kept me around all these years." I paused my blabbering, cringing at my word vomit. God, this was a shitty breakup speech.

"But we aren't engaged..." I rushed out, my eyes closing, waiting to hear him yell.

My eyes popped back open when nothing happened, searching his face for any sign that I might be taking my last breath. The chill in his gaze was as unnerving as the cruel smile that appeared. He stood up, closing the distance between us. His fingers curled under my chin, tilting it to make eye contact.

"Oh, my little Muñeca. Still so naive. You've always been—and will always be—*mine*." He said the last word with a possessive tone that made my skin crawl.

Then his lips brushed against my ear. "I'll share you with no one, Muñeca. I claimed you for myself long ago and have done many things to ensure you stay with me. I suggest you remember that," he whispered.

A chill ran down my spine at his words. Like so many things he said lately, it felt like there was more to what he was saying than the words themselves. Leaning forward, he kissed the top of my head before making his way toward the door.

The feeling of dread was suffocating.

I sat down in my office chair, hanging my head in my hands. What the fuck was happening right now? And why was I most worried about how Gunner had reacted?

"Fuck, I need a margarita and a good lay," I breathed out.

Too bad the person I wanted to fuck me up against a wall thought I was engaged to the heir of the cartel his MC was working for. An heir who was speaking in creepy riddles and didn't seem to grasp the concept of me not being engaged to him.

Oh, and Gunner was probably pissed that I let him flirt with me while *lying* to him about being with Mario. It wasn't true, but I sure as fuck hadn't corrected this whole situation moments ago.

Fuck.

Lotería was closed tonight thanks to Mario needing it for *Dios* knows what. So I was going to go home, binge-watch trashy shows, and pretend to live a normal fucking life.

One season.

I gave myself one season of *The Real Housewives of Beverly Hills* to throw a pity party and get in touch with my emotions. Then it was time to be a bad bitch again. Meaning stabby and aggressive.

Was that healthy? Definitely not, but I couldn't care less. It felt better to put on my strong bitch attitude than my whiny, worry-over-men one. Too bad for everyone else,

I wouldn't be putting up with anyone's shit, so they better come to work on their best behavior.

I strode into Lotería's loading area, ready to assess what flaming pile of shit Mario was leaving on my doorstep now.

"Of course it's fucking chaos in the warehouse," I mumbled in irritation, taking deep breaths and reminding myself it was bad to shoot people.

My eyes caught on Robert shoving his finger into the chest of one of Mario's lackeys. All the men were supposed to work for Los Muertos, but the ones Mario kept close definitely seemed to only bend to his will.

Good thing I loved breaking men.

"Hey, pendejos. *¿Que estas haciendo?*" I yelled out.

They both stopped mid-argument and turned to look at me. Robert's face went from pissed off to relieved. Obviously, he was happy I was here to sort shit out.

"This asshole wants to send the shipment through Reaper territory," Robert said, flailing his arms around in irritation.

My forehead wrinkled in confusion at what Robert was claiming. I didn't even know who this other guy was. I didn't know the names of any of Mario's men; I always just called them Armando. Everyone got the same name because I didn't care to learn their real ones. Plus, nothing pissed off the male species faster than calling them by another man's name.

Striding past the two grown-ass men acting like children, I made my way to inspect the shipment that had arrived while Mario was "using" Lotería. A hand slammed down on the lid before I could pry it open. My eyes cut to Armando.

Who did this asshole think he was? Better yet, who did he think I was? Because I'm not the one.

"Move your fucking hand, Armando. Or I'll remove it from your wrist." My voice cut through the silence, unreleased raged clear in my tone.

He gave me a cocky grin. Fucker thought he was about

to tell me what to do because he was a part of Mario's goon squad. But Mario was on my shitlist, and I didn't care if I pissed him off today. Plus, this *chismoso* overestimated how much his boss would care about him getting hurt at my hands.

"Name's not Armando, and I'm in charge here. Now back the fuck up. I ain't letting some bitch open these crates," he spat out.

A red haze coated my vision, and the whole room could probably hear the grinding of my teeth.

"Don't shoot him. Don't shoot him. Don't...fuck it. Stab him."

Without breaking eye contact, I slammed my switchblade down, pinning his pinky to the wooden top. Armando's eyes widened in surprise before he started shrieking like a total pussy.

"Let's have a little lesson, shall we? I'm fucking in charge here. I run this club, and I run these guns. If I want to open the fucking crate, I can, and I will. And if I decide to cut out your tongue because you pissed me off, no one in this room will stop me." I leaned in closer and bared my teeth. "If you want to test the theory, keep standing in my fucking way. Otherwise, move." My voice was loud enough to carry over the entire warehouse. His head nodded vigorously while his eyes darted to the blade still stuck in his finger.

"Okay, yeah. Now, take that out of my finger." His voice came out whining and desperate.

Rolling my eyes, I yanked out the blade, causing a squelching noise that made Armando turn green.

"Don't you dare puke in my warehouse, Armando," I stated.

With a fearful look, he scurried back to where Robert was giving him a mile-wide grin—clutching his barely injured pinky.

"Who said we're going through Reaper territory?" I called out, lifting the lid.

The crate seemed to look emptier than usual, but I was

overanalyzing everything lately. Something was off in the underbelly of Tucson, and I didn't want to get fucked over when shit when down. So I was keeping my head on a swivel.

Not-Armando-Armando answered, "The MC moving our shit decided the route they wanted to go."

My expression probably looked like I'd sucked on a lime. Luckily, no one was looking at my face. Schooling my features, I turned around. What Armando was saying sure as shit didn't sound right, but the problem was that I didn't know what was going on—yet.

Someone was lying, and it was clear I needed to keep my cards close. Mario's inner circle was only loyal to him, and I didn't know the Skeletons well enough to trust them. And I sure as shit didn't trust the Reapers.

"Okay. So when is the pickup, and where is the drop? I'm guessing this is one of Mario's clients because I didn't schedule this," I said, watching Armando's facial expression as I spoke.

I didn't think he would know anything more. Mario didn't reveal shit to anyone. Half the time, Sergio didn't know what was happening with him.

As if speaking his name summoned him, Mario came striding through the bay door.

"Muñeca, what are you doing here? Shouldn't you be overseeing the dancers?" His cheery tone barely hid the edge in his voice.

What the fuck was up with these men not wanting me to be around my own club?

I folded my arms over my chest, not wanting to deal with Mario's shit. He'd gone too far with the fiancée stunt.

"I'm getting the details for the run, Mario. Details you've yet to share with me," I snarked.

Mario had a long leash when it came to my tolerance of how he treated me. There was some weird Stockholm syndrome going on when it came to him. Because it was hard to let go of the fact that Mario had pulled me off the street, even if it was with a threat. At some point, I'd accepted his treatment. Maybe because he held Sergio over my head or because he would sprinkle in affection...whatever it was, I'd turned a blind eye.

When I moved to Tucson, the distance made me feel free. So, when Mario *was* around, it felt easiest to do as he wanted. But Nikki was right. I lived with my head in the sand when it came to him. Now, I didn't know what to do about it. Maybe being under Mario's thumb forever was the penance I had to pay.

It wasn't like I could go anywhere besides Los Muertos. My soul had splintered at some point, and when it had healed, it entombed the shards. I wasn't a normal woman. Sure, I had a heart; I cared. But my thirst for vengeance and blood was not something I could bond over with the typical suburban housewife.

"Hi, Susan, how's your Starbucks this morning? What's this? Oh, these are just the bloody clothes I now have to burn. Arterial spray is a real bitch to get out in the wash."

No. Those women didn't know what it was like to look over their shoulder at every turn or feel the high of sliding a blade through flesh. They would never know the pleasure of executing men whose victims wouldn't have otherwise seen justice.

Maybe I didn't get to be cared for—to have love. Was this all part of atoning for my original sin? Maybe seeing the blood of evil men on my hands was the only thing my heart deserved.

Ironically, Mario's voice was the lifeline that pulled me out of my contemplative thoughts. "I haven't shared the details with you because I have this deal handled. You can go to the club's main area, and I'll handle everything back here," he stated, his tone flippant.

I bristled a bit at his dismissal. It felt odd. Mario was usually eager to keep me around, taking pleasure in disrupting my schedule and making me heel at his side like a damn dog. A vibration pulled my attention to my phone screen.

It looked like I'd been right to follow my gut and reach out to one of my trusted information channels.

"Sounds good, Mario. You know how to find me if you need me," I replied absently. I turned to leave before Mario became too curious.

I had shit to do.

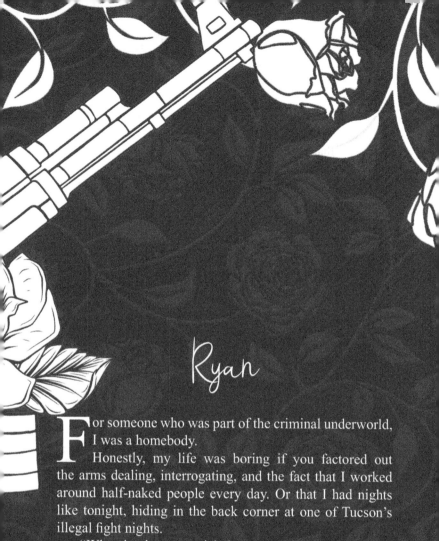

Ryan

For someone who was part of the criminal underworld, I was a homebody.

Honestly, my life was boring if you factored out the arms dealing, interrogating, and the fact that I worked around half-naked people every day. Or that I had nights like tonight, hiding in the back corner at one of Tucson's illegal fight nights.

"Why do they not pick better ventilated venues?" I grumbled, trying to block out the smell of booze, sweat, and marijuana. By all accounts, I looked like I was lounging against the wall. Arms hung loosely by my sides, and my head ducked down, hidden by my hood. But I was on high alert. This wasn't exactly friendly territory.

These fight nights were supposed to be *neutral ground*. But that meant you found all sorts of lowlifes showing up here. Making it the perfect place to scope out information. Not everyone in the criminal world was with a gang or the cartel. Some thrived at being silent and unseen, and for enough money or blackmail, you could get them to tell you what they heard in the whispers.

That was Sam. We came up together on the streets, and I still didn't know her origin story. But I wasn't big on asking about shit that was none of my business. I already knew all I needed about her. She was loyal as fuck and didn't want anything to do with any organization. So the information was unbiased.

"Why are there cats fucking in the warehouse?" I asked in confusion. I searched for where the god-awful noise was coming from, only to find the source was two chicks going at it in the cage. They didn't know what the fuck they were doing, and I rolled my eyes before glancing back around the room.

I never knew why Sam stayed in this world, but that question felt hypocritical. Tonight, I was glad I had a friend and resource like her in my pocket.

The flash of a familiar face caused me to home in on a corner of the warehouse. Reapers. My blood boiled. It wasn't only Lotería they were banned from; it was all of Tucson. They were smarter this time around and chose not to wear their cuts. I wasn't marching over to beat their asses because I didn't want any of them knowing I was here.

Skeletons of Society were here too. Torque and some others were fighting tonight. Good fighters brought in big bucks, and Torque would do well in this circuit. If reapers weren't here tonight, I might've stayed after meeting Sam to watch them. Disappointment hit like a punch to the gut when none of the Skeletons of Society members had piercing green eyes and a mustache I wanted to experience between my thighs.

But then again, I had no clue what it would be like between us now. Not that anything had happened between the two of us anyway. But the physical attraction and chemistry seemed to simmer between us from the very beginning.

"Fuckin' Mario. And his shitty timing. With his shitty non-proposal proposal," I whisper-yelled. There were enough drugs and drinks flowing tonight that no one looked my way as I talked to myself.

A sigh of defeat left my lips.

Gunner treated me differently than anyone else in my life. He gave me respect because I deserved it, not because he was frightened of what I'd do. He was an alpha male, comfortable with himself. He didn't mind standing behind a woman, unlike Mario, where I wasn't allowed to express my opinion if it differed from his.

Hell, it could be the same, and he wouldn't want to hear it.

Out of the corner of my eye, I caught someone hunched over and quickly walking toward me, face covered by a hat. I tightened my grip on my switchblade, ready to use it if needed. But at the last moment, Sam popped her head up, looking me in the eye. A sly smile reached her face as she wagged her brows.

"I know better than to rush up on you, Ryan. Bet your hand is already gripping that switchblade of yours," she said, taking the seat next to me, both of our backs to the wall.

You learned really quick on the streets to be aware of your surroundings. It gave you the best chance of avoiding being jumped or attacked. And that still wasn't always enough to prevent it.

I smiled at one of my oldest friends. "Sam, you look like shit."

She tried to hide the smile playing at her lips with a scowl.

"Fuck off, Ryan. I'm sorry I don't get to sit up in my pretty tower and be entertained all day by beautiful people dancing *bachata* on stage in thongs," she sassed back.

I rolled my eyes at her description of my life as we faced forward to watch the room again. She knew the picture she painted of my life was utter bullshit.

"First off, the men do not wear thongs on stage. I can't get with the banana hammock look. Second off, you know that's not all I do all day; you're the one who delivers information on most of my other…clients. And third, no one is forcing you to get your face bashed in as a career."

In my peripheral, I caught the finger she gave me for that comment. Making me snicker.

"Fuck right off, Ryan. This black eye is the result of a *lucky* jab. I bash the faces in. If you ever came to my fights, you would know," she said.

Sam may have never joined a criminal organization, but her work wasn't exactly legal. She was a well-known name in the fighting circuit. I was good, but Sam was better. She lived and breathed fighting. I knew she could make it out on the legal side, but she never gave me a straight answer to why she wouldn't go.

Her tone changed. Catching up time was over. A grim sound in her voice told me I'd been right. Shifts were happening in the underbelly, and they were trying to stay hidden.

"Word on the street is Reapers had a mutiny. None of the officers are the same. Fresh meat is in power. But these fuckers are worse than the last bunch. And they have some outside involvement. But that bit of information is wrapped up tight."

I nodded slightly, absorbing what she was saying. How did I not hear about a mutiny?

"Had a guy that claimed to know a bit of what's going on, but I never got the info. Found him dead in the alley. They're working hard at keeping their movements quiet. Prepping for something, Ryan." Her voice was low and worried. Sam never worried.

Before responding, I searched for the MC in question. Were they out of their cuts tonight to meet with their outside source? I scanned the crowd but couldn't spot any of them near me.

After a beat, I answered, "Yeah, I feel something

coming. Reapers showed up at Lotería, asking for someone in charge. I wondered why the fuckers thought they would be welcome since I delivered a clear message they weren't. Guess it's because those fuckers are dead." I trailed off, trying to figure out where all the pieces fit.

Sam's gaze burned a hole in the side of my face. I turned to meet her hazel eyes.

"Be careful, Ryan. Their backer is big if they decide to take a swing at Los Muertos…no one has the balls to take on the Mexican cartel unless they're unhinged or well funded. Or both. And all of those options are dangerous," she warned.

I nodded in agreement before turning back to the crowd, feeling like we were being watched.

Sam slipped from the table, disappearing into the crowd without another word. We couldn't afford to spend too much time around one another. Not when she traded information with me. So we always met on neutral ground and kept the conversation under five minutes. Then she would slink away.

A few minutes passed before I left the table to find my way out of the warehouse and back to my comfy bed. Torque's familiar face was over by the cage, cornering for another member I'd never spoken to. I winked at him from under my hood, and a genuine grin appeared when it dawned on him who I was. Thankfully, the guy hadn't turned into a douchebag after our fight. Some men couldn't handle a woman capable of physically taking care of herself.

Goosebumps broke out along my arms as the cool night air hit my face. The alley didn't smell much better than inside the warehouse, but at least the air out here wasn't stale. The former fire exit door slammed closed behind me. I'd wanted to avoid the chaos at the main entrance, so I let myself out a side door.

Sounds of grunts and fists hitting flesh caught my attention. They were too loud for it to be fight sounds from inside. My blood ran cold when I saw four men attacking a small figure partially shielded by their bodies. But the hat on the ground told me exactly who they were attacking. My blade was in my hand without a second thought, and I charged at the one closest to me. They were too close together to use my Sig; I wouldn't risk hitting Sam with a bullet.

Close-quarter knife fight it is.

Sam was attempting to hold her own, but fighting off four grown-ass men was a tall order for one female. Fuck, it would be hard for a man. What kind of assholes jump a woman? Before any of them knew what was happening, my arm wrapped around the chest of the one closest, restraining his back to my chest while I slid the blade across his throat. Hot blood coated my hand, and gurgling sounds were added to the mix.

"Dile hola al Diablo para mí," I whispered in his ear.

The surprise element allowed that maneuver to work, making it a one-trick pony. The other three turned and witnessed his last breath, and the break in their attention allowed Sam to wiggle free and land a solid hook to one of the attackers, dropping him unconscious.

The odds were even, but who knew how long homeboy would stay out. Watching their buddies drop to the floor snapped the two remaining pendejos out of their stunned states. The one at my left lunged forward. The awkward angle slowed my ability to face him head-on, giving him the upper hand. I spun out of his reach but not before his blade slid across the side of my ribs.

"Fuck," I cried out, but the sounds of our fight were being drowned out by the crowd's roar inside the warehouse.

"That's the plan, bitch. Boss doesn't care what we do with the whore. Just as long as we silence her." A cruel grin appeared on the face of the asshole who'd just sliced me.

"But now that you've gone and stuck your nose where it doesn't belong, we get two to play with," he sneered.

I snarled at him. "I'm going to cut out your tongue and shove it down your throat so you choke on it."

I hated men like this. Men who felt they had the right to treat women as property. Limp-dick men who couldn't get pussy, so they decided to take it. He'd sealed his fate. I might've left him lying here injured. But now—now he'd be taking his last breaths in this alley.

Knowing Sam was fine now that the numbers were even, I focused solely on this asshole. A pathetic battle cry left his lips, and he charged like we were in a football game. Head tucked down, arms pumping at his sides like an idiot. Obviously, he hadn't been in many fights. Cocky fucker thought he could overpower me since he'd managed to land the lucky slice.

Using my speed, I side-stepped out of the way while simultaneously throwing out a kick that landed in his gut, knocking the wind out of him and causing him to bend over at the waist, clutching his stomach. Thank God for Mauy Thai lessons. Before he could recover and stand back up, I rushed in front of him, interlocking my fingers at the base of his neck and using my hands to hold him in place.

"Eat. A. Bag. Of. Dicks. Asshole," I yelled out, punctuating each word with a brutal knee to his face.

My jeans were soaked from the blood pouring from his face. His anguished cries drowned out the city sounds around us. Including Sam. I hoped she was doing fine on her own. I hadn't been able to get a good look to see how much damage she'd endured. But my focus was knocking this guy out before his brain caught up and he remembered the knife was still in his hand.

The asshole in my clutches went limp, and I let him slam to the floor before kicking him over to his back, exposing his throat. Seeing the bloody mess on his face brought a smile to my lips. Anyone watching this moment would think I looked like a bloodied, deranged psycho. But they hadn't witnessed the bulge in this piece of shit's pants when he talked about taking advantage of Sam and me. Crouching down, I let my blade spill the blood of a guilty man again, happy to reap another soul and send it to El Diablo.

Sam's voice cut through the adrenaline fog of the fight. But not before a weight slammed into my back, sending me sprawling onto the asphalt. I threw an elbow and got lucky it connected, giving me an opening to flip over so he didn't have my back. The man Sam had knocked out earlier regained consciousness and now had me pinned.

He was a big fucker, and there was no way to get his weight off me. My hips bucked up, attempting to create space and shrimp out, but it was no use. Meaty fingers curled around my neck, cutting off my airway. Black spots started appearing in my vision. I was fucked if I didn't figure out something fast. Shards of asphalt and other shit embedded in my palms as I frantically swept my hands along the ground, searching for my blade.

The moment my hand wrapped around the hilt, I jammed the knife into his throat where I knew his carotid artery would be, desperately stabbing to get him to release my throat, knowing I didn't have long before I passed out.

Moments before I was out of time, his grip loosened. Warm tears leaked from my eyes and ran down my cheeks.

The dead weight of his body was pressed on top of me, and I was too close to losing consciousness to move him. Everything was muffled and hazy, but commotion from the end of the alley still drew my attention.

Please, Santa Muerte, don't tell me these douchebags had backup.

My eyelids strained to stay open, wanting to see who was approaching, but they felt too heavy. Seconds before everything went black, a familiar face popped into view, but my brain couldn't register if it was friend or foe.

I huffed a laugh at the irony of my life being taken in the same place I'd first taken one.

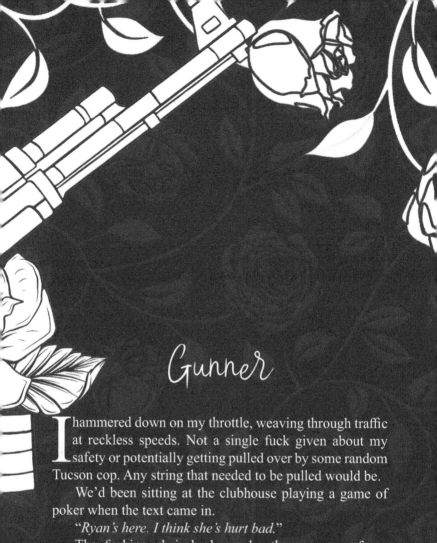

Gunner

I hammered down on my throttle, weaving through traffic at reckless speeds. Not a single fuck given about my safety or potentially getting pulled over by some random Tucson cop. Any string that needed to be pulled would be.

We'd been sitting at the clubhouse playing a game of poker when the text came in.

"Ryan's here. I think she's hurt bad."

The fucking chair broke under the pressure of me shooting up when I read those words. Blood drained from my face, and every rational thought left my brain. Thankfully, Dex took my phone to see what caused my reaction, and he called Torque to get the details of where we needed to go. I wanted them to get her an ambulance since she was lying there bleeding out. But they outvoted me. We were all involved in too much shady shit to call an ambulance or go to a hospital. I let them believe I agreed with them and took off on my bike. I would take her myself if she needed a real hospital, consequences be damned.

I'd acted like a bitch all weekend. Pissed off at the world—and Ryan—for not telling me she was engaged to Mario. A fact that honestly should've brought me relief, but it didn't. So I'd sulked. Not even Dex wanted to be around me. Today was supposed to be about figuring out how to get my shit together before seeing her again. Because regardless of my conflicted feelings, there was still a job to do, and we still needed to get information out of her. But then that text came in, and all plans were thrown out the window. A burning need to make sure she was okay filled my body; nothing else mattered.

The city passed by in flashes, nothing registering. My sole focus was getting to the pin on my map. Getting to Ryan. The mouth of the alley came into view, and I took the corner into the alley at breakneck speeds, not bothering to slow down. Dex's words popped into my head.

"*Asshole, you won't be any help to her if you're splattered across the pavement,*" he'd warned. Neither one of us commented about my reaction to the news—how out of my mind I was for someone I should have zero feelings for.

My breath caught in my lungs, and a chill ran down my spine at the scene in front of me. I didn't even know how I got off my bike. One moment, I was at the mouth of the alley, and the next, I was crouched down, cupping Ryan's face in my hands.

"What the fuck happened?" I hissed out to whoever the fuck was standing around.

My eyes were locked on Ryan, taking in the eerily calm expression on her face as she lay there in a puddle of blood. Scanning over her body, I looked for the source, worried I was already too late.

"It's not her blood. I already checked her over," Torque called out.

The fact that he was so calm pissed me off. Was no one else feeling as if they were being buried alive—suffocating

170

and panicked? Squeezing my eyes shut, I forced myself to take calming breaths, needing to gain control of myself.

You can't shoot everyone in this alley.

"She's got a slice on her rib. Looks pretty shallow, but it'll need cleaning, maybe stitches. Didn't think you'd want me lookin' too close. When I walked out, some asshole was on top of her, choking her out…" His stare burned a hole in the back of my neck. He was waiting for me to snap.

I looked at Torque with a murderous glare. His hands lifted in surrender. Logically, I knew he wasn't responsible for this, but my rage didn't care.

"Hey, Gunner, as soon as I saw what was happening, I started running to help. But your little badass there had it covered. Before I could reach 'em, she pulled a knife out of god knows where and stabbed him in the neck until he was no longer a problem."

"That sounds 'bout right. She wouldn't take a man's bullshit." I pushed her hair out of her face, gently caressing her tanned skin with my thumb.

"There was another chick here when I ran up; she was in pretty rough shape. But as soon as she saw me tend to Ryan, she up and left," Torque said quietly.

That got an eyebrow raise from me. Who was this other woman, and why were she and Ryan fighting off four men? Or maybe it was one against five. The thought of Ryan being outnumbered made my blood boil.

"Where the fuck is the rest of the Los Muertos crew? Why was she out here alone fighting off grown-ass men?" I yelled out before lowering my voice. "I swear when I see that punk-ass motherfucker, I'll kill him."

I was seething.

"I don't know, man. I wondered the same thing. I was surprised when I saw her in there tonight. At first, I thought maybe she was fighting. But she had her hood pulled up over her face and looked like she was trying to blend in."

His words caught my attention. Why was she here tonight?

"I saw her walk out the fire exit door before I cornered Jax's fight. Thank God the fucker got a TKO in the first round. That's the only reason I was out here to see all this shit in time. If the fight had gone the distance, I don't know who would have shown up next." There was a tinge of regret in Torque's voice. Seems my Latin beauty had made an impression on more than just me.

", fucker, I'm glad you were here to help her. But you better only think of her as a sister, you hear? She's off-limits," I practically snarled at Torque while shielding her body from view with mine.

A sly smile crept up on Torque's face, his hands back up in surrender. "You got it, man. She's your woman."

I opened my mouth to argue when Dex pulled down the alleyway in a blacked-out SUV. Not wanting to take any chances if this was turf war-related, I'd made sure he brought the bulletproof vehicle to transport her.

"Thank fuck," I muttered under my breath.

Careful of the wounds, I cradled Ryan in my arms and strode toward the back passenger door and gently laid her on the bench seat before I moved to get in.

Dex's hand on my shoulder stopped me. "You have to check the scene, man," he whispered. The look he gave me was loaded.

My hands rubbed down my face. Fuck, you're right," I groaned, pissed that I was the best person for the job.

The scene needed to be pieced together so we knew what the hell had happened. At least until Ryan woke up and told us her version, but even that wouldn't shed light on the truth. I glanced around the alley. It looked like a bloodbath. Ryan probably wouldn't have details about anything other than what she was involved in. And based on how gruesome and sloppy everything was, this seemed like a heat-of-the-moment attack. Part of me was pissed Torque hadn't gone after the mystery woman, but I would've beaten him to a pulp if he left Ryan lying alone.

"I'll take good care of her, man. She'll be waiting in

the guest room at the clubhouse when you get back," Dex commented when I still hadn't moved.

My head snapped up at the mention of putting her anywhere other than my bed. Dex probably figured I wouldn't want her close after I learned of her and Mario. But her being away from me and unprotected, like she was tonight, made my stomach turn.

"No, I want her in my bed." I gave her one more glance before I strode toward the crime scene, wanting to get started. I called over my shoulder, "And Dex, the doctor and you. You're the only person allowed in the room when he's checking her. She doesn't get exposed more than she has to be. Got it?"

He searched my face, for what, I didn't know. But when he was done, I received a firm nod as a response.

"Go find out what happened, brother. Shit's getting weird, and I've got a feeling moves are about to be made—by all of us," he warned.

He was right—too many coincidences for my liking. Ryan, at an underground fight night, hosted by a neutral party, but not for fighting? And if Torque was correct, she didn't want to be recognized. She was collecting information; I'd put my money on it.

On what? That was the million-dollar question.

I watched as the red-tinted tail lights drove out of sight, carrying the woman who'd clawed her way into my chest. She wasn't supposed to; this fucked everything up. Shaking my head, like that'd clear my confusion, I got to work trying to figure out what the hell was happening.

"Hey, Gunner. We cleaning this shit up or getting Los Muertos to do it?" Torque called out.

"Depends on what we find out. We've got a partnership to run guns, but that doesn't mean we have to share everything we know with them," I replied, crouching down next to the body that'd been on top of Ryan.

Anger thrummed through my veins. If only I could bring this piece of shit back to life and kill him again—slowly and painfully. I looked over at Torque, making sure he got the hidden meaning in my words.

We couldn't trust Los Muertos.

He nodded his head, understanding. "I'll go check those two for anything useful," he answered.

If it benefited us to share the information found in this alley, we would. But if it were better kept in-house, then we wouldn't be telling Los Muertos shit. Sure, Ryan could tell what she knew, but the fact that she showed up without anyone from the cartel said a lot.

The man in front of me didn't look familiar, but that didn't mean too much. He wasn't wearing any colors or a cut.

"You may not be wearing anything, but what's your ink got to say?" I mumbled, pulling up the edges of his blood-soaked shirt.

Reaper. Of course, the fucker was a reaper.

Was this retaliation for Lotería? Did they know she would be here tonight? Were they having her followed? Or was this taking advantage of an opportunity? My mind was whirling with possibilities.

"Gunner, you may want to see this."

The worry in Torque's voice made the hair on my neck stand on end. He was crouched over another body; this one on his side with a clean slit through his throat. If I had to guess, he was taken out first and probably from behind. The guy's shirt was pulled up to under his armpit, and my blood ran cold at what I saw inked on his ribs—a tattoo of La Santa Muerte, the Mexican folk saint of death.

A cartel tattoo.

I tore my eyes from the tattoo and looked at Torque. His face reflected the hundreds of unanswered questions I was also asking.

"Maybe she wasn't alone tonight like I thought?" The tone in his voice let me know he didn't believe that.

But fuck, it would be nice if that was the reality of this situation.

Because if this guy *wasn't* with Ryan tonight…then Los Muertos had a loyalty problem.

Two cartel members.

That's what checking the other bodies revealed. I decided this information better stay in-house until I spoke to Ryan. Sergio wouldn't keep me in the loop if I turned this over to him, and I wanted to know if she had showed up with these guys or not.

If so, did they turn on Ryan or die at the hands of the Reapers and mystery girl?

There were too many unanswered questions, and I wanted to be the one to figure them out. Not Los Muertos.

I left Torque and some prospects we called to cover the cleanup. We decided to dump the bodies elsewhere and hose down the blood. Tucson cops rarely patrolled that part of town; they let the criminals police themselves. And with that alley being outside the warehouse of a known fight ring venue, the remaining blood wouldn't be given a second glance.

My ride back to the clubhouse was almost as reckless as my ride to the alley, conflicting emotions raging through me at the idea of seeing Ryan. I wanted to confirm with my own eyes that she was all right, but the thought of seeing her again while she looked so fragile made my heart feel like it was in a vise grip, and I couldn't get enough oxygen into my lungs. My anger burned to new levels seeing her vulnerable.

Still, a smile crept onto my face when thinking about what Torque described. Obviously, I was deranged, because the idea of Ryan jamming a blade into that asshole's carotid over and over brought me joy.

I hated her being hurt, but I would never want to take away Ryan's need for violence.

"I'm going to spank your ass for not bringing me

tonight, Ryan," I yelled into the wind roaring by my face as I sped through Tucson.

I wanted to bear witness to the beauty of her brutality while letting her know she didn't have to do it alone.

We didn't have to be alone.

That thought was like a bucket of ice water over my soul because she wasn't alone—I was alone—she had Mario. I pushed my bike harder, itching to be with her while I could, like a junkie for her presence. I would take advantage of the time I got to have her before she was taken away from me.

I was off my bike the moment I pulled into the clubhouse. Throwing the door open, I stormed toward my room. But Pres was there to intercept me before I could get to my destination. His large body appeared in my warpath, halting me with one look. I gritted my teeth because I couldn't just tell him to fuck off. That's not how things were done in an MC.

"What happened out there, Gunner?" His eyes were hard, searching my face. "Dex brought Ryan back. Doc cleaned up her side, shallow cut. She's got some bruises on her throat, though. Dex said it looked like a massacre out there..."

I wouldn't be let through until I gave Pres something to work with. I did a quick look around to see who was within earshot, not trusting most people at the moment. Observant bastard picked up the movement, narrowing his eyes.

My tongue wet my bottom lip, buying me a split second to decide on wording. "Too many holes still need filling. Hopefully, Ryan'll have some answers when she wakes up. Two Reapers are now dead," I said.

Pres nodded his head in understanding, thinking that was all the information, and turned his body to let me pass. But I knew he needed to hear this next part.

I lowered my voice. "Two more dead...Santa Muerte tattoos..." I let my words trail off.

His eyes snapped to mine before he looked away, deep in thought. The unspoken implications hung in the air between us. Pres ran a hand through his salt-and-pepper hair—a tell. This information worried him.

His eyes found mine again. "When she wakes up, bring her to me. I want an account of what happened from her mouth." He pointed a finger my way. "Don't tell her beforehand. I want to minimize the chances of her fabricating a story in advance."

I nodded my head, attempting to hide my clenched fists. "Got it." My tone was clipped.

I didn't like Pres insinuating Ryan might be a liar. Logically I knew she might not share all she knew since we were from different organizations. I mean, I sure as hell didn't tell her the whole truth, but it still grated on my nerves. Moving past Pres, I was careful to keep my emotions under wraps, not wanting him to think I wasn't level-headed enough to be around her.

Cracking the door open, I poked my head inside, noting Dex sitting next to the bed in a chair he must have grabbed from downstairs. His head was in his hands, and he rubbed his tired eyes.

"How is she?" I asked, making sure to keep my voice low so I didn't wake her.

Dex looked up and caught my gaze. "She's good. Doc cleaned her up. Gave her a sedative and pain medication. Given what the alley looked like, homegirl's relatively unscathed. The cut and bruises on her throat are the worst of it all. She's got some other cuts and scrapes, but nothing major. She'll be knocked out for a bit and will probably be groggy when she comes to," he replied.

I nodded my head while moving to the bed. She looked so peaceful lying on my pillow with her dark locks splayed across it. I tucked a strand behind her ear before leaning forward and kissing her forehead.

"What did you find?" Dex prodded as I walked over to my dresser to strip out of my clothes. Thankfully, he didn't comment on my show of affection.

Dex would burn all our shit from tonight. Looking over

a scene was messy work, and we didn't want any evidence linking us to the alley.

A deep sigh left my chest. "You ain't gonna like it." Our eyes locked. "Feeling it's 'bout to get messy for us, Dex."

He straightened in his chair, prepping for the blow to come, nodding for me to continue.

"First guy I checked out was a reaper. Thought maybe Ryan got caught up in some retaliation shit. But Torque called me over to check out what he found. His dude... tatted with a cartel tattoo..."

Dex's jaw dropped slightly, his eyebrows scrunching in confusion as mine had.

"So was she there with him, and they fought off three reapers?" he asked.

I shook my head before continuing, "Thought the same thing at first, but there were two of them. Two reapers, two cartel members. I think Ryan and this other chick managed to kill all four." A sense of pride filled my voice.

A cruel smile played at my lips. "I bet my balls the one with the slit throat came from my girl," I said. My blood still boiled at her going up against them alone, but I couldn't deny she had the talent to do so. My mood turned when I remembered the object stuffed in my boot.

"Then there was this," I said.

Dex caught the small burner phone I lifted off one of the cartel members. I made sure no one saw me do it, wanting to keep this find under wraps.

"The last text message came from an unknown number—burner. Says, 'Take out the nosy bitch before she gets too close.' I don't know if that's referring to Ryan or the chick with her. But someone is pulling some strings," I commented, rubbing my forehead.

All the secrecy shit gave me a headache. We were being left out of the loop, which meant people would get hurt until we uncovered this shit. Dex stood and moved toward me, collecting my ruined clothes while holding up the burner.

"I'm guessing no one knows about this..."

I gave him a single nod. "*No one* knows…" I let the implications hang in the air.

The look Dex gave me said he knew what I was trying to say, and then he was out the door, leaving me alone with my sleeping beauty. The last thing I should have done was get in bed with her, but after seeing her lying lifeless in a pool of blood, I didn't give a damn about what I should be doing.

I would enjoy knowing she was pressed against me all night and not her asshole of a fiancé. Soft sheets brushed against me as I eased myself under. My calloused fingers met the silky smoothness of her skin. A growl left my lips. She was wearing nothing but a bra and panties. I didn't know if I was pissed or excited. Dex better not've looked at her, or I would dump him in the same grave I put the reapers.

Pushing my irritation down, I molded our bodies together, trying to convince my dick it needed to chill out because she was in no condition to entertain him. Fuck, being around Dex for so long had me talking to my dick like it was a whole other person.

The moment her back touched my chest, she let out a satisfied sigh and wriggled in close. Filling me with masculine pride. I told myself that even in her unconscious state, she knew I would watch over her. I didn't know if I was right, but it's what I would go with.

Fuck the rest; right now, all that mattered was Ryan.

Ryan

Great, I was for sure spending too much time around Gunner while not getting laid enough, and it was affecting me mentally. Because now I was having horny dreams and waking up wet and unsatisfied. Sleep was fighting to take me back under, and I was willing to go if it meant returning to the dream that had my body feeling so hot and overly sensitive.

Apparently, I fell asleep wrapped around my body pillow because something solid was against my front. My hips ground against the pillow in hopes of finding relief for the ache between my legs. A moan fell from my lips at the pulse of pleasure I experienced when pressure was applied to my clit. My teeth bit down on my pillow, knowing the orgasm I was planning on bringing myself to might wake Nikki up if I didn't silence myself.

But instead of soft fabric, I was met with the saltiness of skin, making my nipples pebble and increasing my need to reach my climax.

Great, now my brain was conjuring up the taste of his body.

A heavy hand landed on my ass, slamming my clit farther into the hardness of the pillow. The slight bite of pain almost put me over the edge. Damn, was this what lucid dreaming was like?

"Fuck, Gunner," I whispered his name, something I would only allow myself to do in the safety of my room.

"Ryan, if you continue to grind your wet pussy on my leg and bite my chest, I won't be able to keep myself from flipping you around and fucking you."

My eyelids flew open at the sound of his deep voice. His green eyes stared intently into mine, his tongue swiping along his bottom lip. Like he was getting ready to devour me.

My adrenaline spiked at the idea.

"I'm all for us fucking, babe, but make sure that's what you want. Because when I fuck you, I'm not planning on being gentle. I'm locking you away in a room all day and night until I have had my fill of this sweet pussy," he said, making sure to grind the thigh I was straddling against my clit at the last part. The corners of his delicious mouth curled as my body rebelled and let out another moan.

"What the fuck are you doing in my bed, Gunner?" I tried to bite out, but my words were breathy and desperate. God, I was going to need a cold shower. I attempted to untangle myself, but he gingerly wrapped his arm around my waist, pulling me closer. His thumb softly skimmed the skin at the bottom of my ribs, which I realized were bandaged. The intimacy of the moment caused my heart to stop. This wasn't what happened to me; men didn't tend to me or show me they cared.

Not even Mario did that.

It was dawning on me that I was more of a possession than a person to Mario.

"First of all, you're in my bed, babe. And second, I

know that look. You look like you want to run." He buried his nose in my hair, drinking me in. "But there's nowhere to go I won't find you, Ryan." His words were like a caress on my soul, and my body reacted. Everything tingled with an emotion I couldn't place. My eyelids fluttered closed, and my fingertips dug into his chest.

"Now, Brujita, stand at the edge of the bed like a good girl and let me check your cut," he commanded.

"Whatever, Gunner, make it quick. I have places to be," I snarked, attempting to sound unfazed. But it was utter bullshit. Gunner had the evidence of my feelings coated on his thigh.

Should I be concerned with hot I thought that was?

He pulled his face back, eyebrow raised. "How hot what is?" he asked.

My eyes widened at the realization that I'd said that thought out loud. Wanting to avoid his question, I scrambled out of his bed like my ass was on fire. I told myself I was doing as he said so I could sort out last night's shit show. Or I hoped it was last night. It dawned on me that I didn't know how I got here or how much time had passed since meeting Sam.

Fuck, Sam.

I went to open my mouth, but Gunner beat me to it. "We need to talk about what happened last night, Ryan," he said.

"Yeah, like how the fuck did I get here?" I asked, my voice trailing off the moment warm hands grasped my hips, guiding me to stand between his legs. I was trying to avoid looking at the massive bulge barely being concealed by his black boxer briefs. But looking at the tattoos snaking up his muscular thighs wasn't much better.

"Stop staring at my dick, Ryan. Just ask for it if you want it," he said while leaning forward and inspecting my newest scar. I was about to sass back some bullshit about me not wanting him or his body, but his dangerous growl stopped me in my tracks.

"Fuck, Ryan." His eyes met mine. They held an intensity

that shocked me. "How many times have you gotten hurt? What the fuck is your beautiful body doing with this many scars?" he seethed. His tone made me defensive. It sounded too close to how Mario spoke to me. "Fuck off" was on the tip of my tongue when his hands gently cupped my face.

"I can't risk worrying about you, Ryan. I have a job to do, and I can't do that and be worried about you." He ran his hands over his face before looking at me again. "And before you tear me a new asshole, I know you're more than capable of taking care of yourself. But I need you to stop doing things solo. Okay?" His hands traveled up my abdomen, leaving goosebumps in their wake and heat pooling at my core. "You call me when you go do things like you did last night—for my sanity." The sincerity in his voice sent me into a panic. I didn't know how to react to tenderness.

Stepping back, I tried to distance myself, feeling too exposed. And the feeling had nothing to do with me only wearing a red bra and thong right now.

"Gunner..." I blabbered, lost on what words to say. With a soft smile, Gunner wrapped his hands around the back of my thighs, pulling me so our bodies almost touched.

"I found your body in a fucking alley, babe. Lying in a literal pool of blood, I didn't know if it was yours or not. It pisses me off that no one was there to help you. That *I* wasn't there to strip the flesh from the motherfucker who thought he could mark you." His thumb rubbed across the bandaged wound. "You didn't call me to tell me what you were doing. We have a partnership now, remember?" he asked. His stare was so intense it was hard for me to keep eye contact.

I was taken aback by the rawness in his voice, like I'd hurt him by not telling him where I was.

"Gunner, we have a partnership when it comes to running guns. I don't have to involve you in everything I do. Besides, the look on your face the last time I saw you told me you didn't want to talk outside of work," I shot back. A yelp followed by a moan fell from my mouth as his calloused hand slapped my exposed ass cheek before rubbing away the sting.

God, what was wrong with me?

"Wrong answer, babe. From now on, you don't make a move without letting me know. Got it?"

"Gunner…"

His hand once again landed on my already sore cheek. My eyes closed as my toes curled against the floor. When I opened them back up, Gunner's face was inches from my ribs, unwrapping the bandage I didn't remember getting. The reality of my situation set in. My hussy side would have to chill until I could sort out what happened after losing consciousness.

My voice came out barely above a whisper. "What the hell happened? How did I end up here at the clubhouse?" I asked. On my side, I now donned a cut about four inches in length, not deep enough to need stitches. It'd been cleaned and wrapped. Gunner nodded his head in approval, apparently happy with how the wound had been cared for.

"I got a text from Torque last night saying he found you lying in the alley," he replied, his eyes again meeting mine, but the emotions from earlier were now gone, replaced by a neutral expression.

We were in a standoff, trying to figure out how much we should reveal to one another. Seconds passed, with neither of us doing anything more than assessing. Finally, Gunner sighed and patted the bed next to him.

I crawled back onto the soft, gray comforter, sitting across from him to watch his body language. I wanted to trust Gunner, but old habits died hard. So for now, this was all he would get: a truce and exchange of information.

Deciding I needed to show good faith. I revealed a little nugget of intel while fishing for my own.

"I was there last night meeting with an informant. Like always, we left separately. But when I entered the alley, I saw four assholes attacking. So I jumped in."

Gunner's eyebrows scrunched in confusion, making me wonder what information he had. But instead of asking about that, I asked the question on the tip of my tongue since I'd woken up.

"Was there…was there another female body?" I whispered.

Gunner shook his head, and a sigh of relief left my lungs. As long as Sam made it out of there, she could take care of herself and reach out when it was safe.

"Torque said she ran away as soon as she saw you were being cared for," he supplied.

Torque. Thank God he'd been the one to find me.

"Remind me to buy him a shot. I wasn't sure who was approaching right before I lost consciousness," I commented.

Gunner was staring off, deep in thought, since I mentioned why I was at the fight night. Not wanting to chance him not sharing what he knew, I sat quietly until he finally broke the silence.

"Why were they attacking her?" he questioned, suspicion thick in his voice.

I rolled my eyes at his question. Didn't he hear me say I walked out to them attacking her and just jumped in?

"I don't know why they were attacking her, Gunner. I was too busy trying not to get my ass beat to play twenty questions with them."

"Always a smartass," he replied, a smile now on his lips.

"Only when asked dumbass questions," I threw back.

He pinched the bridge of his nose, working through some internal debate. When he looked up at me, it felt like a shift in our relationship was about to happen. Somehow, I knew, once he spoke these following words, we were agreeing to be partners in more than arms dealing for Los Muertos and Skeletons of Society. *We* would become partners. His eyes searched mine for a sign that I even wanted that.

I pulled at my bottom lip, gnawing on it with my teeth. Did I want that?

"You show me yours, and I'll show you mine, big boy." My heart and mouth decided before my brain could keep up. A stab of insecurity hit me. What if I misread his body language? But the feeling was stamped out when he smiled at his words from our first meeting being thrown back at him.

"Okay, here's what I know. The four assholes who attacked your informant, two were reapers," he supplied.

That didn't come as a surprise.

"Makes sense. She told me her former source was found dead in an alley. He was probably tortured for information on who was asking too many questions," I responded.

"Yeah, well...the other two had cartel tattoos. Santa Muerte, to be exact..." he added.

My face drained of color. "Those were Los Muertos's men working with reapers? Muertos tried to kill me?" I pried, my voice thick with emotion.

Gunner squirmed uncomfortably, like he wanted to console me but didn't know how, so he continued, "One had a burner phone in his pocket. The last message was from a blocked number, said to take the bitch out. At first, I thought it was you, but I guess it was this informant chick."

"Sam, her name's Sam. She was getting me information on moves in Tucson's underbelly. I thought someone was intentionally trying to keep moves quiet." I looked up and met Gunner's eyes. "She told me the Reapers had a mutiny. Now there're all new players involved, worse than the last. She thinks they have an outside backer..." I let my words trail off, not wanting to voice what I knew we both were thinking.

Gunner did it for me.

"Someone in the cartel."

I nodded my head, not ready to say the words aloud.

"Did you know Mario has us doing a run later today? Says there's a specific route we gotta take, and guess what territory it takes us through?" he asked.

I scowled at Gunner's statement, remembering what Armando had said about the route.

"Well, it seems someone's trying to set you up because

Armando said your MC chose the route. And Mario told me I wasn't involved in this run," I said—mistrust for Los Muertos members seeping in.

A sly smile made its way up onto Gunner's face before he spoke. "Well, I say fuck Mario and his orders. Let's show up with you on the back of my bike anyway. The element of surprise may help us find who's fucking with us. Now, go get your cute ass in the shower."

Ryan

I rested my head against the cold tile of Gunner's shower, watching red water run off my body.

The Reapers were planning something big. Last night's attack felt like confirmation there was at least one rat in Los Muertos. My inner thoughts were interrupted by the sound of soft footsteps. Turning toward the noise, I was met with the sight of Gunner opening the shower door.

Holy Jesus, Joseph, and Mary. That body's a fucking work of art.

My eyes had to be blinking like I was having a seizure, drool probably collecting at the corners of my mouth. I'd yet to see the man naked, but this morning gave me an idea of what he was working with. Damn, he was glorious, standing there covered in tattoos. I watched as his eyes roved over my body. His cock hardened the longer he looked at me.

Never knew watching a cock harden was such a confidence booster.

I bit my lip in anticipation, breaking the already damaged skin. If we moved forward, it would change everything. He stepped closer so we were only inches apart.

"I couldn't handle knowing you were in here naked. So close, yet so far. I'll ask you this one time, Ryan," he said, voice coated in lust.

He was making me squirm with the intensity of his presence. My fingers itched to run down his chest. To trace the V leading to his cock, but I didn't dare move. Afraid I would break the moment.

"And what's so important, Gunner, that you needed to interrupt my shower?" I asked, my chest heaving in anticipation.

The corners of his mouth inched upward at my words. The man loved my attitude.

"I want to fuck you, Ryan. To absolutely destroy you, put you back together, and do it all over again." His hands were clenching and unclenching at his sides. He was restraining himself from touching me, probably equally as afraid to shatter the moment. "I want to own every part of you. But I want it all, Ryan. If you give yourself over to me, you will be mine. Understood?" he asked, voice so possessive it made my core clench.

My head nodded in response, moisture pooling between my legs with every word he'd spoken. But in the back of my head, I knew he was asking for more than this moment. There would be no going back from this, and I didn't care.

"Words, Ryan. I need you to tell me you're giving yourself over to me," he replied.

"Yes, Gunner. Fucking shatter me," I said, my voice coming out breathy.

The moment the words fell from my lips, my back slammed against the shower wall. Gunner's hands wrapped around my hips while he shoved his muscled thigh between mine, applying pressure to my clit, mimicking the position I'd woken up in this morning. The desperation and brutality alone felt like it could break me.

I was like a goddamn live wire.

Calloused hands roughly grabbed my jaw, forcing my mouth open. Gunner leaned forward, biting my bottom lip before licking away the blood I'd drawn a moment ago. My moan echoed off the shower walls.

"Yes, baby, grind that pussy on my leg. Use my body to bring you pleasure." He nipped at my jaw as I threw my head back, desperately trying to relieve the ache. His hot breath hit my ear, making my nipples pebble, aching to be touched.

"I thought I lost you last night, Ryan. Before I got to sink my cock into this sinfully delicious pussy." He bit down on my earlobe, drawing a moan from me. "Fuck your psycho fiancé. I'm not staying away from you, babe," he growled.

"Not my fiancé, Gunner. He never was," I breathed out, writhing against him. Somehow feeling too much and not enough. He let out a satisfied grunt before running his tongue up the hollow of my throat, fingers gripping tighter on my mouth, holding it open. My eyes flew open when he spat in my mouth before shoving his tongue inside.

Holy fucking Christ. I did not know I was into that.

My brain was busy recovering from the short circuit he caused, and Gunner took the opportunity to flip me around. The sensation of the cold tile against my sensitive breast caused me to cry out. I arched my back, firmly pressing my ass against his hardness.

"Fuck the lying, Ryan."

His calloused palm met my ass cheek with a brutal smack, causing my pussy to clench. But there was nothing there to fill it. Before I could reach down and do the job myself, Gunner snatched up my arms and wrenched them behind me.

"Tell me you want my cock. Tell me you're mine," he whispered in my ear, the vulnerability and anger in his voice almost too much to handle.

"Yes. You're the only man I've ever wanted to let close. I don't know what voodoo you've worked on me, but I want you, Gunner," I replied, shocked I'd showed my emotions.

"You're the one known as La Brujita, Ryan." His lips landed on the back of my neck, sucking gently. "You bewitched me." He slid one hand up to my throat, his other held my arms, before he growled in my ear. "I'm going to make it so you only think about my hand around your throat and the pleasure it brings you. That asshole from last night doesn't get space in this pretty head of yours. Now, you keep these right here. Do you understand?" he asked, my cheek rubbing against the tile wall it was pressed against as I viciously nodded my head.

"Remember, words, babe. I want your words."

I tried to recall how to even form words. My brain was overloaded with all the stimulation and deprivation I was feeling.

"Yes, Gunner, I won't move them. Now fucking touch me," I ground out.

The hand that held my wrists made its way down my body. Over my hip, my thigh, until he was centimeters from my clit. I squirmed, trying to force his fingers to touch me where I wanted, but his hand just tightened on my throat.

"Ryan," his voice dragged out my name like I was a naughty child, "don't be a brat. You're not going to rush me. I'm going to take my time with this sweet pussy," I cried out when he slapped my clit, reprimanding me. "Behave. Now, let's see how badly you want me."

I could hear the smile in his voice as he ran a finger along my slit.

"Fuck. You want me so fucking bad, babe." Lust coated his words.

He thrust two fingers into my wet pussy without warning, making me moan in pleasure. The pressure from his hand tightening on my throat increased the sensations. I let out a cry of protest when he removed his thick fingers.

"*Chinga tu madre,* Gunner. Fuck me," I growled out, hardly recognizing my voice. It was hard to tell if I was in pleasure or pain. I sucked in a breath as he dragged his fingers coated in my arousal and prodded at my ass.

"Soon, Ryan. Soon, I'm going to fuck you. And when I do, you'll never get away. Understand? You've ruined me. Changed all my plans, altered the very fabric of my future. So as punishment, I'm going to drag you along with me," he whispered in my ear. "I'm keeping you, Ryan. You hear? When all the shit hits the fan, when you fight me, when you question everything, 'cause you will. None of that will keep you from me. You won't get away."

His words were spoken as a promise. But I was too desperate to try to analyze what they meant. I did know that those words made me feel complete when spoken from his lips. There was a stark difference between this and the caged feeling when Mario said something similar.

My head hit his shoulder while my hands wrapped behind Gunner's neck—fingers entwining in his hair. Gunner groaned as my nails dug into his scalp.

His hands moved to my breast, pinching my nipples hard. I didn't know what I was being punished for, maybe for making him care, but he was just as guilty. I wasn't supposed to fall for anyone. Especially Gunner. Opening up meant heartbreak, and I already knew he would shred my war-torn heart to pieces. But I was learning I liked the pain and pleasure Gunner gave me.

Turning in his arms, I took in his face. His pupils were blown out with lust mixed with a look of longing and an emotion I couldn't quite place. Our eyes stayed locked as my tongue dragged down the ridges of his abdomen, my knees hitting the tile in front of him.

Dicks were not good-looking, but fuck me if Gunner's didn't look like the hottest thing I'd seen in my life. I leaned forward and lapped up the precum collecting at the head. The moan he let out had me reaching down to rub my clit. But my fingers never made it to their destination. Gunner tangled his hand in my hair and yanked back. Water ran down my face, making it hard to see and breathe.

When did waterboarding become hot?

"You are not to touch yourself, babe. Your hands are on me or behind your back, but that dripping cunt of yours doesn't get touched," he commanded.

I whimpered at his words, fucking whimpered, never having been more turned on in my life. He allowed me to move my mouth back to him but didn't remove his hand from my hair. I pressed my tongue flat along the underside of his cock and ran it up to his tip. A huge smirk appeared on my face when Gunner's free hand landed on the shower wall—using it for support. It was all the encouragement I needed to reach up and roll his heavy balls in my hand while circling his tip with my tongue.

I peeked up at him through my lashes, finally pulling him as far down my throat as I could handle. The hold on my hair tightened, and he shoved in a few more centimeters, causing me to choke and my eyes to water.

"That's a good girl. Let me hear you choke on it," he said.

The growl in his voice had me moaning around his cock. I didn't know if a woman could orgasm without even being touched, but Gunner sure was getting close to helping me accomplish that. My mouth worked up and down for a few strokes before moving down to his balls, taking each one in and softly sucking. Gunner let out a moan and moved his legs apart slightly to give me more room to work.

He used my hair to pull my mouth off, forcing me to look at him. "I want that dirty mouth around my cock, Ryan," he claimed before ramming his dick back down my throat.

The bite of the tile on my knees and the aching of my core added to the experience. Through my lashes, I took in the look of pure pleasure on Gunner's face, making me decide to take this further. My hand found its way back to his balls before moving to his backside.

"Fuck," he called out, slamming his palm against the wall the moment my finger prodded his ass.

But he didn't stop me; he widened his feet, giving me

better access. I sucked harder as he fucked my face. Saliva dripped down to the hand wrapped at his base. This was the sloppiest blow job I'd given, and I loved every moment he held me in place—fucking my face.

Actually, I'd never loved giving a blow job until this moment.

I felt his balls tighten as he got close to his release. His pace increased, and I watched in fascination. His head was hung back, a look of ecstasy plastered on his face while droplets of water rolled down his chest. The whole act was erotic, and I chose that moment to push my finger past his tight rim.

The hand entangled in my hair disappeared, and I heard both fists slam against the wall.

"Fucking hell, Ryan," he cried out in pleasure.

His cock pulsed in my mouth, spilling his cum. I tried to swallow it all down, but I felt some escape and run down my chin. After a moment, I removed my finger and pulled my mouth off. But not before giving his overly sensitive cock a suck and watching him shiver.

"Brat," he said, his tone filled with lust as he yanked me off my knees and slammed his mouth on mine. His tongue thrust inside, not caring that it was coated in his cum. It was so hot; I was desperate to get him inside me.

"Gunner, if you don't fucking touch me…I swear I will stab you," I threatened between kisses.

I felt as he smiled against my mouth, unfazed by my threat.

"Turn around. Hands on the bench, Ryan. Now. I plan on feasting on this pussy, and I already know it will be the best thing I've ever tasted."

His words sent chills down my spine.

I'd never been a prude, but there was something vulnerable about bending at the waist and putting your pussy on display. But then there was the thrill of knowing he was seeing all of me. The feather-light touch of his knuckles traced up and down my slit, caressing me and sending chills coursing through my body.

"I was right, Ryan," Gunner whispered. "You have such a pretty pussy. And at some point, babe, when you're ready, I plan on taking you bare and watching my cum run down your legs."

I looked over my shoulder at him. The man was a God when it came to dirty talk, and I was so tightly wound that it would not take much to push me over the edge.

"Fuck you, Gunner. You can't say shit like that and not fuck me bare. My finger was in your asshole, so I know you're not hiding a condom there. And I want you in me— now. I'm good for ten years in the birth-control department," I stated before adding on, "If you don't stick your dick in me, I'll murder people."

The genuine laugh Gunner let out made my heart clench; I was so fucked when it came to this man. And he hadn't even given me an orgasm yet.

"Turn back around, Ryan. Hands don't leave the bench." His warm breath tickled my ear as he shoved the top half of my body down, ensuring I was fully on display.

"Ah, fuck you, Gunner," I moaned as his tongue traced me, clit to ass, before he moved back and pulled my clit into his mouth, biting down on the sensitive bundle of nerves.

I could feel him smiling against my pussy, obviously pleased with the reactions I was giving him. I didn't know how I would survive him; everything he was doing was ruining me for anyone else.

"I could lick your pussy every day until I die, Ryan. Your dripping cunt is now my all-you-can-eat buffet," he groaned.

"*Sí por favor,* let's make that happen..." I barely got the words out before he shoved his tongue in, and his thumb circled my clit. I shut my eyes on the brink of my orgasm. But before I could reach it, Gunner stood up.

"What the hell?" I seethed, whipping my head around, wishing I'd brought a knife.

"There's no fucking way I'm letting the first orgasm I

198

give you be around anything other than my cock," he stated, as if I was being unreasonable.

"Then put it in me already, assh..." I was moaning before I could finish my sentence.

Gunner shoved every glorious inch inside me. His rough hands gripped my hips as he thrust at a dizzying pace.

"Touch your clit, Ryan," he demanded. "I can't do that while I smack your ass and use your hips to fuck you harder."

To prove his point, his hand came down on my ass cheek seconds before he slammed into me again. This time, when my pussy clenched at the bite of pain, it was around Gunner. His name fell from my lips the moment my fingers found my clit.

"Say it again, babe. This time louder. Let all these assholes know who you let fuck you," he growled.

I'd never had a man dirty talk to me the way Gunner was. It provided another level of stimulation I never knew I wanted in sex.

"Fuck me harder, Gunner. Ruin me for anyone else," I begged.

He let out a dark laugh at my words while thrusting harder. "Babe, you were never going to be anyone else's. The moment your mouth opened when I first saw you, I knew I was fucked. We are destined to burn in chaos together, so we might as well have great sex while doing it."

Of course, his fucked-up words were what brought me right to the edge. Gunner somehow saw my jagged edges, and instead of trying to smooth them out, he wasn't afraid of running his tongue over them—even if it meant getting cut.

"Gunner, I'm so close. Don't change anything."

Every man I'd been with chose the milliseconds before I found release, if I found it, to change what was working. But not Gunner. Instead, he decided to give me the same special treatment I'd given him.

"Fall apart, Ryan," he commanded as he pushed his finger in my ass, sending me over the edge while I yelled his name.

"Fuck, babe," Gunner cried out, finding his release inside me.

I'd never let a man fuck me bare, and now I didn't think I could ever go back. There was something so erotic about feeling his cum filling me up. Gunner pulled out, letting his last few spurts hit my pussy lips.

"Goddamn, I knew watching our cum leak out of you would be hot as fuck."

I turned around to face him, and without breaking eye contact, I scooped up the cum making its way down my thigh and brought it up to my mouth to lick clean.

Gunner's nostrils flared, and I swore I saw his cock twitch. Unable to help himself, he tangled my hair in his hand and slammed our lips together.

When he pulled back, we both were breathing hard.

"I'm fucked, Ryan. Utterly fucked. And I can't seem to care," he whispered.

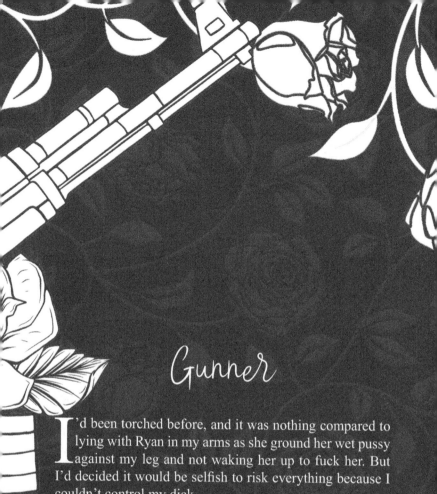

Gunner

I'd been torched before, and it was nothing compared to lying with Ryan in my arms as she ground her wet pussy against my leg and not waking her up to fuck her. But I'd decided it would be selfish to risk everything because I couldn't control my dick.

That commitment sure lasted long.

I watched her lithe body ride against my thigh for about five minutes before I couldn't take it anymore. But I didn't think through what slapping her ass would do. The Reapers cockblocking me from their graves was a blessing until my restraint broke at the thought of her naked, wet body standing in my shower just feet away.

The internal war I had going on was brutal. On the one hand, her supposed engagement to Mario gave me a clean break, but on the other, I couldn't get the image of Ryan lying in a pool of blood out of my head. And the heartache and regret that gripped my soul at that sight. Those feelings made me question everything. I didn't know if what I was doing was worth a damn if I didn't get to keep Ryan at the end of it.

I broke.

And now I was more fucked than before because I would never be able to leave her after having her. Part of me hated her for that, hated that she made me feel so much in this life. She was so beautiful, with her scarred, caring heart and attitude as sharp as the blade she wielded. We were one and the same, she and I. Our hardened hearts beat only for those we felt needed caring for. And we didn't blink an eye when violence was required to punish those who deserved it.

"The irony of my other half being in the Los Muertos Cartel..." I mumbled.

The bathroom door opened, and I couldn't help the smile on my face when Ryan walked out, her long locks wrapped in a towel precariously perched on her head. Her eyes narrowed, daring me to comment.

"Don't give me that look, Gunner," she warned, her hands resting on her hips. "Today was *not* supposed to be a hair washing day, but as usual, asshole men ruined my plans. So now, instead of my nice microfiber towel, I have this." She gestured to the top of her head while letting out an exasperated sigh.

I didn't have the balls to tell her I had no clue how most of those towels had gotten into my bathroom. The only one I bought and used was the navy towel around her body. Closing the distance between us, I wrapped my arms around her. I didn't think I could be around her and not touch her.

"Babe, I fucked you while dried blood that was not your own ran down your body. You and this towel thing won't scare me away," I said, leaning down and gently sucking on her bottom lip. Her hands moved to my chest. I loved that they were rough. How had I thought she was a cartel princess?

My tongue prodded the split in her lip, knowing she

204

loved a bite of pain. She hissed, digging her nails into my skin, our tongues going to war. I needed to break away if we were going to get to Pres's office on time. I stiffened at the thought of Ryan being interrogated by Pres.

Breaking away, I cupped her face in my hands.

"Ryan, when you see Pres, you can't say anything about the burner or that we think someone from the cartel may be involved," I warned, watching as she assessed my words, searching for tells of deceit from me.

I refrained from grimacing at the idea of her not trusting me because why would she? This world was built on deceit and betrayal. If you wanted to survive, you had to sus out the lies.

And I had a lot of lies. More than I was able to share with her. But I wasn't lying on this matter, and she seemed to believe me.

"Okay. So you don't want your pres to know. But let me guess, Dex knows?" she asked.

God, was she sharp.

"Yeah, Dex knows." I chuckled. "Pres knows about the bodies, and Torque was with me when we discovered the tattoos. But at the moment, they think they might've defected. Pres asked me not to tell you shit when you woke up, so you'll have to pretend you don't know anything other than the fight…Pres thinks you might be lying to us."

"But you don't," she stated.

"No. I think you are more trustworthy than anyone here," I responded.

I couldn't quite read the expression she gave me, but it made my heart beat faster. I knew she was trustworthy. Because at her core, Ryan was filled with good intentions. And I was all too aware that good intentions were often achieved with sins.

I placed a chaste kiss on her lips before walking to my dresser to find shirts for both of us. I'd thought it was idiotic when men talked about loving women in their shirts, but now I got it. The thought of Ryan walking around wearing my shirt, covered in my scent…I would be rocking a hard-on the whole meeting.

"McGregor? What does that represent?" Her voice cut through my thoughts, and I stilled as her fingertips traced the tattoo on my tricep.

Closing my eyes, I attempted to shut out the memories the old tattoo brought. I should've covered it up entirely but could never bring myself to do that. So I had it worked in as an attempt to keep it hidden from sight. Of course Ryan's perceptive eyes would find the cursive lettering camouflaged in the other artwork.

I swallowed, desperate to get moisture back in my throat. "It's the name of someone I once knew. From an old life," I responded, yanking a shirt over my head to hide the ink and end the line of questioning.

Ryan stared at me with a look of understanding and acceptance. Making my heart ache even more. We both had scars and stories better left unsaid. I wondered if she would still feel the same way about me if she could see all the skeletons in my closet. A chill ran down my spine at the thought that she someday might. But I couldn't afford to go down that rabbit hole at the moment.

A knock at the door broke the moment.

"Freshly fucked friends, open up the door. I come bearing gifts for the good-looking one," Dex yelled from the hallway.

Ryan arched an eyebrow and looked over at me. "I'm not entirely sure if he's talking about you or me."

Before I could answer, the asshole strode in.

"What the hell, Dex? What if we were naked?" I yelled.

"That's honestly what I was hoping for," he answered, wiggling his eyebrows.

A growl escaped my lips. The thought of him seeing Ryan naked pissed me off. Dex's smile widened. The asshole knew exactly what he was doing. He winked at me as he placed a pair of black leggings and a sports bra in Ryan's arms.

"What, no shirt?" Ryan asked, inspecting the stack.

"Caveman over there insists you wear his shirt so he can parade you in front of the other assholes and claim you. Basically, the modern version of pissing on you." He paused his insane speech and dropped his voice to a whisper yell. "Unless you have a thing for being peed on. Is that why y'all were in the shower so long?" Dex asked.

Ryan's mouth opened and closed a few times before words finally came out.

"No, I'm not into Gunner peeing on me," she shrieked. "Dex, you're lucky I'm not hiding a knife in this towel because I would stab you in the forearm."

My crazy brother shrugged his shoulders like this was the most natural conversation. "Don't knock it till you've tried it, chica," he sing-songed.

Ryan's head snapped to me, her eyes wide as saucers. Laughter erupted from my chest because the woman didn't bat an eye at a knife fight, but Dex had put her in a stunned state.

"Oh, you haven't been around long enough to know; that's on the milder side of shit Dex says about sex. He once told me an Aussie girl asked him to pretend to be a magpie and 'Dive bomb her pussy.'" I used finger quotes around the phrase because I still didn't know what the fuck that meant.

"The worst part of that story was that it wasn't a one-time hookup," I added.

"I have so many questions, but I'm afraid of the answers. So I'll go change now and try to erase all the mental images I'm currently experiencing," Ryan responded.

Dex's smirk fell the moment Ryan closed the bathroom door. It was scary how he could switch; he and Ryan had that in common.

"Well, the whole no fucking her plan is out the window. Do you know what you're doing here, brother?" he questioned.

My fists clenched and unclenched at my sides. I was sure I was leaving indents in my palms. I didn't like this line of questioning because the truth was that I had no answers.

"Don't worry; the job will get done." My tone was clipped as I responded.

Dex's gaze felt like it was peeling away at my skin, searching for my soul. But I was beginning to think my soul was in the hands of another, which was a danger to our plans.

"I'm sure the job will get done, but are *you* going to be able to do it now?"

I gave him a swift nod because I didn't know that I could say those words aloud and claim they were truthful.

Ryan

Gunner warned me not to give anything away at this meeting since Pres didn't feel I was trustworthy. Not that I blamed him. Until Gunner, I didn't trust anyone outside of Los Muertos and Nikki. How ironic. Now Los Muertos members were who I shouldn't trust.

"Ryan, so glad to see you up. As you can imagine, I have some questions about what the fuck happened last night," Pres called out as I entered.

I eyed where he sat behind a large wooden desk, looking for his tells. His face and body language didn't give a thing away. The man was a statue.

Color me mildly impressed.

He sat there waiting out my silence, assessing me the same way I assessed him. Mario would've already stabbed someone for not answering. It's why I did all the interrogating for Los Muertos. Dead men give little information.

My arms folded across my chest as I leaned against a

wooden chair.

"With all due respect, I don't owe you shit. I didn't call you for help. Your club members decided to do that of their own volition." I pressed my palms to his desk, leaning in so we were at eye level. "Really, I think it's me who should be asking *you* for an explanation. Like why is it you decided to bring me to the clubhouse and not call in Los Muertos? What is it you know that you wanted to keep hidden?" I prodded, smirking when I caught Gunner and Dex stiffen.

Gunner said to play it off like I didn't know anything. Well, this would've been the answer and attitude I gave if I'd woken up at an MC and hadn't been told shit. My acting skills were giving authenticity, and those boys should be appreciative, because the only people being suspicious were them.

Pres and I locked eyes, neither willing to break contact. I won most dick-measuring contests. Pretty good for someone who didn't have a dick. When he realized I wasn't going to relent or cower, Pres broke out in a cold smile. Not quite threatening, but definitely not kind either. That didn't matter to me; I wasn't here to be liked.

"You may not be Sergio's blood, but damn if you aren't just like the bastard. I'll take your reaction as a sign that you didn't orchestrate any of last night's events." He gestured for me to sit. "We brought you back here instead of calling Los Muertos because we wanted to be sure we could trust who we were working with," Pres answered, his gaze cutting over to the wall where the boys were standing.

"Seems these two believe you aren't going to betray us. Boys, I need a moment alone with Ryan here."

"Pres…" Gunner all but growled out his name.

The two locked eyes, and I could see the ticking of Gunner's jaw as he clenched his teeth. After a moment, his eyes cut over to me, his facial features softening. I could read the unspoken question on his face and gave a slight nod toward the door. Pres waited for the door to close behind them before continuing the conversation.

"Now, to get to current affairs. We have a gun run today. One Gunner says you claim not to know about," Pres stated.

"That's right. I wasn't brought into the loop on the details of this run. Let me guess, Mario was the one who contacted you about today's run?" I meant to come across as nonchalant, but I could hear the irritation in my voice.

Pres nodded his head and steepled his fingers. He was now looking at me with a curious gaze. Like hearing me speak about Mario in such a tone gave him something else to consider.

"Yes, Mario reached out to me. Said we were needed for a run, two crates full of guns going to a buyer on the outskirts of Tucson. He told me the guns would be loaded up in a box truck, and only two men were needed. Strangely enough, he only had one specific name he asked to be present..."

"Gunner," I supplied.

He nodded his head at my answer. "Also mentioned this was his client. No need to contact you for information because you wouldn't be involved." He eyed me, seeing if I was picking up on all the unspoken allegations. It wasn't wise to bite the hand that fed you, especially if the hand was the Los Muertos Cartel, so this was Pres's way of sussing out information.

"Who decided the route?" I asked, keeping my tone light and my face blank. His answer would determine the direction of our conversation.

"Mario. He said the destination and route would be on the map he provided."

A chill ran up my spine at Pres's words. Mario was sending Gunner through Reaper territory on purpose. I had more questions than answers. Mario was a possessive bastard, but this prompted the question of how Mario knew Gunner had taken an interest in me. The meeting at Lotería was the first time Mario had seen Gunner and me together, and it was his lap he'd forced me to sit on.

Memories of the texts I received on fight night flashed in my mind.

After last night and this morning's revelations, there was a nagging voice in my head wondering if Mario could be the one involved with the Reapers. But that didn't make any sense. Los Muertos was his. If it was a business deal with the Reapers he wanted, he could arrange that. All the cloak and dagger shit was unnecessary.

Maybe the ringleader was a disgruntled Muerto? But I didn't think there were any who would have enough money to fund the Reapers. My hand came up and pinched the bridge of my nose as I tried to sort through which problem to solve first.

After a few seconds, I locked eyes with Pres. I didn't like to waste time thinking about the what-ifs and what-to-dos. I was a take-action type of bitch, and to execute my next plan, Pres needed this nugget of information. My gut told me he was loyal to his brothers, and I could trust him. But I wasn't naive; I didn't matter to him and would need to stay useful, or he would leave my ass behind.

"Send Dex with Gunner today. I've got a feeling Mario is hoping Gunner will run into problems, and Dex is who Gunner trusts to have his back. I plan on throwing another wrench in the fucker's plan," I stated.

"I can do that. Just know, I'm telling those boys they're free to handle threats however they see fit."

The smile I gave Pres probably made me look ruthless, but that's how I was feeling.

"I would be disappointed if you didn't," I answered, standing up and making my way toward the door. But the moment my hand touched the handle, I turned back.

"Mario didn't know I was at the fight last night, and since you didn't reach out to Los Muertos, no one knows what went down. I suggest we keep it that way. This conversation never happened." I gave Pres a stern look, the one I usually gave my men. This was his one moment to back out of this little secret, but I figured he was already withholding shit from Los Muertos. What's a few more secrets?

The man gave a curt nod, and Gunner's words from

this morning instantly came to mind, causing me to blush. I shoved the image of Gunner's naked body out of my mind before speaking.

"I need words, Pres. Our agreement doesn't work if the words don't leave your mouth," I demanded, pulling a genuine smile from him.

"Beautiful and smart. I can see why Gunner is taken by you. Let's hope you prove to be worth all he will lose. I agree."

I flinched at his words like I'd been physically slapped. I wanted to argue that I wouldn't cause Gunner to lose anything, but I knew that would be a bigger lie than whatever Pres was keeping from me.

Without another word, I turned and left to find Gunner.

Gunner

Dex and I pulled up to Lotería around noon. Mario had at least gotten that part right. A box truck leaving the club during regular business hours was less likely to draw police attention than one lurking around in the dark. But it wasn't the cops I was concerned about for this run. It was what we had waiting for us when we entered Reaper territory. Because my money was on this shit being a deliberate move on Mario's part. The petty bastard didn't like the attention I was giving Ryan. Or at least that was a portion of his motive.

"How would you react, knowing I had my cock in her this morning, fucker?" I mumbled to myself as I pulled up to Lotería, coming to a stop a few blocks away from the back entrance.

I was on edge because Ryan was coming with us. I knew she could handle herself. Hell, she'd survived out on the streets and in the fucking Mexican cartel way longer than I'd been around this world. But that didn't lessen the shot of fear that ran through my body when I thought about the danger she might be putting herself in by coming.

She took special care to make sure Mario didn't know about what she had planned last night. As far as Mario knew, Ryan hadn't left her apartment. She Ubered to the warehouse, leaving her car at her place to keep wandering eyes under the impression she was home. Dex let Nikki know last night what happened to Ryan to avoid the woman sending out a search party. But I guessed she didn't take the news so well by the bruise on his cheek.

My eyes cut over to Dex as his bike pulled up beside me, and I snickered at the thought of the petite blonde managing to assault him. The noise caused him to look over with a raised brow.

"I was just thinking that I would've paid money to see Nikki beat up your giant ass," I said.

He rolled his eyes as we started walking toward the club. "I already told you, I bruise easy. And she didn't beat me up…" He threw back with a huff, his cheeks taking on a pink tint. "She threw her stripper shoe at me when I told her to let the men handle this," he mumbled.

Laughter burst from my chest at Dex's confession. That further proved he must have a good dick game because his interpersonal skills with women were not it.

"Listen, it's not funny. Those fuckers are heavy, and they hurt, and homegirl has got a wicked arm," Dex whined.

I had to try to compose myself even to respond. "Dex, be glad she doesn't store weapons on her body like Ryan does. Because she probably would've shot you instead." The grunt he let out told me he agreed. "You're an idiot. You know that, right? Did you tell her to calm down too?" I asked jokingly.

When all I heard was silence coming from my right, I looked over in disbelief. The fucker had told a woman, who'd been informed that her best friend was injured, to calm down. He had to have a death wish.

"Seriously, Dex? You're terrible at talking to women," I claimed.

"Listen, they love my dirty talk, and that's all that matters," he stated, his voice taking on a cold tone.

I nodded in response, ready to move on. Emotions were a sore subject for Dex, but there seemed to be something going on between him and Nikki. I didn't know what it was or if it was even romantic, but he needed to figure his shit out or ghost the chick.

I winced at the verbal lashing we would get from Ryan if Dex fucked things up with Nikki. But before I could warn him, Lotería's metal roll-up door came into view.

Here we go.

Our MC personas clicked into place as we walked in. No more joking and laughing, just a focus on not murdering a cartel heir. Robert gave me a slight nod as we walked past.

Good, everything went smoothly on his end.

I didn't bother nodding back, not wanting to bring attention to the exchange. Especially knowing there was a rat in Los Muertos and Mario had some secret plans of his own with this drop.

"Buenos tardes, gringos." The asshole in question's voice cut through my thoughts. "I hope you're ready to work today because this run will determine whether I keep you working for me," he claimed, arms raised out to his sides, looking like he was about to yell out "Are you not entertained?" The madness in his eyes spoke volumes about how he thought today would go.

Dex and I responded with a curt nod. We couldn't piss the psychopath off, and if I had to speak to this asshole, I'd more than likely fuck that up. So we'd decided Dex would ask the questions about the suicide mission.

"So, what do we need to know about this drop? Namely, time and location. Has payment already been made?" Dex asked, his deep voice commanding attention.

Mario dismissively waved his hand. "You do not need those answers. The cargo is loaded in the box truck graciously provided for you, and the navigation is programmed with the location. I didn't know if you were familiar with doing a job correctly, so I took it upon myself to give you the best chance of success," the condescending ass responded. "As for the payment, forgive me if I don't trust a bunch of outlaw bikers with collecting my money. The client has already paid," he added on.

I fought to keep my face neutral at the bullshit this man was spewing.

No one in their right mind would pay for the product in full before receiving it. There *might* be a wire at the exchange time, but I knew damn well Los Muertos kept everything cash. They wanted no electronic footprint when it came to money or any illegal shit. It was why authorities had such a hard time nailing them to the wall. To get to Los Muertos, they would have to get close and get proof of dealings because they weren't going to find shit online.

So Mario's claims—utter bullshit.

Dex's fists clenched and unclenched. "Perfect. So glad you thought about all of that for us," he answered, making his way over to the driver's side. It sounded like he was swallowing broken glass trying to get those words out. If the situation wasn't so fucked, I would be cracking up at the level of restraint Dex had to use.

Man's asshole is probably clenched as tight as his fists.

Mario's hand appeared by the passenger door, holding it shut. "Gunner, I do hope there are no hard feelings about you being rejected by Ryan. I wouldn't want that to impact the working relationship we have."

I glanced over to where he was standing and imagined ramming my fist into his face—replacing his manic grin with a bloody mess. The man was fucking delusional, and his head was so far up his ass that he didn't even realize the shit that came out of his mouth. Ryan told me about their exchange after I left. How he insisted she belonged to him after she told him they weren't even a couple, much less engaged. I could see it now as he stood in front of me; Ryan was his obsession, and he felt he owned her.

I shook my head. "No, I'm not impacted by the relationship Ryan has with you," I responded, deadpan.

His smile widened as he opened the truck door for me to get in. Fucker thought he'd won. Before Dex fully backed out of the loading dock, I rolled my window down.

"Hey, Mario, you might think she's your girl, but it's my name she yells out when I fuck her. And she does it so beautifully," I yelled out, flipping the man off.

His face morphed into a snarl. I wasn't entirely sure he wouldn't pull out his gun and shoot me right here, but before he could retaliate, Dex gunned it.

"Really, man? And y'all say I'm the one with communication problems?" Dex said, his head shaking in disapproval, but the smile on his face let me know he wasn't actually pissed.

Seconds later, my pocket buzzed, and I winced. *She* might be pissed, though.

Ryan: Seriously? You had to antagonize him, didn't you? Now he's going to be texting my ass.

I caught Dex shaking his head at the goofy grin on my face as my fingers flew across the screen, typing out a response I knew she would hate.

Me: Oh, baby, I just wanted him to know what he was missing out on. Besides, if we're about to be ambushed like you think, I already had it coming from him.

All I received was the middle finger emoji and a muffled "fuck you" coming from the cargo area. Ryan would make me pay for announcing how loud she was when fucked. But her wrath was worth the pleasure I got calling Mario out on his bullshit.

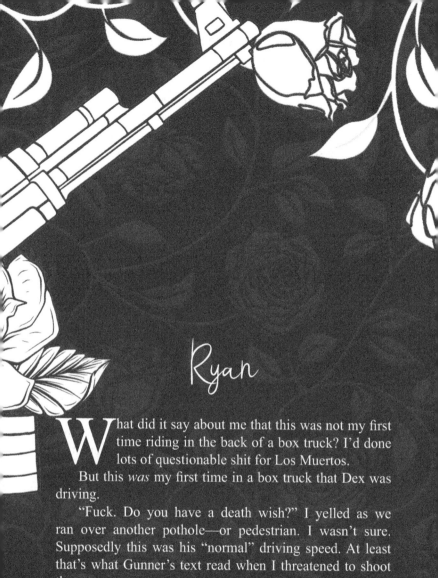

Ryan

What did it say about me that this was not my first time riding in the back of a box truck? I'd done lots of questionable shit for Los Muertos.

But this *was* my first time in a box truck that Dex was driving.

"Fuck. Do you have a death wish?" I yelled as we ran over another pothole—or pedestrian. I wasn't sure. Supposedly this was his "normal" driving speed. At least that's what Gunner's text read when I threatened to shoot them as soon as we came to a stop.

It was decided that I would be at the drop today because it was too much of a coincidence that Mario kept all the details from me while insisting Gunner deliver the cargo to its destination. Mario knew I hated the Reapers, so I guessed he would stage the attack to look like their MC was responsible, but my money was on his Armandos doing the actual attack. And I was going to kick their asses when I saw them. Mario may be the cartel heir, but they knew Sergio would be pissed at this temper tantrum he was throwing. Didn't Mario consider what would happen if I had decided to retaliate, thinking this attack really was the Reapers?

"Why didn't I have Robert load a pillow?" I mumbled, bracing myself with the two crates so I didn't get a concussion from Dex's driving.

I had texted Robert this morning, telling him to leave the box truck unlocked so I could climb inside. Mario still thought I was at home, and I hoped he didn't send anyone looking for me. If he did, Nikki agreed to run interference, but it would cost me. She was pissed at me for almost dying and making her deal with Dex. So I would be eating, and paying for, Chinese takeout for the next week.

The screen on my phone lit up, illuminating the dark truck.

Gunner: Ok. We're on that long stretch of road we talked about.

Immediately, I was on high alert. I'd snuck a look at the route that Mario provided. There was a long stretch of desolate road leading to the destination. My guess was that the truck would be hijacked before it ever got there. Who knew if that destination was an actual drop location. A failed drop would make it look like the Skeletons, and more specifically, Gunner, were incapable of running guns. That's how I would plan it if I were in Mario's shoes.

Dex hit another pothole, sending me careening into one of the crates. The hairs on the back of my neck stood on end when it moved so easily. I loaded enough of these shipments to know the crate shouldn't be this light.

"There's no fucking product," I whispered in horror.

This wasn't a setup to show Gunner couldn't handle the job. Mario wanted Gunner leaving in a body bag. The thought of there being a hit out on Gunner sent me into a rage. The emotion pumped through my veins, and I knew I would put a bullet in the skull of anyone who tried to harm him.

It was like the wool had been lifted from my eyes, and the blind loyalty I'd given Mario was severed. Somehow the man I'd only known for a few weeks had managed to burrow his way into my soul in such a way that I was willing to betray the only other family I'd come to know. Deep down, though, I knew Mario never thought of me like family, only his obsession—an object to possess. And my affection-starved heart locked on to the first person that provided me any semblance of a family, of belonging.

Why I let myself be held under his thumb for so long, I didn't know. But Mario never counted on a man coming along and showing me genuine affection. Gunner showed me a man shouldn't demand you chain yourself to their feet. I didn't know what Gunner felt for me, but I did know he didn't keep me caged.

He held the safety net at the bottom of the building as I jumped off and attempted to fly.

Freedom. He gave me freedom, and I would protect him with every fiber of my being.

My fingers wrapped around the grip of my Sig, removing it from where it was holstered at the small of my back. Pulling back the slide, I checked the round in the chamber. My gut told me to be ready.

Me: Get your guns ready, boys. Crates are empty. We are about to play my favorite game: who's the better killer?

Gunner: It's so hot when you say shit like that. I should have ridden in the back with you. Could have let you ride on me...

The corners of my mouth turned upward. Typical. I just told him we were about to be in a firefight, and he was thinking about me naked. This man may have been as deranged as I was.

Gunner: We have someone tailing us.

The calm that came with the promise of violence slid over me like a second skin. My fingers brushed my switchblade tucked into my jeans, and I checked for the extra mags attached to my thigh. Good thing I hadn't counted on using any of the guns in the crates. The Armandos were about to find out how accurate a shot I was and how much I loved the feel of my blade slicing through flesh.

Gunshots pinged against the left sidewall, riddling it with holes. My body slammed into the floor as I threw myself behind a crate, hoping no one would land a lucky shot. It felt like hours, rather than seconds, for the truck to stop—muffled shouts mixed with the echo of bullets against metal filled the cargo space.

My blood ran cold at the distinct sound of motorcycles approaching.

"Fuck. How did the Reapers keep showing up at shit?" I questioned. "Or were they asked to be here..." Now I wasn't so sure my assessment of Mario's plan was correct.

We were in their territory, but it was too coincidental that they would show up without a hint. It felt like a rock sank into my gut. I had been hoping this run didn't have shit to do with last night or the other stuff going down in Tucson. But my hopes were quickly being dashed.

"Looks like I need to collect a reaper for questioning. Because I want to know what the fuck is happening," I mumbled.

Staying in a low crouch, I made my way over to the roll-up door before fulling lying on my belly and lifting it just enough to peek out and not draw attention. The sounds of gunfire and approaching motorcycles drowned out the groaning metal.

How many of you fuckers are here? And where are you all at?

Directly behind the truck was clear, and without the metal echoing the shots, it was easy to tell that the action was happening to my left. Sucking in a breath, I squeeze through the narrow opening, my hips catching on the metal bumper.

"Fuckin' Latin baby birthing hips..." I muttered, finally managing to squeeze out. Dust billowed at my feet as I hit the ground, and a sigh of relief left my lips when I spotted

Gunner and Dex down toward the driver's side door. Gunner was using the engine block as cover, popping up every few moments to get off a shot. Dex had a similar strategy, but he was positioned farther toward the front, looking around the hood rather than over. And the two worked seamlessly.

"Calm down, hussy. We are literally in a firefight," I told myself.

Rather than head toward them, I dropped to the ground, crawling under the box truck. Making sure to stay behind the tire, I peeked out to assess where our attackers were. Motorcycles were a shit form of cover, so we had that advantage. Their advantage was their numbers, but those were quickly diminishing. I had just finished counting three downed men when I saw a reaper's head snap back seconds after he peeked his head up over the gas tank of his ride.

Headshot. Right between the eyes. Damn, these guys were good; that was a difficult shot to make.

A coppery tang filled my mouth as I broke the skin of my bottom lip. I needed to fix that habit. But the more pressing issue was deciding the best course of action. Going to Gunner in Dex would only reveal there were three of us, taking away that advantage. But we were out in the fucking desert, and there wasn't even a damn cactus to hide behind. And with five Reapers still standing, it would be a dumbass idea to go running toward them. So, while not an ideal shooting position, I'd work with what I had.

None of the reapers were expecting a third shooter, so they were leaving themselves exposed to the back portion of the box truck—a perfect opportunity for me. Thank Santa Muerte I'd practice shooting as much as I did. Including shooting off my back and side. The reaper closest to me would be the hardest for Gunner and Dex to take out from their vantage point.

Rolling over to lie on my right shoulder, I curled my body into a *C*, bringing my arms between my knees. Using them to brace as I aimed to shoot. I steadied my heart, mentally drowning out the commotion around me. I let my lungs fill with air before slowly releasing and pulling the trigger.

"Fuck yeah," I whisper-yelled the moment the bullet connected with the side of his head. He collapsed, causing his club brother to cry out as blood splattered over him.

Aiming again, I pulled the trigger, hitting the squawking man. His freak-out caused him to move last minute, and the bullet hit him in the neck. If he wasn't a reaper, I might feel bad that he was about to have a slow, painful death. But if he chose to ride with the Reapers, he knew the type of business they had their dirty hands in. So all of these men were guilty by association.

I didn't stay in my position to watch the chaos break out. I didn't want to be pinned down if they determined my location. Hot sand scorched my palms as I crawled toward the side of the truck Gunner and Dex were on. Shots and yells of a potential third shooter sounded behind me. Popping back up, I ran in a crouch toward the boys. All of Gunner's attention was on the threat in front of us, but he called out over the noise the moment I neared.

"Ryan, if you don't get your cute ass over here so I know where you're at…" He took a brief moment to glance over at me. "Fuck. I'm pissed, proud, and turned on all at once, babe," he growled.

Unable to help myself, I slammed my mouth on his, biting at his bottom lip before pulling back to look into his eyes.

"You're welcome. Now, keep one of these assholes alive. I have questions," I commanded.

At that exact moment, Dex moved back behind the truck. "There's only one left, boys and girls, and he's running away. Gunner, will you do the honors?"

I popped my head up to see a man booking it. He was probably a hundred yards away now.

"Someone started running before the firefight ended. Coward," I spit out. "Gunner; he's too far. Let's just go run him—"

I didn't get a chance to finish my sentence, because in the next second, the man's arm flew up as he fell. My eyes cut to my left. Gunner had his Glock propped on the hood of the truck.

"You shot down a moving target from a hundred yards away—with a Glock," I said in awe.

"I know you like me in your mouth, babe. But now's not the time," Gunner whispered, his thumb brushing along my bottom lip and gently closing it. Dex started busting up at my expense.

"Why did you think we call him Gunner? The man is an assassin with a firearm." Dex looked like he was about to say more but snapped his mouth shut. I rolled my eyes. MC clubs and their whole "no one without a dick can know" bullshit.

Who cared if I knew Gunner's kill count? Or maybe he thought that might scare me away and didn't want to be a cockblocker. If only Dex knew it turned me on to learn how proficient this man was with a gun.

"Let's go pick him up. I was aiming for his spine, so if my shot was true, he shouldn't be feeling his lower half at the moment," Gunner casually announced, like he was talking about the weather.

I blinked up at him for a few moments, stunned.

I was fucked when it came to this man.

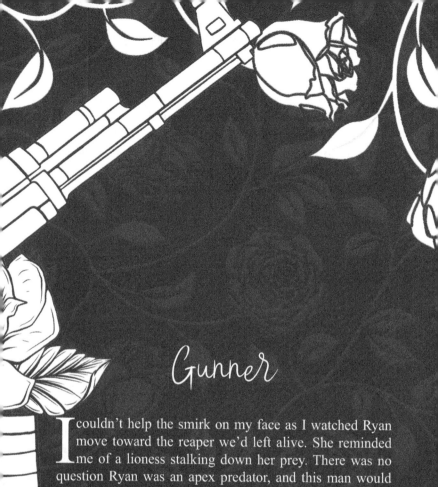

Gunner

I couldn't help the smirk on my face as I watched Ryan move toward the reaper we'd left alive. She reminded me of a lioness stalking down her prey. There was no question Ryan was an apex predator, and this man would be eaten alive. The confidence she walked with would have me adjusting a hard-on soon if I didn't focus on something else. Her ass looked great, but what had me worked up was the dust coating her clothing right now. Because I knew that dust was from her taking out threats from a fucking lying down position under a box truck.

"You know, she kind of scares me. But also, low-key, I want to be her," Dex piped up from beside me.

A genuine laugh fell from my lips, drawing Ryan's attention.

"This guy must think we're deranged with how you two are acting," she said, shaking her head and focusing back on whatever she had planned, but I spotted the smirk on her

SKELETONS OF SOCIETY

face.

Groans of agony hit my ears. The reaper I'd shot attempted to drag himself away from us. But the bullet severed his spinal cord, so his legs were useless. He clutched a gun in his hand, but it wouldn't do shit for him. Ryan strode up to him, slamming her boot down. The sound of crunching bones and cries filled the desert air.

"Oh, I'm sorry. Were you planning on using that?" she asked. Her sugary sweet tone did nothing to hide the malice. She lowered to a squat, her boot still pinning his hand to the ground. His gaze lifted toward her.

"I swear to God, Dex. If you get a hard-on watching my girl work. I'll shoot you in the spine too," I whispered to my brother.

This was Dex's first time seeing this version of Ryan. A peek into the darkness that surrounded her. The same darkness that encompassed our souls. The darkness needed to handle shit others couldn't. The world had good because people like us could handle doling out the bad.

Ryan's cold voice cut through the agonized groans. "Glad you're still alive because I have some questions I need answering. If you cooperate, I'll shoot you in the head and end your pathetic life quickly. Which is more than you deserve, honestly. Since you fuckers sell women like cattle."

I caught the sinister grin spread across my brother's face at Ryan's words. Maybe now he would understand why I couldn't walk away from her, why I was willing to alter my whole path for this dark goddess.

"But if you decide to be an asshole about this, I'll make our time very painful." She emphasized her words by digging her heel farther into his ruined hand. His yells were so loud that Ryan had to raise her voice to be heard. "And then, when you inevitably give me what I want, I'll leave you lying out here, half dead, so the scavengers can pick you apart. I hear they start with the eyes," she hissed. Her face held no kindness.

The reaper dry heaved.

I didn't know if his reaction was due to the pain or how fucking scary Ryan was.

"Oh, I definitely want to be her. She's so fucking cool," Dex stated, his mouth opening up to ask a question.

"Before you even ask, Dex, because I know you're about to, I wouldn't fuck you," I announced. Dex's shoulders sagged like he genuinely was hurt by my statement.

Ryan's eyes met mine. Warmth had returned to her smile as she winked, causing my eyebrows to raise. This woman knew how to switch in and out of her calculated mode, which was a skill few possessed and most learned in high-level training. But Ryan's teacher was life's trials and tribulations.

The sound of strangled coughing pulled Ryan back to her task. She lifted her foot and plucked the pistol out of the Reaper's ruined hand, using the toe of her boot to kick him over onto his back. He yelled out in pain as his gunshot wound hit the earth, but Ryan ignored him. Dex and I moved closer in case she needed us, but it was apparent she knew what she was doing.

"Why were the Reapers out here? Did you spot us entering your territory or get a tip?" she asked.

"You dumb bitch…" the reaper spit back.

The sound of a gunshot filled the air as Ryan shot off right next to the Reaper's head.

"Babe, what the hell are you doing?" I called out over the noise. But she was already crouched back down, pressing the hot barrel to the underside of his chin. The aroma of singed flesh hit my nose.

"She's done this a time of two, huh?" Dex questioned, eyes drinking in her every move.

My head nodded. I saw her working that night at Lotería, but seeing her now; it was clear she wasn't new to this line of work.

"That's fucking brilliant. It's painful enough to hurt, but not so bad he'll pass out. I'm going to have to pick her brain on interrogation methods," Dex said while I shook my head.

Of course my best friend and the woman of my dreams were psychos. In the best way.

Ignoring Dex, Ryan continued. "Let's try again. Why the fuck were you out here?"

She kept the gun digging into his flesh as she waited out his reply. He seemed to realize he was fucked and better off focusing on how to lessen the pain he would endure.

"You have no fucking clue what's going on, do you?" His question was genuine and lacked the mocking tone he had moments ago.

Ryan's face stayed neutral, not giving away a single emotion or thought. But I knew her, and she was pissed that this asshole was right. She didn't know what was going on. It was why she'd carried out this plan in the first place. Because someone was fucking with her, and she didn't know who or why.

"We were hired to attack the box truck. Got a call saying to take out the two guys making the run."

I watched as Ryan's brows furrowed. "Who gave the order?" she demanded.

The Reaper locked eyes with her before letting out a long sigh. He knew his time was up.

"Mario Jimenez."

Her eyes searched his, looking for any signs of deceit. But I could tell he was telling the truth. She gave a nod before standing up. A single shot rang out. A bullet through the head, just as she'd promised. Her voice came out cold and menacing.

"Mario is the Reapers' backer." She started marching toward Dex and me. A perplexed look on her face.

I ground my teeth together. I hated to see the flash of betrayal in her eyes, especially knowing I would probably see more of that look as truths came to light about Mario.

"Yeah, it seems that way, babe," I answered. My words caused the crease in her forehead to deepen.

"Here's what I don't understand. He's the heir to the cartel, second in command. He could've arranged to not work with your MC. Why keep his dealings with the Reapers a secret? And where the fuck has Sergio been in all this?" she pondered.

Dex and I exchanged looks. We had it on good authority that Mario was in on some of the same shit as the Reapers. We'd wondered if the rumors were true. And if they were, was Los Muertos involved? Ryan's reaction confirmed Mario must have been acting on it alone.

I looked back to find she had her phone pressed to her ear.

"Scar, I have a favor to ask. But we need to meet at one of your places." A sly smile crept onto her face. "We both know you eat men who disrespect you for dinner. Just get your pampered ass on a jet and get over here." Her smile fell at whatever was said on the other side.

"Yeah…shit's shifting. Don't text me anything. Call the burner you gave me. See you tomorrow."

Before I could even ask who Scar was, Ryan tossed her phone on the ground and shot it.

"Girl!" Dex yelped, throwing his hands up to cover his ears.

I rolled my eyes at Dex's theatrics. The man never used ear protection and had way bigger caliber guns go off near him.

"Dex, you can't even hear, so stop being dramatic. And babe, a little warning next time before you decide to pop off on your phone," I called out.

She tucked her Sig into her back waistband before flipping Dex off. But her face quickly sobered when she started speaking. "This is more fucked up than I thought. I figured Mario was going to try to take you out, but the fact that he hired the Reapers to do the job—seems he's working with them behind Los Muertos's back, and I want to know why and for how long," she answered, her hand coming up to pinch the bridge of her nose.

"Sure, but you didn't have to go all trigger-happy on your phone, chica. What if you had shot me?" Dex whined.

I failed at holding in my laugh at the look of annoyance she was giving Dex.

"Dex, when I shoot you, you won't have to wonder if it was intentional or not," she threw back, her hands hitting her hips.

"What do you mean *when*? You meant to say *if*, right? Right?" Des asked, his eyes looking back and forth between Ryan and me.

My hands raised in surrender. "Hey, don't look at me. I have no interest in getting you into bed, so you're on your own," I said, blowing a kiss to Ryan, which only got me a middle finger back.

"Dex, stop pissing me off. Gunner, stop trying to get me naked. I have important shit to say." She let out a deep sigh. "I shot my phone *because* something's going on. And Mario has enough resources to get my phone traced and information pulled from it. It's not going to be long before he realizes I'm not home, and I don't want him to know where I'm going. Or, more importantly, who I'm going to see. Scar is…secretive like that…" She gnawed on her bottom lip.

My hands wrapped around her waist; the feel of her body against mine was heaven on earth. My lips brushed against her hair as I spoke. "Damn, I love a woman with street smarts." I stiffened slightly at my choice of words.

Would she take them as me saying I loved her? Did I love her?

I'd been a shell for so long I hadn't thought I would ever feel alive again. But being around Ryan gave me the same sense of freedom I was constantly chasing.

Pulling back, I cupped her face as I tried to imagine leaving her behind. A stab of pain shot through my soul, and my tongue swiped across my dry lips. Ryan was oblivious to my internal debate.

"So Gunner, mind if I move in for a bit? Oh, and Dex, text Nikki and tell her I said to leave town for a bit."

"Why is that my job?" he whined from behind me.

Ryan just arched an eyebrow and cocked her hip. "Don't play with me, Dex. Nikki already told me you drunk sexted her, so I know you have her number," she called out.

He mumbled his agreement while he walked off to make the call.

My fingers wrapped in her hair, and I brought our mouths crashing together. She tasted of dirt, sweat, and all of my fantasies.

"Yeah, babe. You can be naked in my bed for as long as you want," I answered, searching her face in hopes of answers to all my problems. This situation with Mario left me not knowing what our future held, whether I would get to keep this Latin beauty in my arms at the end of this.

Or lie in my bed having nightmares of the things I'll miss out on with her.

Her hand traveled up my chest, trailing along my collarbone until she reached my jaw, gently cupping my face.

"You're tensing your jaw, Gunner. Relax, this whole situation may be fucked, but you can get me back to the clubhouse, and I'll let you see my boobs," she teased.

I didn't know how she knew I needed that moment of laughter, but she did. And for just a moment, I could put all the bullshit coming our way out of my head.

A scoff left my mouth. "I'm insulted, Ryan. What, do you think that because I'm a man, that's all I want from you?" I asked in mock horror.

She studied my face for a second before bringing her lips so close to mine they were almost touching.

"No. I think you want my pussy too," she whispered before turning around and striding toward the box truck and carnage. I stood there shaking my head because she was wrong.

I wanted so much more than just those two things from her, and I didn't know what to do.

Gunner

Today we were meeting whoever this Scar person was. Ryan refused to give me any information on her or why we were meeting. All she said was that Scar was the best at what she did, and she might be able to give us the insight we needed to get a leg up.

We left the box truck out in the desert, along with all the bodies. Figured it would be a clear enough message to the Reapers and Mario; we weren't to be fucked with. Whether they figured out we knew Mario was working with them— only time would tell. The whole situation was a shit show, and I felt like I was being backed into a corner.

Because now I had Ryan to consider.

The moment she opened up that beautiful mouth of hers and told me to go fuck myself, I was hooked. She had a heart that bled for helping those she felt would never see justice. The more I was around her, the more I realized I would burn down the world for her. Take the head of anyone who tried to harm her and offer it to her on a silver fucking platter. And those types of feelings had no place in this life of mine.

We were at a crossroads now. The deal between the Skeletons and Los Muertos was over, but since Pres hadn't heard from Sergio. We didn't exactly know if we were supposed to keep up the charade or not. And Ryan...Ryan was a whole other complication. Not addressing all the hurdles between us, I didn't know what she would do now that Mario was working with the Reapers. I was hoping whatever this Scar chick told us would help give insight into what to do.

I raked my hand through my hair as a heavy sigh left my chest. As I pushed my door open, my eyes were met with a sight that made my dick twitch, and all my worries floated away. Ryan stood there, her pretty pink tongue poked out, running across her bottom lip before she pulled it between her teeth.

I was rock fucking hard, and she hadn't even touched me.

I cleared my throat. "Is there a reason you still aren't dressed, Ryan? You know we have places to go today." Like a predator hunting its prey, I stalked toward her.

But Ryan was no prey; she was my equal, who granted me the pleasure of dominating her.

"You're eye fucking me again, Gunner," she whispered, raking her eyes down my body.

She was right.

"How can I not with you standing there in the middle of my room in my shirt. I can practically see those pretty pussy lips peeking out." I tried my damnedest to sound calm and unfazed, but I had a visceral need to fall to my knees and worship her.

Her eyes narrowed in on my clenched fists. If she breathed on me, I would blow my load like some virgin. I strode forward, threading my fingers through her hair, and pulled—giving her the bite of pain she craved.

"I'm not sure if you've ever looked into a mirror, Ryan. But you happen to be very. Fucking. Hot," I breathed against her throat, running my tongue along her skin.

Her fingertips gripped the front of my cut, and she had a mischievous glint in her eyes. "You said we don't have time, Gunner," she responded, her hand snaking to my dick and squeezing.

"Brujita, you're asking to get laid across my lap and spanked."

"How about you slap my ass while you shove your cock in me? Pretty please," she asked.

The air was thick with sexual tension, and my resolve broke at her words. Her hair slid through my fingers as I tugged so we made eye contact. A moan left my lips the moment her blown irises met mine.

"Babe, I'll always have time to service that leaking cunt of yours. On the bed, Ryan. All fours. Face me," I demanded.

Her eyes widened in excitement. "Fuck," she whispered, her words breathy and low.

This woman was a goddess among mortals. I didn't deserve her and should let her go, but I was addicted to her special kind of poison. I didn't want the war of emotions she stirred in me, but I was powerless to stop them.

We'll never work out; we were destined for failure from our very start.

My depressing thoughts vanished when her lithe body climbed up onto my bed and scrambled to get into place. Ready to submit to my every word.

"I'm not walking away from her," I mumbled to myself while I watched her wait on all fours on the bed. The sight was so painfully delicious that I took my time making my way over to her, not ready for it to end. My shirt had ridden up and was now resting at the small of her back, leaving her plump ass on display. A groan escaped my mouth when I spotted a black lace thong barely covering her pussy.

Fuck, was I hard.

"We can't be late, Gunner." Her face was inches from

my cock, and I knew what she was thinking as she looked at me through her thick black lashes. "But you don't look like you'll last long anyway." A sly smile graced her lips.

My fingers wrapped around her chin. "Don't be a brat, babe. Or I'll make sure that pussy of yours doesn't get an orgasm," I warned as my hand met the lace of her underwear, yanking the fabric toward me, pulling a moan from her pouty lips as the lace bit into her clit.

I smirked at her reaction. "You fucking love some pain with your pleasure, don't you, Ryan? I bet your pussy is already drenched, waiting to be fucked. Do you want to be filled with every inch of my cock?" I asked—my free hand wrapping around her throat.

"Yes, I want you rough and fast, Gunner."

"You're too fierce to be treated delicately. It's why Mario would never have you. He doesn't see you. And I'll break every bone in that man's hand if he ever touches you again." Her eyes widened. "And that would be the start of what I'll make him endure." My words were spoken as a promise. Mario was lucky that he never physically hurt her, because I would make his death long and drawn out for that offense.

"Gunner…" Her voice was thick with emotion I wasn't ready for, so I switched the subject. Bringing us back to focusing on the physical attraction between us.

You know you're already emotionally attached, asshole.

I shook my head, attempting to clear my thoughts. "You aren't even ready to go yet, Ryan." Another pull on her thong. "You knew we had places to go. Your poor planning means you're in for a quick and dirty fuck." Her pupils were blown, and a whimper left her lips at my words. Fuck, did I love the little sounds she made, and I didn't even have my cock in her yet.

"Face the other way. Ass up in the air, chest on the bed, babe. I want to feel how your cunt drips for me."

She took one last peek down at my cock, I knew she wanted it in her mouth, but she did as she was told.

242

Fuck. Such a good girl...

This position seemed like a good idea at the time, but now faced with her glorious ass and her pretty pussy, I didn't know how I would be able to torture her in the way I wanted. It was a good thing I had already told her it would be quick and dirty because I wasn't sure I could deliver anything else with the way she had me wound up.

Leaning forward, I pulled her clit into my mouth, lace and all, living for the full-body shudder it drew from her before I yanked her thong to the side and parted her lips with my tongue—lapping at her wet pussy. I knew my fingers were probably leaving indents in her thighs with how tightly I was grasping them. The wet sounds of me eating her out mixed with the soft whimpers falling from her sinful lips had me ready to come.

"Fuck, Gunner." She moaned, slamming her fist down on the bed.

I smiled into her pussy. God, the way I wanted to hear her say my name, to listen to her yell from the rooftops who she'd chosen to give her body to. With a plop, I pulled my mouth from her clit, running my fingers along her wet lips.

"Would you like my cock, babe?" I asked before biting her ass cheek. "Because I'm going to fuck you and then watch as my cum drips down your body while your ass turns red from me smacking it." As I spoke those words, I thrust my fingers into her without warning, pulling a loud moan from her. "What a good girl you are, already wet and ready for my cock. Come undo my belt, Ryan," I commanded, removing my fingers so she could do as she was told.

The moment she faced me, the little vixen leaned forward and took my fingers into her mouth, cleaning off the juices coating them. Fuck. My dick twitched as her warm wet tongue circled the digits, as her hands were busy undoing my pants.

Fucking with jeans stuck at your thighs was a pain in the ass, but I was too eager to bother taking them off. The moment she fisted my cock, all restraint was gone. I needed in her immediately.

My fingers dug into her jaw, tilting her head to look at me as my thumb grazed her bottom lip—slipping into her mouth, meeting her warm tongue. The sight of her kneeling on my bed in front of me had my heart in a vise grip. I leaned forward and slammed my mouth onto hers. I wanted her to feel all the emotions I couldn't find words for. Feel all the things I wanted to say to her, how she fucked up my plans, and how she made this life better.

"Gunner, if you don't fuck me this instant, I'll do it myself." Ryan huffed in anger while pulling on my dick.

I smiled against her lips. That sharp tongue of hers delivered the type of pain I liked.

"We will revisit you showing me how you like to fuck yourself. But right now, you are going to lay on your back like a good girl, and I'm going to drive my cock into you until you beg me to stop."

Her tits bounced with the force of me pushing her back on the bed. Gripping her thighs, I yanked Ryan to the edge of the bed and buried myself inside her. Her cries of pleasure filled my room. Hands gripped the sheets, attempting to anchor herself against the relentless thrusts of my cock. The walls of her pussy fit me like a goddamned glove. I wanted to be buried balls deep in her sweet cunt forever.

"You're mine, Ryan. You fucking hear me? Every goddamned thing about you calls to my soul, and I'm never letting you go," I promised as my fingers reached forward and circled her clit. Pulling another breathy moan from her while *Gunner* continued to fall from her lips.

"Santa Muerte, I'm going to come, Gunner...please keep fucking me like that, or I swear I'll stab you," she cried out.

I laughed at her inability not to threaten people. "Is that your version of praise and degradation, Babe?" I asked, my fingers meeting her wet tongue. Her eyes popped open and gave me a questioning glance. But my good girl obeyed, moistening them with her mouth.

"What a good fucking girl you are, Brujita." I praised, watching as her eyes rolled back at my words.

Who didn't have a bit of a praise kink?

A pop sounded as I pulled the digits from her lips. Leaning over her body, I trailed my tongue along the shell of her ear.

"Come for me, Ryan. Right. Now."

I pushed a lubed finger into her ass. Perks of having her hanging off the edge of the bed. A gasp choked fell from her lips, and her pussy pulsed around my cock. I groaned at the sensation of her riding out the aftershocks of her orgasm before flipping her pliable body over and bending her over the bed. My cock sank back into her warm cunt.

"Fuck, you're going to have me seeing stars, Ryan," I exclaimed, as my hands grip her hips while I fucked her.

She let out a breathy laugh. The beads of sweat on her back caught the light and tempted me to lick them up. A full-body shiver took her over as my tongue trailed up the back of her neck.

"Is that what my name is? Because you fucking emptied my soul with that orgasm," she responded.

A smile pulled at my lips. "Your tanned ass is begging to be reddened, Ryan," I claimed as my palm lands on the smooth skin. The impact caused her to clench down on my cock, sending me into an orgasm.

"You feel so fucking incredible, Brujita."

The pleasure she brought me was evident in my tone. Her pussy was trying to milk my cock of everything it had. I pulled out, watching as my cum landed on her ass, leaking between her cheeks down to her pussy. I didn't know how she managed to make me cum so hard, but fuck, she drained my balls.

"Gunner, we have places to be…" the rest of her words were lost to her moaning into the sheets as I slapped her ass once more, coating my fingers and shoving them into her warm cunt, before dropping to my knees and lapping up our release.

"Holy, fuck. That is the hottest thing a man has ever done."

I smirked into her pussy as I watched her stand on her toes, attempting to escape my assault on her sensitive clit. My hand met the small of her back, shoving her back down and biting on the sensitive bundle of nerves. Her yells of pleasure were music to my ears. A growl rumbled from my chest.

This was where I wanted to be, always—worshipping this fallen angel.

A visceral need to let her know, as much as I could, how I felt about her took over, and I pulled back, spinning her around.

Looking up at her from my knees, like a knight swearing his fealty to his queen, I whispered, "Say you're mine, Ryan. Tell me that even when the world burns in chaos, you'll trust me, baby."

A moment of surprise flitted across her face. Like she hadn't expected me to say those words. I didn't miss the irony. So far, our whole relationship had been not getting what we expected, and that would more than likely be the way it ended.

But I would enjoy every part of this woman for as long as I could. She was beautiful, and it had nothing to do with her looks.

A soft smile appeared on her lips. "I'm yours, Gunner. I don't know why you want my damaged soul, but I'm yours."

Ryan

"**W**here the fuck are you taking me, Ryan?"

I let out a chuckle at the exasperated tone coming from Gunner. He was always so cranky when left out of the loop. In his defense, this was a sketchy-looking neighborhood I had us going to. The walls of the alley were covered in grime and stains that looked an awful lot like bloodstains. But the best places to hide were in areas like this. Areas no one wanted to go into for fear of the people who would have the balls to live there.

Intuition was something left over from our ancestors, a warning system Mother Nature put in place for the prey. And then there were people like Scar, the predators. She was the boogeyman of the slums she held safe houses in—the person setting off their alarm bells.

"Come on, the inside is much nicer than the outside. And you don't have to worry. Everyone knows not to fuck with Scar's section of the slums," I called over my shoulder.

I still hadn't let him in on who Scar was. She was complicated to explain, and it was better if he just met her. I ducked under a rotted two by four with a ratty blanket nailed to it. The makeshift curtain reeked of urine and scents I couldn't begin to identify. All the trash was a security measure in itself. Scar didn't even need the biometric scanner I knew she had on the smooth metal door in front of me. A camera positioned to capture everything was up in the corner of the small doorway. Scar could tell me how many chin hairs I needed to pluck with that thing.

"Seriously, Ryan. Where the fuck are we going, and how will anyone living in this shit hole be able to help with Mario?"

Before I could even answer, the door popped open with an audible whoosh, revealing a nondescript antechamber. I peeked back and smirked when I saw Gunner's furrowed brow.

"What the fuck?" Gunner whispered under his breath. "I'm now guessing Scar is not some transient we are meeting in a sketchy back alleyway. Also, what the fuck kind of name is Scar?"

I cut Gunner a glare while letting out a harsh *shh* sound.

"Do *not* talk about her name. It's a very touchy subject we will not get into before entering the Fort Knox of Tucson. A Fort Knox ran by the woman you are insulting," I scolded.

Men. Do they ever think before they speak?

Scar took her security very seriously, and she was the best when it came to installing it, and she was the best at getting past it; what better person to sell security systems than the person who beat them? Of course, she didn't tell any of her clients her side hustle was breaking and entering.

"Nothing I love more than fucking over rich men. I rob them blind in the middle of the night and then take their money when they hire me to keep their remaining shit safe."

Scar had issues with the upper crust of New York, and she took every opportunity to fuck them.

Gunner and I stepped into the antechamber. The

slamming shut of the metal door caused Gunner to flinch slightly, bringing another smile to my face. I wasn't going to tell him I let out an audible yelp the first time I was here. The moment the door sealed, a red light came on overhead.

"Seriously, Ryan?" he yelled, his arms wrapping around me, pistol drawn. My heart fluttered at the show of protection. Sure, I could handle myself, but the fact that Gunner would put himself in front of me filled me with an emotion I'd never experienced for a man. My hand patted the firm muscle of his bicep, and because I couldn't help myself, I trailed my fingertips down his arm, tracing the inky lines. When he noticed I was calm, he tucked his Glock back into the waist of his jeans before grabbing my jaw.

"I swear, the moment we're alone, I'm smacking that ass of yours until you can't sit without being reminded of the consequences of not filling me in on this kind of shit. How do I keep you safe if I don't know what the fuck's going on?" he whispered.

His words made my heart and pussy flutter. Which was a first. Until Gunner, I didn't even know my dead heart could feel enough to flutter.

Focus, bitch, unless you're going to give Scar a show.

"*Cálmate,* Gunner. This room is like an at-home TSA checkpoint. We are being scanned for weapons, which, clearly, you have. And she's probably running your face through her program to find out who you are. Scar's a bit anal when it comes to this shit…" I said.

Gunner stiffened. I could understand; it was a lot, especially if you weren't prepared for it.

"Don't worry. She'll let you keep your gun. She knows I always carry, and that I trust you if I told you about her." His eyes locked on mine. "Not even Mario and Sergio know about Scar. I wouldn't have brought you if I didn't think I could trust you, Gunner," I stated, the emotion in my voice taking me by surprise.

Telling Gunner I trusted him felt like breathing fresh air for the first time. I hadn't realized how few people I trusted, how few I cared for in the way I was beginning to care for Gunner. My parents were on that list at one point, but now it only consisted of Nikki. I couldn't even say I ever cared for Mario or Sergio. I craved their affection, but now comparing my feelings toward Gunner to what I felt for the Jimenez men, caring for them was never something I felt.

His green eyes met mine for a brief moment before quickly looking away, a flash of *something* on his face.

"Ryan…"

Gunner looked conflicted. But how could I blame him? He was probably still wondering if I was playing him. Mario announced I was his fiancée a short while ago, and I didn't say shit to correct that. It made sense that he had lingering doubts about my loyalty. Not telling him about Scar's security OCD was not helping smooth things over. At least she wasn't so crazy that he would have to go through a cavity check. Hopefully.

I wanted to tell him not to feel guilty for not fully trusting me yet, but I never got the chance to because a discreet door slid open, and in popped Scar's face. She had cut her hair since I last saw her; the brunette locks now landed slightly past her shoulders. Her blue eyes were as piercing and intense as always. She quirked her head to the side, looking us both up and down in a way that always made me feel like she was determining how she could kill me before I could get to her. She was a world-renowned thief, but I had a feeling she took on more *unsavory* jobs as well.

She was intense. Her face was always unreadable when in the presence of those she didn't trust, and I didn't know if there was anyone she trusted. Scar had her emotions locked down tight. It was a product of her upbringing.

"He's cute," she stated matter-of-factly.

A masculine growl came from behind her, causing her to roll her eyes at the exact moment that my brows went up. I'd never known Scar to bring anyone to her safe houses with her.

"Come on, follow me. And ignore my pest problem. I

252

keep trying to exterminate them, but they continue to come back like roaches. Or psycho criminals," she mumbled over her shoulder.

I was about to ask her what she was talking about, but the moment we walked into the small but lux apartment, her "pest problem" became apparent—three massive and intimidating men from vastly different backgrounds.

From beside me, Gunner spoke in a low voice. "Why do I feel like she means literally when she says 'tried to exterminate'?"

"Because I did mean literally," she replied without missing a beat.

I smirked when I saw that Scar's words caused the scowl to deepen on the brooding man leaning against the wall. He must have been responsible for the growl. His eyes tracked Scar's every movement, and by the look on his face, I was guessing he wanted to either fuck her or fight her. Maybe even both—at the same time. I studied them a little closer, curious about the three men invading her space.

"Bringing clients home, Scar? An interesting group here; we've got what? Yakuza, Bratva, and…Irish Mob?" I asked, using my head to indicate to tall, pale, and brooding.

Gunner's whole body suddenly was on high alert.

Maybe the Skeletons of Society and the mob had beef.

The two men locked eyes for several seconds. The moment was so intense that I thought I might need my Sig. Scar's eyes pinged back and forth between the men, assessing their body language. Finally, the brooding male spoke, but he never broke eye contact with Gunner.

"How did you say you knew these people, Scarletta?" he asked in his prominent New York accent.

He's from Scar's city. Interesting. But using a woman's full name like she was a petulant child? That never goes well for men.

I caught the minute movement of Scar's shoulders relaxing before she walked over and placed her body in front of Mr. Broody, arms folded over her chest in the classic woman's power stance. His eyes peeked down at her cleavage. Men, so easily distracted by boobs. Ironically, they say women are too emotional to do certain jobs, yet all it takes is a set of tits, and men are putty in our hands.

"I didn't say, Callahan. Because it's none of your fucking business. Now, stand there quietly like a good boy. Maybe you'll get a reward," scar answered, a million unspoken words passing between the two.

Damn, now I know what Dex means when he says watching us is like foreplay.

Obviously, they were by no means friends, and the tension between them had me doubting this man was one of her clients. The air of professionalism that always surrounded Scar was missing, replaced by a simmering rage I'd only seen her have toward her "family." I didn't have time to get into whatever was going on here, plus it was none of my business. But damn if I wasn't curious.

Scar gave Callahan one last scolding look before turning to face us.

"Sorry about that. Still trying to train them on knowing their place." She looked over her shoulder to glare at Callahan. "Some are dumber than others."

A chuckle came from the man sprawled out on the couch, sharpening a Katana. He seemed to be completely at ease lying around in Scar's space. The same couldn't be said for the giant sitting in the armchair. He looked as if he was ready to attack at any given moment. The buzz cut he was rocking showed how his tattoos ran up the back of his neck and onto his skull.

These men were no fucking teddy bears.

"Okay, let's get down to business," Scar called.

My blood ran cold, though, when the look she gave me was filled with pity. Scar never gave anyone pity. It was one of the reasons I liked her so much. Her take on life was like mine; we take the hit and keep moving. There was no room for pity or wishful thinking.

I walked over to a table cluttered with papers and

photographs. My jaw ached with how hard I clenched my teeth when I saw what they were of.

"How far does this go back?" I asked, desperate to keep a handle on my rage. Betrayal seeped into my veins. Gunner put his hand on my hip, pulling me flush against his side, sensing my need to be grounded to reality. I was moments away from barging out and going on a murder spree. The bloodlust was yelling at me to exact revenge.

"How did you get all of this?" Gunner asked.

If I hadn't been so enraged, I would've laughed at the horror and admiration in his tone. He didn't know anything about Scar's talents in getting information. The woman was a genius and dangerous, which was why I was so intrigued as to why these four were together. But that curiosity was trumped by the facts laid out before me.

"I keep tabs on all of my clients," she replied. "It's a good security measure to have dirty details on people for when they become…difficult to deal with."

Mr. Katana piped up from the couch. "That strategy didn't go well for Epstein."

Scar's delicate fingers pinched the bridge of her nose, a sigh leaving her lips. Despite my anger, I smirked at the fact that these men, or at least that man, were capable of breaking her icy facade.

"As I was trying to say, I keep tabs on all the people I work with or may work with." She nodded to the files on the table. "I've been watching Los Muertos, the Jimenez men in particular, for years. That's how I discovered they had a fellow woman running shit in this toxic paradise that is the criminal world. But I've kept a closer eye on Mario since deciding I liked Ryan. I didn't care for the way he treated her." She let her words fall off, locking on to my eyes and giving me a glimpse into the emotional turmoil she kept tightly tucked away.

Meeting Scar taught me that losing my parents was tragic and brutal, but sometimes having no family was better than constantly being fucked over by your blood.

"Anyway, some of these go back years. But these—these are what I could pull from the last few months. This picture was from earlier this month," she said, pushing a photo forward.

Saliva pooled in my mouth—nausea hitting me like a freight train.

"Fuck. Can we keep these?" Gunner asked, reaching out and plucking another piece of damning evidence from the table.

"Of course. I have my copies," Scar answered.

The photo in my hand shook—my emotions battling for the top spot. After the initial horror, I settled into my comfort. Rage. The picture was taken at Lotería, the night he asked for the club to be emptied. Mario and his crew, with members of the Reapers, hosting an exclusive party. But we already knew he was working with them. What made my skin crawl was the women being auctioned off on the stage. The mascara streaking down their faces and the restraints around them were all the evidence I needed to know what was happening in the picture.

"He's selling skin," I seethed. The emotion was so thick in my voice.

I needed to shut down my feelings immediately. I would not let this stand, and I wouldn't be able to do what needed to be done if I let my emotions rule my decisions.

I reaped the souls of guilty men, and Mario wouldn't be given a pass.

"Look's like he's been doing it for months. He's trying to get the attention of the Circle. Nasty bunch of assholes, let me tell ya." Scar looked over at Mr. Broody, a silent exchange happening. "But Mario will never get it. He's got too many eyes from law enforcement agencies looking at him, but no one's been able to pin shit." Scar let out a humorless chuckle. "If only they would be willing to break a few rules, he would've been taken care of months ago. I mean, look at all the shit I found."

Callahan walked over, plucking the photograph from

Gunner's hands and examining it.

"They would never do that. Citizens would freak out if they thought government agencies were spying on them…" Callahan remarked, laughing at the irony.

"Snowden tried to tell them, and look what happened to him," Mr. Katana piped up. "People don't want to know how trackable and hackable their shit is. Buncha sheep."

Callahan continued to speak, not remotely perturbed by the interruption. "It's why we end up cleaning up this kinda shit," he said as he glanced over at the other men before looking at Gunner and me.

Anger filled my veins that these women were enduring this, and no one was fixing it.

"Fuck the police or FBI or whoever the fuck it is that's failing their job. I'm going to kill Mario since they won't." I turned back to Scar. "Where is he now? And where the fuck is Sergio in all of this? Why set up the deal with Skeletons of Society to let all this other shit go down?" I asked, throwing up my hands in anger.

Gunner piped up. "Unless Sergio doesn't know about any of this." He grabbed another document from the table, his brows furrowed.

"Then where the fuck is he? He hasn't answered any of my messages in days. If he wasn't a part of this, why is he avoiding me?"

Callahan seemed to look at me for the first time, assessing me in a way that felt eerily similar to Scar. I didn't think they realized how similar they were. Or they didn't want to admit it. Fuck, it was going to be fireworks between the two of them. They were either going to kill each other or kill others together.

"You're Los Muertos's arms dealer." He looked over at Scar, narrowing his eyes. "So Ryan doesn't have a dick," he stated as his eyebrow hit his hairline.

Scar pulled her bottom lip between her teeth and looked at the tabletop guiltily.

Gunner chuckled. "No, she doesn't, but you're just

finding that out, huh?"

Callahan glanced at Gunner before turning back to me, giving me a single nod and leaving the small room. Scar rolled her eyes at his departure.

"He's always annoyingly vague and asks questions that make you wonder what the fuck he's going on about." She looked over toward where he'd left the room before lowering her voice. "The annoying part is usually he's on to something, and normally he's right. Fucker."

The statue in the chair made a sound that I thought was a laugh, be he covered it up with a cough. Scar's head whipped toward the noise.

"Told you the big guy laughed. You just hadn't said anything funny until now," Mr. Katana said, getting a glare from both of them.

"Anyway…" she said as she pulled out her phone and typed in something. "I don't know where Sergio is. I've been watching for any activity, but it's radio silence. His phone hasn't moved from his place in Sinaloa. And that fucker is either a genius or too old, but he doesn't have cameras at his compound. Nothing to hack if there's nothing there. I pulled this feed from Lotería's security system this morning."

She pushed the phone toward me, a video playing on the screen. Mario was ransacking my office and breaking whatever he could get his hands on.

"I'm guessing he knows you're missing. And he doesn't look too happy about it, Ryan," she stated, pulling the phone back.

Gunner pinched the bridge of his nose in frustration. "Fuck. What are we going to do now?" He turned to look at me, his fingers curling around my shoulders. "You are going to have to leave town. Go to another one of Scar's safe houses or wherever you told Nikki to go. But you can't stay in Tucson."

"The fuck I can't, Gunner. I'm not letting Mario—or Sergio—get away with this. He was auctioning off women in *my* club. The club I built as a haven for women, and he tarnished that." Angry tears welled in my eyes, my voice cracking under the emotion. "He knew, Gunner. He knew I saved women, housed them and employed them if they wanted it."

The room blurred as my tears reached the breeching point before rolling down my cheeks. I looked away, unable to look at anyone in the room. Ashamed that I was unable to keep a lid on my emotions.

Strong arms surrounded me. Gunner's hard chest felt like coming home, and a new set of emotions rose inside me.

"Lotería was a haven because of *you*. The building had nothing to do with that. You are not responsible for the actions of others. His sins are not your own, and you are not guilty of them. Do not punish yourself for something that was never your doing."

A sniffle came from Scar's direction, and I saw her discreetly wiping away a rogue tear. If only Gunner realized how healing his words had been to more than just me. From over her shoulder, I saw Callahan staring down Scar. I wasn't the only one who had caught her reaction.

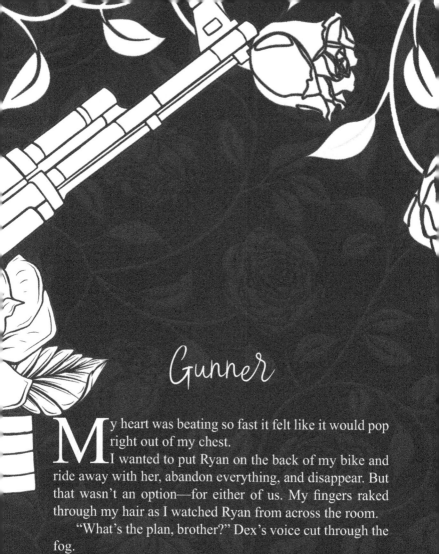

Gunner

My heart was beating so fast it felt like it would pop right out of my chest.

I wanted to put Ryan on the back of my bike and ride away with her, abandon everything, and disappear. But that wasn't an option—for either of us. My fingers raked through my hair as I watched Ryan from across the room.

"What's the plan, brother?" Dex's voice cut through the fog.

"I've got no fucking clue. But we've got proof of Mario trafficking women." I caught the tightening of Dex's fists. "You'll need some more alcohol for the next part," I commented, using the end of my beer to point to his drink. His eyes narrowed in suspicion as he chugged.

"Babe," I called out, catching her attention. "Get your cute ass over here…and bring the tequila."

After meeting with Scar, we rode back to the clubhouse. The beautiful thing about being on a bike was that I didn't have to figure out how to fill the silence—because I was in my fucking head after all I'd learned.

The bottle slammed down on the table, followed by her ass in my lap seconds later. Good Lord, how was I supposed to focus with her soft curves pressed against me?

"What's the plan, boys?" she asked, taking a swig from the bottle, her eyes pinging between Dex and me.

"I thought you were the woman in charge here, chica. Shouldn't you be answering that question?" Dex asked. His tone was light and playful, but I could see the tension in his back and how his eyes had that caged animal look. This was a sore subject for him, but he would need to pull it together.

"Well, my plan got denied. Grumpy here said we couldn't go in and shoot the bastard in the head."

My eyes rolled at the sass in her voice. "Ryan, we can't just march into Lotería and shoot people and just hope it will work out." My fingers came up and pinched the bridge of my nose as she and Dex shrugged their shoulders as if to ask, *why not*?

"Not happening. You two hear me?" I exclaimed, not trusting either of them.

My question was answered with disheartened yeses.

I shifted in my seat, trying to put more space between Ryan's ass cheeks and my dick. My hard-on was going to be the fourth member of this meeting at this point. As it was, the scent of Ryan's coconut shampoo was tempting me to bury my nose in the crook of her neck.

"Ryan, do you know anything about the Circle Scar mentioned?" I asked, hoping the grim conversation we needed to have would calm my dick down. The way her back went rigid told me she knew at least *something* on the subject.

"Yeah." She took another pull from the bottle, her eyes staring off. Wherever her mind was, it wasn't here. With a slight shake of her head, she started speaking again. "I don't know too much. They're too high up on the criminal ladder for me to interact with, but the Circle is the elite of the elite.

Old *dirty* money."

Her eyes met mine. "My hands are so clean they're sterile compared to theirs. Sergio knows a few of them but never wanted to associate with them too closely. You get an invitation if you kill enough people, make enough money, or commit enough evil acts…like selling skin."

"Wait, wait, wait." Dex's fingers were pressed to his temples. "There's an elite circle of assholes *within* the criminal world? Like all the organizations we know aren't the only ones?" he asked, disbelief in his voice.

Ryan's hair brushed my arm as she nodded, tempting me. All I could imagine was her locks splayed across my pillow. But her following words killed that line of thinking.

"Yeah. The top of the top runs everyone else. Our organizations bow to them, whether you realize it or not. They're the overlords with billions. Their dirty fingers are wrapped up in different things, both legal and illegal. These assholes are still trading their daughters and nieces like chess pieces," she seethed.

"Up here, you have the Circle. Elitist assholes—untouchable." Ryan used her hands to represent the order of power. "Then you have this level. That's the Four Families in New York and Los Muertos. But Sergio doesn't rub shoulders with them…or he didn't."

I interrupted her lesson. "How is it that you know all this?"

"Yeah, I've been with the Skeletons for five years, and I've never heard this shit," Dex threw in.

The corners of her plump lips pulled up into a smirk. "The Four Families run New York, Dex. You've got the Yakuza, the Bratva, the Irish Mob, and the Italian Mafia." She ticked each one off on her fingers. The hair on my arms stood on end at the information being dropped. "Their organizations are so big that they caught the attention of the Circle. Same as Los Muertos. The Circle has demands that we play their games…or face the consequences. They've got lots of power. For example, Sergio has cargo planes that are given unrestricted airspace and a cleared-out runway to land right at billionaires' estates. Blow makes the best party favors for the rich," she commented.

Dex's brows furrowed. "How did I not know any of this? Well, minus the Families. I know who those fuckers are."

"Because the Skeletons are third on the power hierarchy. I only know about this because Mario has complained for years about Sergio not taking advantage of the opportunity... looks like he finally did." Her tone was bitter and full of rage.

"You think the girls in those pictures were being sold to the Circle," Dex stated, his fist balled up on the table, knuckles turning white.

"No." Ryan shook her head. "I think Mario's trying to become a big enough name in the skin trade that he gets noticed by the Circle. He wants to be invited to the table too. Only Sergio has had the offer extended to him."

"But he's not going to because he's caught the attention of law enforcement," I stated, nodding as all the pieces were coming together.

"Supposedly. That's what Scar thought, at least. But I don't know if those fuckers are doing anything," Ryan seethed, throwing another shot back.

Dex met my eyes over the top of Ryan's head. "Well, this is a bit of a shit show now," he commented.

"Good news," Ryan piped up, "is that when we kill Mario, we won't be assassinated by the Circle since the asshole hasn't been initiated," she said in mock cheer.

I opened my mouth to answer when Lolli came striding up.

"What's this bitch doing here again?" she called out, words slurring.

When we got back, the clubhouse had been relatively empty, but I knew it wouldn't stay that way. Over the last hour, more and more brothers and bunnies had trickled in, but we were tucked away in a corner where we *should* have been left alone.

"Stick your tits out a little more, Lolli. Maybe someone will want to touch them." Ryan drew her eyes up and down the intruder. "Probably not, though. Now run along and sexually harass someone else," Ryan said, shooing her away with her hand.

A scoff left Lolli's lips while a bark of laughter left Dex's.

"Listen here, you trashy bitch. These two don't want you around. They have to be around you because Pres is forcing them. But they won't have to for long," Lolli spewed out.

What the fuck was she going on about?

My hand traveled up Ryan's back, landing on her neck, my thumb tracing along her skin. Lolli's gaze darted to the movement, a flash of insecurity in her eyes.

Ryan's eyebrow quirked up, her eyes lighting in mischief as her elbows hit the table and her chin came to rest on top of her hands. "Lolli, you think your Pres also asked Gunner to fuck me until I saw stars? Oh, you didn't know that part, did you? I didn't think so, based on the shade of red your face is turning. Well, let me tell you, it's a *pleasure* to work on Gunner," she said condescendingly.

I chuckled at her choice of words while my dick twitched.

"You fucking whore," Lolli shouted, her eyes wild.

Her reaction put me on alert, but Ryan was unbothered.

"Well, that's a bit ironic, isn't it? A little like the whole pot calling the kettle thing," Ryan mocked, utterly unfazed by the tantrum Lolli was throwing.

"Are you fucking both of them?" she shrieked.

"No," Ryan and I answered simultaneously.

Dex set his beer down, eyebrows furrowing. "There is nothing wrong with a throuple, assholes. But to mimic what they said, fuck no...Gunner would cut off my balls, not suck on them," he stated.

Ryan's eyes cut over to Dex. "You've given this thought, huh?" she asked.

"Eh, I don't care whose mouth sucks my balls, as long as it happens." His eyes quickly cut to Lolli, pointing at her. "Not your mouth, though."

Lolli's eyes bounced between Ryan and me, her mind trying to figure out whether Ryan was lying.

Let me show you then, Lolli.

My fingers threaded in Ryan's hair, and I yanked her head back, giving me access to her mouth. Our tongues fought for dominance before I pulled hers into my mouth and sucked. A moan escaped her, and she scrambled to straddle me without breaking contact. Her peaked nipples brushed my chest, and my free hand snaked up to pinch them, pulling another moan from her throat.

I barely registered the yell from Lolli or her stomping off.

"Fuck, I'm gonna go find someone to suck me off," Dex called out before disappearing.

My fingers released Ryan's locks, both hands resting under her ass. "Lock your ankles, babe," I said against her mouth before standing, carrying her off to my bedroom. "I'm going to strip off every piece of clothing and worship you like the goddess you are."

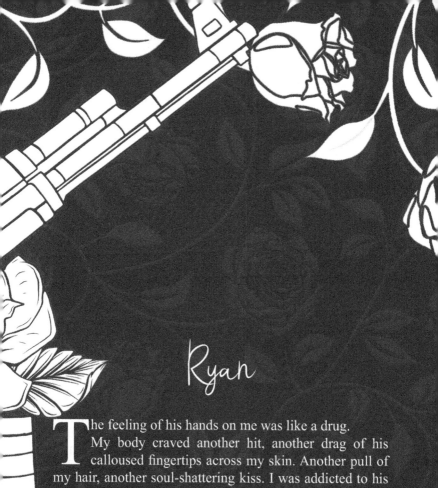

Ryan

The feeling of his hands on me was like a drug. My body craved another hit, another drag of his calloused fingertips across my skin. Another pull of my hair, another soul-shattering kiss. I was addicted to his presence.

Addicted to him—and that was a problem.

My breath whooshed from my lungs as he slammed me against the wooden door of his bedroom. His cock ground against my clit, pulling a moan from my lips. My fingers threaded through his hair, yanking him closer, our tongues sliding across each other.

"Door. Get the door," Gunner said between rushed kisses, his fingers digging in to my ass as his hips thrust into me. I didn't think he realized he was doing it.

Our bodies were ready for each other. "My thong is soaked for you, Gunner," I taunted while fumbling for the handle, unwilling to break my lips away to see what I was doing. A frustrated grunt left my mouth.

"Fuck it. Fuck me in the hallway," I mumbled against his lips as my hands trailed down to his belt buckle. But he yanked his face away, horror in his eyes.

"The fuck I will. You think I would let any of these assholes see what's mine?" he growled, setting me down to jiggle the handle and get the door open.

I rolled my eyes at his dramatics, trying to ignore the sense of loss I felt now that he wasn't touching me. "Gunner, you're acting like I told you I killed your mom," I responded, walking into his bedroom. A firm hand landed on my ass, pulling a yelp from me.

"Naw. My mom was a bitch. I wouldn't have batted an eye at that," he responded nonchalantly.

His words reminded me there was so much about him I didn't know. For most people I crossed paths with, I didn't care to know about them. But suddenly, I wanted to know everything about Gunner.

I turned to face him, my hands landing on his chest. "What's your favorite color, Gunner?" I asked, feeling a bit silly that it was so important for me to know. His brows furrowed. Two seconds ago, I wanted to fuck him in the hallway. Now I wanted to know his favorite color. His rough hand came up and stroked my cheek. There was a tenderness in his eyes.

"Green...my favorite color is green," he said against my lips.

I nodded my head, nibbling softly on his lip. "Yeah, you're not a blue person," I whispered—no clue why I knew that. I just did.

His lips left mine as he pulled back, searching my face. "No, I'm not...Tell me you're mine, Ryan?" he asked as his hands found the bottom of my shirt, lifting it over my head.

"All yours, Gunner," I whimpered as his teeth nipped at my throat before soothing the sting with the pad of his tongue. His hands hooked under my ass, and he deposited me on the edge of the bed, stripping me of my jeans so fast that the friction warmed my skin. His hands pulled down the lacy cups of my bra, pinching my nipples. I could feel the heat of his gaze on my body.

"Fuck, Ryan. I wish I could look at this beautiful body forever," he said as a thick finger slipped past the lace of my thong, his knuckle caressing my wet pussy. Something about his tone set off a warning bell in my head, but I was too turned on to pay it any attention.

Ripping sounds filled the air, and suddenly I felt cool air. I lifted onto my elbows and was met with the sight of Gunner kneeling between my thighs. My thong was ripped away, and his inked fingers were wrapped around his throbbing cock—stroking it in languid pulls.

"Fuck, that is the hottest thing I've ever seen," I whispered as my tongue swiped across my bottom lip. His precum glistening at the tip made me want to lap it up.

"Spread your legs, Ryan. Let me see that dripping cunt of yours. Let me see what's mine," he growled.

"Is this what you want, Gunner?" I taunted as my knees fell open and my hand snaked down my body. I dragged my fingers down my center, dipping them into my pussy, watching how his throat bobbed as he swallowed. His eyes locked on to the thrusting motion, our paces matching. I pulled the soaked digits out, offering them to him. A moan fell from my lips when he pulled them into his mouth, sucking them clean.

"Fuck, you taste like heaven, babe. Now be a good girl and move your hand because I'm going to bury my face between your legs," he said, his tongue already trailing up my inner thigh, his facial hair adding to the sensations.

I cried out as his mouth sucked on my throbbing clit while three of his thick fingers plunged into me—stretching me. He knew I loved the bite of pain. His name fell from my lips, causing him to groan into my pussy. Suddenly I was empty. His heat disappeared.

My head shot up, only to be slammed back down with his hand wrapped around my throat. The action was so primal I almost came from that alone. His fingers dug into my jaw while he used his other hand to rub the head of his cock up and down my pussy.

"Open up, Ryan," he demanded, his pupils blown out with lust.

I did as I was told, my tongue lapping up the saliva he let drip into my mouth, tasting the lingering flavor of my pussy.

Fuck. I did not know I was into that shit.

"Such a good fucking girl for me, huh?" he asked as he sunk his cock into me.

A groan fell from my lips. All I could do was nod, too enveloped in pleasure to form coherent words. The hand on my throat tightened as he pumped into me at a dizzying pace, his balls bouncing off my ass. The slapping noise filled the room, mixing with the wet sounds of my pussy and our moans. I couldn't tell if my fingers were digging into the sheets or his ass. Reality seemed suspended, pleasure overwhelming all my senses.

Suddenly his lips were on mine, our tongues warring for dominance, my hands trying to pull him even closer.

"Come for me, baby. Let go with me," he muttered against my lips.

Warmth filled me as he came inside me, the pulsing of his cock sending me over the edge. I barely recognized that the moans of pleasure were my own as my body rode through the aftershocks of my release.

"Fuck, Ryan. Your greedy pussy is milking me of everything I've got." He groaned against my throat, nipping at the skin as his body shuddered.

Suddenly, his body hovered over me as his hand cupped my face. "You have to leave, Ryan. It's too dangerous to stay here." His brows furrowed. "You changed my every plan. God, I want to keep you," he whispered. So low it felt like those words weren't meant for me.

I trailed my fingertips along his jaw, taking in his beauty. "You can keep me, Gunner. I'm not going anywhere," I answered.

His eyes searched mine, indecision flashing across them.

"I don't want to worry about this tonight. Not when I have your perfect body against me." He pressed a kiss to the top of my hair. "Tonight, I'm going to enjoy having you in my arms."

He stood up and walked toward the bathroom, muttering under his breath.

"Since I don't know how long I'll have that."

My gut clenched because those words felt like an omen.

Ryan

T he sound of vibrations woke me up.

In my sleepy state, I thought Gunner had forgotten to turn my vibrator off, but then, as some of the fog lifted, I remembered we were at the clubhouse, so there was no way that would cause the noise. I peeled my eyes open and found the screen of my burner phone illuminated. My brows wrinkled in confusion.

No one has this number. Fuck, Nikki.

A feeling of dread sank in my stomach, and some instinct made me look over at the sleeping man. I always had a strong intuition, one I learned to listen to long ago. It was now telling me to commit everything about Gunner to memory. The way his calloused hands felt on my skin, the rough sensation of his facial hair against my thighs, the tugging of my hair in his hands. The way he spoke to me as an equal and saw all my rawness and found beauty, not flaws.

The way I knew I loved him.

Another round of vibrations pulled me back to the phone. My hand shook as I reached for it.

Nikki: Muñeca. Why are you hiding from me?

I muffled my gasp. A picture of Nikki restrained to a chair in a room I was all too familiar with. He had her. The bastard had Nikki.

Nikki: For Nikki's sake, I hope you're reading these. Because if not, she's about to make someone a very happy man when they buy her. Will you fail Nikki like you did your parents? Didn't you tell me it was your fault they were out that night, Muñeca?

Nikki: Come to me. Now.

Nikki: Alone, Muñeca. I'll know if you don't.

My fingers were on the keyboard, ready to respond, when a soft knock sounded at the door. My head whipped to the noise, wondering if the shock had me hearing things. But after another *thud,* I tiptoed to open it. Queen bitch stood on the other side. She peered around my body, taking in Gunner's sleeping form, making me want to knock her ass out on the spot.

What the fuck does she want?

I was about to slam the door on her and her shit timing when her words stopped me in my tracks.

"Oh good, your whore ass is awake. Mario wanted to make sure you got his messages and remind you that he was watching," she taunted. A cruel smile was plastered on her face, delighting in the shock on mine. "He didn't say this part, but I'll be glad when he sells your ass. Gunner was always supposed to be mine," she seethed.

I was so stunned that I didn't even swing at her or demand more answers.

She called over her shoulder as she walked away. "You've got ten minutes to get to Lotería, Muñeca. Alone... those were his words." Laughter left her lips. It was clear she was taking great joy in this whole situation.

"Bet you the bitch he's holding deserves it too if she

276

friends with you," she added.

My vision flooded with rage. She should've run when she had the chance because now the initial shock had worn off. And if she'd done her research, she'd know I was amazing at recovering quickly and retaliating with a vengeance.

I watched my fingers disappear into the bleach-blond rat's nest, grasping hard on to her locks and yanking. I felt as hair pulled free from her scalp. She was lucky she wore some cheap-ass extensions, or the damage would have been worse. A shriek escaped her mouth before I clamped my free hand over it, fighting back an inner gag at the thought of where her mouth had been. Her flailing proved she didn't have a clue how to fight. She was hoping digging her talons into my arms would set her free.

Had she forgotten she'd watched me fight a big-ass man? Who threw literal punches at my face? What did she think her nails would do besides piss me off more? I shoved her up against the hallway wall, careful to avoid any doors. If I was going to get to Mario's alone, I needed to be sure not to wake Gunner or any of his club brothers.

I leaned forward, whispering in her ear, "Listen here, you sorry excuse for a woman. I have more important things to do than beat your ass, but I'm going to hurt you. I'm going to give you a taste of what is to come after I go handle Mario," I said, making sure she heard the menace in my voice—got a picture of the killer I was.

A whimper escaped as I pulled harder.

"How many women have you helped him sell? Huh?" I asked, shoving her face farther into the wall. "Do the Skeletons know you're double-dipping into the Reaper MC? My guess is no. See, your fuck up, Lolli, was not knowing who the fuck I am. *I* run shit for Los Muertos here in Tucson. *I* run Lotería. And I know for damn sure you didn't meet Mario there. So where did you meet him, Lolli?"

I let my question sit in the air between us. Her body went rigid at the accusation of her disloyalty. She knew club rules, and as a club whore, she was Skeletons' property. Being with the Reapers in any way would be cause for extermination.

Warm tears hit my hand, and I let out a cruel laugh.

"Yeah, you chose the wrong bitch. La Brujita de Los Muertos. Do you know what that means, Lolli?" Her head shook no, tears continuing to flow. "I'm the witch of the dead, chica. And I'll be back to reap your soul for El Diablo," I whispered in her ear. The bloodlust thrumming through my veins demanded I answer the call of violence.

Without warning, I spun her around, landing a solid punch to her orbital, the fragile bone crushing under the force. Before she could alert anyone, my left hook hit her chin, knocking her out on impact. I stared at her crumpled form for a few moments before realizing I needed to get a move on if I was going to make Mario's timeline. My stomach turned at the memory of me bending to his will. Now I would have to do that again.

I cracked Gunner's door open and peeked in, hoping his sleeping form hadn't moved. The sliver of light coming from the hallway showed his chest rising and falling under the sheet. A sigh of relief escaped my lips, but my heart clenched at the thought of what I was about to do. It was better this way, his still being asleep. It meant I could sneak out of here and show up alone, as Mario demanded.

And he would know. He wasn't dumb enough to only have Lolli as a mole. Someone else would be watching, waiting to see how long it took me to leave the clubhouse and who left after.

It always pissed me off in movies when people split up or characters didn't communicate what was happening. But now I understood. Now I could see how shoveling the burden on your shoulders seemed better than risking your loved ones. And I loved Gunner. I wouldn't get him into this mess, but I wouldn't risk Nikki either. Not going wasn't an option.

On silent feet, I gathered up my clothes and anything

else I needed. They would check me for weapons eventually, but I would keep my Sig on me for as long as possible. I gnawed on my lip, and against my better judgment, I crept over to Gunner's side of the bed. My fingers longed to touch him, but I knew I couldn't do that. I was already pushing the limits. My vision blurred the longer I stared at him. Despite the threat I gave Lolli, I didn't know if I would be coming back. I didn't know if I would survive whatever Mario had planned. Unable to resist, I leaned forward and brushed my lips against his forehead, choking down a sob while whispering into his skin.

"Fuck. I'm sorry I never told you I love you. But I guess, given the circumstances, it's better this way. I hope you find someone who makes your soul sing the way you did for me."

I gave myself seconds to have my breakdown before tucking the emotions into my inner box. Cold and calculated was what I needed if I was going to get Nikki out. Because while I didn't know what my fate would be, I was going to make damn sure she was freed.

Ryan

Crazy how many things can change in such a short amount of time.

I had never felt dread when coming to Lotería. It was always like coming home. Walking in felt like a warm embrace, but that had shifted. Now it felt cold—hostile—no longer the place I loved.

Tarnished and broken by the vile acts of a man I thought had saved me.

That moment in the alley was beginning to haunt me. The rose-colored lens I'd given the memory stripped away, leaving the broken and bloody reality. Now I could see how I was like so many girls I saved. Captured. The other women may have been bought and sold with money, but Mario bargained for my life with an offer he knew I couldn't reject.

Silence was the currency of my captivity.

My jaw clenched, and anger pulsed through my veins.

Mario's downfall would be that he'd caged a predator in his quest to own something dangerous wrapped up in a pretty package. He'd brought me into Los Muertos and allowed me to prosper, giving me a place to live in the shadows and hunt. Somewhere to feed the bloodlust that called to me when I watched the guilty slip through the cracks. Arrogant of him to think I would never realize my strings were held by one such guilty party.

Muñeca. I was no longer his doll. Now I was coming to reap the souls of guilty men and revel in the blood I spilled.

The crunch of gravel felt deafening in the silent parking lot.

"Hopefully, you make it back to your owner," I mumbled, tossing the keys to the stolen bike into one of the worn leather saddlebags.

The Skeletons apparently never feared their rides would be stolen from the compound. Then again, you would have to be a psycho to attempt that. Or desperate. But with a full-face helmet hiding my identity, the prospect at the gate didn't bat an eye. Or, since the prospect manning the gate was that bitch-ass kid Roy, Mario probably told him to let me through.

The arched entrance loomed in front of me, dark and dead.

"How poetic." A sigh left my lips. "Ironically, this is exactly what Gunner told me not to do. No point trying to hide my arrival," I mumbled as I shrugged out of my jacket. I was going to need room to move.

Mario knew I would come. He'd dangled the one of the few things I would drop everything for. This was what I got for letting him know about her. Being close to me brought danger and heartache. My heart clenched at that thought.

"Time to take out some assholes," I said as my fingers wrapped around the grip of my Sig.

No one ever believed a woman could be bloodthirsty. And all of Mario's stupid Armandos were so damn misogynistic that they never bothered looking at a woman as a threat. Too bad they wouldn't be alive long enough to correct their mistakes.

"Armando," I called out to the asshole manning the door.

The moment he turned his body, I put two in his chest. The smell of gunpowder was like an aphrodisiac to my revenge-filled mind. Stepping over the fallen body, I raised an eyebrow at the dying piece of garbage.

"Having a good night? It would've been nice if your boss informed you that I was a crazy bitch, huh?"

There was no response other than the blood trickling from the corner of his lips and a gurgling noise sounding from his chest.

"I saw you in that picture. You were holding the restraints of that woman. Tell El Diablo I'll see him soon," I spat before moving farther into the club.

I put bullets in three more guilty men, painting the walls with their blood, before a small army met me in the pit where the main stage was housed.

"So nice of you all to gather in one spot for me. Although, I truly love the hunt, so if your cowardly asses decide to run…I'll gladly come to find you," I called out, wanting every one of them to hear the truth of my words.

My sinister grin only widened as Mario's men shuffled uncomfortably.

I wouldn't be able to pick any more of them off. They were too jumpy. I couldn't afford to get injured or die before freeing Nikki. But I committed each of their faces to memory, promising to take out as many of these motherfuckers as I could before breathing my last breath. A wave of grief hit me at the thought of likely never seeing Gunner again. I closed my eyes, trying to block out the pain.

I couldn't afford weakness. Nikki couldn't afford for me to be weak.

I locked my feelings down, embracing the cold killer that lurked just below the surface.

Nikki's ass better be smart enough to get herself to

Gunner and Dex after I got her free. I was sure the Skeletons would keep her and my other girls safe. Because despite referring to Lolli as a club whore, the club girls were well taken care of. Consent was something the Skeletons of Society took very seriously. It's why I thought Sergio wanted to partner with them to begin with. Now I didn't know what to think.

"Muñeca, stop taunting my men."

His voice caused my gut to clench, a million different emotions flashing through me. Mario came forward from behind the wall of expendable bodies. My knuckles went white as the grip on my gun tightened. He dragged Nikki by her hair, and it took every ounce of restraint I had to keep my arms down by my sides. I'd have to use all my skills to get Nikki out of here as unscathed as possible.

Damn, it would have been nice to have Scar here. If my theory on her was right, that bitch would've already picked off every asshole in this room.

I was more brute force, whereas Scar was finesse.

Blue eyes met mine; not a tear was in sight. Instead, Nikki had a murderous look painted on her face like a bloody warrior goddess. My chest swelled with pride.

"Muñeca. Good to see you can still follow instructions. Although, I think it was unnecessary to shoot four of my men. No need for a temper tantrum," he tsked, not an ounce of sorrow in his voice for the fallen.

The fucker was delusional. I shrugged my shoulders nonchalantly, refusing to rise to the bait.

"I didn't like their faces, so I shot them," I threw back, folding my arms over my chest while keeping a tight grip on my gun. They would strip it from me soon, but I wanted time to assess the situation. There hadn't been a whole lot of time to preplan an escape. Thank Santa Muerte Nikki worked here too. She would know all the ways out when I gave her an opening. Finding the opening would be the tricky part.

Anger flashed across his face, fists tightening, but he

284

quickly recovered his composure.

"I'm here now, Mario. Let Nikki go. Or do you no longer tell me the truth?"

The implication hung heavy in the air. He hated being questioned. His word was law, and no one was allowed to go against it. Or question it. How had he managed to force my submission for so long? I was like a caged animal; failing to see the hand that fed me was the same hand keeping me tethered. The hand I was about to bite the fuck off.

"Muñeca, you can't be that stupid. Why would I let her go when I can have both of you? And you do not tell me what to do. I'm in charge." Spittle flew from his mouth as he raised his voice. The men close to him carefully inched away while trying not to draw his wrath toward them.

"No, I'm not that stupid. I was hoping for your sake you wouldn't be either," I stated.

An unhinged look appeared in his eyes. "You've given me no other choice than to remind you who you belong to."

Bile filled my mouth at his words. "Fuck right off, Mario. No one owns me; the fact that you thought you could will be your downfall."

I could sense men coming up behind me to disarm me. The urge to roll my eyes at their attempt was strong, but I held off, letting them get close. Yells rang out seconds after I turned and shot the guy on my left in the head.

In the chaos, Mario called, "Don't shoot her; restrain her."

Nikki shrieked in distress for me. But I was too busy dealing with the man I'd given my back to. He'd pinned my arms to my sides, restraining me while another Armando ran up to retrieve my gun. Dumbass. The moment he got close, I landed a solid kick to the middle of his chest, sending him flying.

"Fuck," I gritted out as my arms were wrenched behind my back. The telltale sound of zip ties cut through the noise, and hard plastic bit into my wrist. At the last moment, I shifted the positions of my hands. Leaving a little room to work with.

Cigarette stench hit my nose as the asshole behind me leaned in close enough to whisper in my ear.

"We may not be able to touch you for now. But when Mario is tired of you, I plan on fucking you over and over again…"

The coppery taste of blood filled my mouth as I bit my tongue to stay silent. I needed to bide my time and choose the right moment to act out. But knowing that didn't make having restraint any easier.

"Nothing to say now? Shame, I like to hear a woman scream for help." He jerked my body to the side, sending me stumbling to my knees in front of Mario. His words played on repeat in my head. These men had all signed their death warrants.

I mourned for the women who thought there would never be justice for what they endured. I wished I could tell them their monsters had just met their slayer. These fuckers had no clue who they were dealing with or the levels I was willing to go to for revenge.

I made a silent vow. By the end of this, my hands would be stained in blood, and I would make a crown from the bones of my enemies to wear while I sat on my throne. Right next to El Diablo himself.

I bared my bloody teeth at Mario, wanting him to see the monster he provoked. *"Te voy a matar Mario."*

His jaw ticked, making my smile widen. "Bring her to the interrogation room. It's time my Muñeca remembered her place." The tremble in his voice betrayed the emotions he was trying to keep hidden. He was rattled.

As I was yanked from my knees, I called out, "You ready to play, Mario? Because this is my favorite game, and you should have chosen an easier opponent."

Anger blazed in his eyes, but so did doubt. Mario hated not being in control, and he didn't expect me to fight back since I never had before. I always stayed inside the lines he drew for me. But now I knew my power.

286

He hadn't betrayed me, because he'd never had my trust—only my blind obedience.

What would save him now?

Gunner

"**W**here the fuck is she?" I roared out.

The pain and anger in my voice were almost tangible. My hands held Lolli under her armpits, pinned up against the wall, feet dangling. Her eye was swollen shut, and the popped blood vessels had colored her skin a deep purple.

"I don't know what you're talking about, Gunner," she whimpered as I leaned my face in closer.

"Don't insult my intelligence, Lolli."

"Gunner, please. The bruise is from a club brother," she claimed, fear evident in her voice.

I let out a guttural roar, slamming my fist beside her head. Drywall coated her already messed up hair as she stood awkwardly now that I was only holding her by one hand.

"I know damn well a club brother didn't do that," I seethed.

By this time, all the noise drew others to the hallway, all bearing witness to my rage. I saw Dex approach from the corner of my eye, but he didn't intervene.

"While another club brother wouldn't hurt a woman. I have no issue causing you pain until you tell me what the fuck you did to Ryan. That's who did that to you, right?" I asked, fighting to speak calmly.

Another whimper left her mouth as she looked around at the brothers, waiting for someone to come to her aid.

"Don't wanna talk? Then tell me which brother hit you, Lolli." I raised my voice and gestured to the crowd behind us. "Tell us all who hit you like you're saying."

Her one good eye widened. "Gunner…"

She'd used that excuse before there were other ears to hear it, but now, she'd have to name a brother if she continued with this lie. Her body began to physically shake, but I couldn't drum up an ounce of sympathy for her.

Not when I knew she had something to do with Ryan being missing. I saw the burner my baby left behind with a single line of unsent text typed out on the screen.

Mario has people watching from within the Skeletons. I'm sure you can find the one I left for you. I'm sorry. Te quiero.

Those were the only words Ryan left behind. But I could piece together enough of what was going on by the messages she'd deleted. She probably didn't anticipate me looking in her deleted file. Or maybe she did. The woman was cunning and seemed to think quickly on her feet. Leaving the burner behind certainly felt planned.

My fingers dug into Lolli's jaw, forcing her to make eye contact. All semblance of restraint was disappearing, and the predator being kept at bay was pacing the cage to get out. I wanted her to see that in my eyes. A large hand landed on my shoulder, attempting to ground me. I turned and met Dex's questioning gaze. A million unspoken words were written upon his face. But I knew his most pressing question, and I gave him one quick but sure nod.

Yes, I was going to see this through. I was going to go rogue.

His gaze lingered a moment longer before turning to Lolli.

"I suggest you tell him what he wants to know. Because you are standing between him and the woman he loves, and believe me when I say he's willing to give up everything to keep her," Dex stated. His tone was icy.

A sob left Lolli's lips. "She's at Lotería. Mario told me I needed to make sure Ryan got the messages and went to Lotería without anyone following. He said she would follow directions since he had her best friend or some shit like that."

Dex's entire body went rigid at the mention of Nikki.

"What the fuck did you just say?" The low growl was terrifying, and it wasn't directed at me. Tears and snot ran down Lolli's face, making her look pathetic.

"He's selling her best friend. Said that's the way he would take back control of Ryan," she sobbed, her words barely decipherable.

Another presence appeared at my side. Pres's arrival made Lolli's skin turn ashen. His deep voice rang out, silencing everyone.

"Why do you even know Mario, Lolli? Where did you meet him?" Pres asked, his tone menacing.

The panic-stricken look on her face told us everything we needed to know. She'd been working with the Reapers too.

"Gunner, you and Dex do what you need to do. We'll take care of Lolli here." Pres turned to face me. "You let me know what you need from me and the Skeletons."

I gave a quick nod before stalking off to my room. A million scenarios about how this would go down and the aftermath of these decisions ran through my head. I didn't have to look behind me to know Dex had stalked after me, ready to act in whatever way I decided.

The door slammed into the wall as I charged into my

room, on the warpath to gather what I needed. Coherent thoughts escaped me. My brain was like an oil slick; anything remotely useful was refusing to stick. The only mental picture I could form was Ryan strapped to the chair Spinner had been strapped to. His bloody and broken face was replaced with hers.

I dug my fists into my eye sockets, trying to physically remove the vision. A guttural yell sounded, and it took me a minute to realize it was coming from me.

"Fuck!" I cried out, sending the contents on my dresser crashing to the ground. "I know this fucker. I know what he's capable of. The psychotic tendencies of his brain. Mario's obsession with Ryan may have saved her before, but now…"

My body shuddered when I thought about what he would do to her now that he felt she wasn't his. The punishments he would put her through—was putting her through.

"Brother. You need to get your shit together. Now. Save your fucking breakdown for another time."

I peeled my eyelids open and stared down the giant man I called my brother. He was right, of course. And fuck, I'd never had an issue with this before.

His stony face softened. "Hey, don't even go down that line of thinking. I can see it on your face. You are completely qualified and capable of getting her out of there." Dex's voice tightened. "Them, out of there. Because I'm not about to go through losing two more women in my life." The pain in his voice tore into my tattered soul even more. But instead of making me weaker, the pain fueled my need for vengeance.

"You've never had this reaction before because you've never loved a woman before, Gunner," Dex said. His words hitting me like a truck.

I probably looked like a gaping fish the way I was opening and closing my mouth. He'd said those words in the hallway, but I'd brushed them off in the heat of the moment. But he was right. I'd fallen for the Latin beauty whose mouth could cut down the most confident of men and whose heart bled for others so strongly she'd run off into the den of a psycho. Her beauty came from the strength to weather the storms life had thrown at her.

"Fuck, I love her," I muttered. Emotions clogging my throat.

How could she feel she wasn't worthy of love and affection? And why did I never tell her those things? Because now it might be too late. Dex's deep rumble pulled me back to reality.

"How are we playing this, Gunner? Lotería is Mario's territory, and we have done zero recon on the place. But, fuck, if we wait for them to move the girls, we may be too late."

My hand hit the false bottom of the dresser drawer, pulling it off to reveal my stash of supplies. I liked to keep my shit hidden in a house full of people. Never knew when someone would get ballsy and go looking.

"Ryan's." I turned to face Dex, tossing him a couple of flash-bangs. "It's Ryan's territory. That asshole is just temporarily occupying it. And we are going to make a call."

Dex's brows shot up in surprise, not at the flash-bangs but at my words.

"To…"

A wicked grin worked its way up onto my face as I stripped off my shirt. "A chick named Scar, who just so happened to install all of Lotería's security. She's the same person who hacked in days ago to get us the evidence and video feed."

I didn't think Dex's eyebrows could get any closer to his hairline, but they did. I hadn't gotten around to filling him in on the specifics of the meeting. We talked about what we learned but not how Ryan's contact had gotten it. To be honest, I didn't fully understand Scar's capabilities. But I knew she was talented. And based on who was at her safe house, she had connections.

"Eyes and ears on the inside. Wow, that's a better contact

than who I thought you were going with," Dex said.

A grunt of agreement left my mouth as I walked over to my bed and reached underneath, pulling out a black case. "The interrogation room is behind a steel door with a biometric lock." I pulled on a black long-sleeve shirt before putting on my cut again. "I'm guessing that fucker thinks he's safe because of that. He probably figures when I come—because he knows I will—I'll never actually make it to her. Unfortunately for him, I know just the person to override that lock."

I slid the magazine into my Glock and tucked it into my holster before picking up another handgun and several extra mags and strapping them to every available spot on my body.

"Well, fuck, this whole mission just got interesting," Dex replied.

Picking up Ryan's burner, I ran through the call log to find what I was looking for.

"Gear up, Dex. We have shit to go fuck up," I announced, having found it.

My brother's grin was unhinged as he reached for the supplies on my bed. A whole tactical candy store to choose from.

Mario chose the wrong fucking woman to mess with. Because Dex and I weren't the rescue party; we were the backup. And he should be scared of the fox he'd let into his henhouse; I had no doubt she would cause a massacre.

MARIE MARAVILLA

Ryan

The irony wasn't lost that I was the first woman to have been tied up in the interrogation room I designed. The plus side was that all the elements made to intimidate didn't affect me. The stark tiled walls and ceiling didn't bother me, the drain made to wash down blood didn't bother me, and the fact that I sat on a metal chair with my hands zip-tied behind my back under the fluorescent lights didn't bother me.

"You good, girl?" I asked.

Mario had Nikki and I deposited in here and then left us alone—a stupid move. I peeked at the corner of the room; there was no green light on the camera there, so we weren't being watched or listened to for the moment.

"I always knew I hated that fucker. But yeah, I'm good," Nikki replied.

I peeked at her from the corner of my eye, unwilling to take my eyes off the door and camera.

"Injuries? And why the fuck didn't you leave town like I told you?" I asked. I hadn't been able to look at her when we were out in the main part of the club.

Nikki let out a deep sign, sounding utterly exhausted. Which made me wonder how long she'd been here with him.

"He found me, Ryan," she said, sounding resigned.

Pain shot through my jaw as I clenched my teeth, upset that she'd had to endure Mario.

"No shit, Nikki. I can see he found you." My eyes rolled. "What I want to know is how. You know what? It doesn't even matter. Now we need to work on getting out of here…"

Nikki whipped her head to the side to look at me. "No, bitch. Not Mario," she fired back. "My ex-husband found me."

"*Espera, ¿Qué dijiste?* What did you say? Ex-husband?" I asked, dumbfounded.

"Well, he might not be my ex? I might still be married to him. I couldn't exactly mail him the divorce papers, you know?" She paused for a moment. "Then again, my father essentially sold me to the asshole, so who knows if I was ever legally married…"

"What kind of telenovela am I living in right now? Okay, we'll get back to that bomb you just dropped, but what does it have to do with you being here?" I asked.

"Oh, right. There was a note at my safe house from my ex. And when I was trying to figure out where else to go, Mario showed up. Threw me into your upstairs office, and now here we are," she replied.

I turned my head to look her in the eyes.

"Nikki, I'm going to get you out of here. But you're going to have to follow my lead. And you're going to leave me when an opening arises."

She opened her mouth to protest, but I shut her down.

"No, Nikki. You have to leave me behind and find Gunner and Dex. Listen, babe, I love you, and you're fierce and a fighter. But not a literal fighter."

"Yeah, but I can shoot," she protested. "Your drill sergeant ass made me practice until I could shoot off a grouping. Consistently."

I smiled at the memory of making her run through shooting drills repeatedly until she did them correctly. But I knew Nikki, and she probably hadn't shot in months.

"Babe, I love you. But I'll be worried about your ass the whole time. So, when you get the chance, you leave me. Okay?"

Tears welled in her eyes. The thing about people who'd been through some shit in their lives was that we tended to be able to see things how they were, not how we wished them to be. She knew as well as I did that the chances of us both getting out weren't great.

"Stop, Ryan. We're going to get out. Gunner will come for you; that man is crazy about you. He won't let this happen," Nikki said, not ready to face the facts.

I gave her a somber smile.

"He doesn't know where we are, Nikki. I left the burner so he couldn't trace me. Mario threatened to sell you if I didn't come alone, and he had people on the inside. I left some clues for Gunner so he didn't think I had betrayed him and left him in the middle of the night. But I had to make sure he wouldn't find me too quickly. I won't risk him or you," I said quietly.

Nikki hung her head, giving me a single nod. A sniffle sounded from her side of the room. But there was a look of determination when her eyes met mine.

"Got it. Fuck up these cocksuckers and then take the opening," she said.

The corners of my lips pulled upward, but the door opened before I could comment. I wished I could've given Nikki more details, but honestly, the plan was fluid at this point. We'd have to react on the fly and pray to Santa Muerte that it worked.

The asshole who'd whispered in my ear walked through the door.

Well, fuck yeah. This made getting Nikki out so much easier.

I kept my face neutral as I flexed my shoulders and repositioned my hands under my shirt with the tops flat against my back, keeping my movements discreet.

"Well, well, well. Look at the new toys I get to play with. Well, toy." He walked over to Nikki and tucked a strand of her blond locks behind her ear. A nasty snarl left her lips.

He tsked at her. "It's too bad your ass is already spoken for; some big wig with the Russian mob." His words drew a small gasp from my friend. The noise made the asshole's smile widen.

"So it's true. We have a case of a runaway bride. Maybe I should sample the goods and tell him how they are. I mean, he can't be expecting a virgin anymore, right? Not since you became a whore." He leaned forward, inhaling the scent of Nikki's hair. She gagged at the proximity of the vile creature.

The fucker was dead.

My hands inched up my back, sliding under my sports bra. The feeling of cold metal met my fingers when I reached the blade stored in the band. Fuckers figured since I came in guns blazing, I only had one weapon. They didn't bother checking. Working for Mario made them lazy and weak. Traits I'd been banking on. Thank Santa Muerte, I was right.

The moment I grasped the blade, I cut through the zip tie. Uncaring that I was going through the material of my shirt or that I may catch some skin in the process. There were about to be a lot of cuts and scrapes, so I might as well start mentally blocking them out now.

"Hey, asshole. Leave her alone," I called out.

Obviously, I was the only one doing interrogating for Los Muertos, or at least doing them well. Otherwise, they would've known to string my arms up above my head. Or, at the very least, they should have strapped my legs to the damn chair. Their mistakes would lead to their demise. And hopefully, Nikki's salvation.

"What the fuck did you call me, bitch?" The ogre's attention turned toward me. "You, I get to play with as soon as the boss is done." His large hand struck my cheek, causing my head to snap to the side and throb in pain. My tongue probed at the split on my lip as I slowly turned back to face him.

"Fuck you," I seethed, spitting a mouthful of blood at his face.

He let out a roar and threaded his fingers in my hair, wrenching my head back.

Nikki let out a cry, and I wished I could clue her in on the fact that I was fine, but I couldn't do anything other than stare into the eyes of a dead man.

"Bitch. Now that you've gone and pissed the boss off. I get to hurt you and can say you weren't cooperating." His free hand reached for his belt buckle, and flashbacks of Jimmy in that alley came flooding back. But they didn't pull out the scared girl I once was. No, those memories fueled me.

"We can call this part of your retraining," he said, leaning in to run his tongue up the side of my face.

"Lesson one, *pendejo*. Check a bitch for weapons," I whispered, ramming the blade into his throat. Warm blood splashed across my face when I ripped the blade out to stab him again.

The squelching and gurgling sounds were music to my ears. He stumbled back before collapsing on the floor by my feet, clutching where blood was seeping from his body.

Nikki let out a cry of surprise. She'd never been part of Los Muertos, so I didn't know how many dead bodies she'd encountered, but today she'd already witnessed me kill several. I hoped she would be able to keep it together long enough to get out of here.

I crouched down, watching him gasp for air.

"Hard to breathe with a hole in your throat, eh, Armando? None of you did your research, did you? Figured

I was one of Mario's bitches; some weak little girl he *saved*. No…I'm the one you should've been scared of." I laughed at the widening of his eyes.

"While I would love to spend time making you regret all your life choices, we don't have time for that." Standing up, I landed a kick to his ribs as I moved to Nikki. "By the way, you dumb motherfuckers really should learn how to restrain a captive properly."

Nikki had a wild look in her eyes as I approached.

"Look, this is perfect. You can cut me loose, and we can both escape. Then you can run into your man's arms and tell him you love him and rip each other's clothes off. Hell, you can get it on in the parking lot and unlock your voyeurism kink. Point is, we can both get out of here, Ryan," she rushed.

Nikki was rambling, a last-ditch attempt at getting me to go with her.

"Nikki, babe. All we've managed to do is get the zip ties off. Mario's men might be dumbasses, but the numbers help even the odds. Fuck…"

I looked up to check the camera; the light had been turned on. It wouldn't be long before he stormed in here if he was watching us right now.

"But, Ryan…" she whispered.

I gripped Nikki's shoulders. Tears streamed down her cheeks, the moisture making her eyes bluer. My thumbs flicked away the runaway tears, but they were replaced with more. Unable to bear looking at my sister's face, I pulled her into my chest, wrapping my arms around her. Nikki held on to me like I was a life raft, the only thing keeping her afloat in the storm. I just hoped I could live up to that.

"Nikki, babe. Tell him I loved him. Okay?" I choked out, my vision getting blurry.

Her whole body shook as she sobbed into my chest. Silent tears slid down my face, their saltiness mixing with the coppery taste of blood.

She couldn't get out any words, but I felt as her cheek

rubbed against my chest.

"Okay, I'm going to check pendejo for weapons, okay? And you need to try to remember how to shoot properly," I said into her hair, happy to hear the small chuckle leave her lips. I needed Nikki to have some fire in her if I wanted to get her out of here.

"God, it would've been nice if you had two guns," I mumbled as I patted down Armando.

I thrust the Glock I found into Nikki's hand. "Don't shoot me. Or yourself. Got it?"

She rolled her eyes. I didn't think she would do any of those things, but given our situation, I needed to address every possible pitfall. We paused next to the door, listening for any commotion outside. I was shocked no one had come bursting in here yet.

Did they not see the giant man lying in a pool of blood and two women making an escape attempt?

I peeked through the crack in the door, seeing no one. But I couldn't see shit through the half of an inch I had.

"Well, Niks, we're about to fuck around and find out," I whispered.

"My favorite way to live life, babe. It's not guaranteed, clearly, so let's take the fucking risks...and fuck who we want," she replied.

I scrunched my nose up and peered at her over my shoulder.

"We are literally captives of a psychopath, and your *possible-last-moment-alive* speech is about fucking who you want?"

"Yes, Ryan," she sassed. "Were you almost forced to have a same-dick-forever marriage you didn't want? And then forced to run away and then get captured again with the threat of selling you back to said Russian crime boss? No? Then you don't get a vote on my last-moment-alive speech."

"Hold up," I whisper-yelled, "you didn't mention he was a Russian crime boss or that Mario was selling you back to him." My fingers pinched the bridge of my nose.

"I was a bit too busy for a proper story time, Ryan," she answered, as if I was the one being unreasonable.

We were seconds away from potentially dying, but still having this conversation. It was so us. I couldn't help the sad smile it brought to my face because I didn't know if I would have another talk like this with Nikki.

"Fuck who we want," I responded.

The smile on Nikki's face mirrored mine. We ignored the fact that as soon as I opened the door, Nikki would run down the hallway to the exit, and I...wouldn't.

Shouts pulled my attention back to the cracked door.

"Time's up," I called over my shoulder, yanking the door open. We rushed into the hallway. I shoved Nikki toward the fire exit as voices got louder.

"Run, Nikki."

I turned to distract the men rounding the corner when a shot rang out, hitting its mark, dead center.

"Babe, that was great and all, but don't ever do that again when I'm standing in front of you. Now go!" I yelled over my thankfully noninjured shoulder.

Not waiting to hear Nikki's response, I ran forward to hold off the remaining guy. He was a big fucker but slow, so I would have to use my speed to make sure I gave Nikki enough time to get to the end of the hallway. He drew his firearm but cursed and tucked it away. Guess his orders were to make sure we were alive. That moment cost him, and I landed a right hook to his temple.

"Fucking bitch," he yelled out, slamming into the wall.

A blaring alarm sounded in the hallway, and I sighed in relief. Nikki had made it to the fire exit door. Scarlet had placed alarms on all the external doors in this portion of Lotería.

Fuck. Time to get captured again.

I stood still, letting his meaty fist slam into my gut, flexing at the last minute to lessen the blow.

It still made me double over, and I tried to move to avoid

the knee aimed at my head, but I was too slow. Everything went black as flashes of Gunner ran across my mind.

Gunner

Dex was right.

I was capable and qualified for this type of situation. So I shoved every emotion in a box and locked that shit up tight. A level head was needed for this because I was throwing all my plans out the fucking window now. But just because I was going off-plan didn't mean I could run into this situation half-cocked. Mario had the upper hand; I was going to need to do whatever I could to even the odds. The shit that happened after would be a future me problem because God knew there would be fucking problems.

Dex silently followed as I stormed off toward the SUV. A motorcycle provided shit coverage in a firefight, and it would be hard to ride with the small arsenal I was bringing. Slamming the door, I slowly let what I was about to do sink in. Dex's rough hand covered mine over the keys in the ignition.

"You sure this is what you want to do? I'm all in, brother,

but I need to know if this is what you want. I'm sure Pres would be willing to…"

I cut him off before he could finish. "That would be a bloodbath, Dex, and Ryan is mine. I'm not fucking throwing away the one thing I want for once. I've given up everything. I'm not giving her up too," I answered.

A proud smile bloomed on his face as he removed his hand. For years we hadn't seen eye to eye on the idea of justice. But now, it all clicked into place. Bloody hands sometimes got the job done better than clean ones.

"I'll paint the walls with anyone who gets between Ryan and me and bring her their heads," I promised.

"You know, for normal chicks, I'd say not the best gift idea. But for Ryan…no better way to that woman's heart than bringing her severed body parts," Dex replied cheekily.

Ringing sounded through the car as I silently pleaded for Scar to pick up. I didn't know anything about the woman, but from the little bit of her work I'd seen, she knew what the fuck she was doing.

"Ryan. What's wrong?" Scar answered, a slight note of panic.

"Not Ryan. But she's in trouble."

The silence on the other end was deafening, but I took it as a good sign that I didn't hear a dial tone.

"What do you need from me? I'll help however I can, but you should know I'm no longer in Tucson," she replied.

I sighed in relief at her words. "I need access to the parts of Lotería biometrically locked, and I need camera feed access so I know where Ryan is in the building." I grimaced, knowing I needed more than that but unsure whether I should ask. Ryan and Scar were friends, but the definition of *friends* in the criminal world was different from the definition to everyone else. I didn't know where Scar's generosity would run out, so I started with the must-haves.

"Psh. You're going to need more than that. I know you're used to working with shit resources and intelligence, which is ironic, but that's not how I work. A message is coming through. You'll find the blueprints to the club and a link to watch the live feeds of all the cameras." The sound of a keyboard clicking could be heard. It was like the woman had twenty fingers with how fast she was typing. "Well, our girl is currently blowing holes in people," Scar announced casually.

My eyes widened as I scrambled to click on the link. It was a highly inappropriate time to get a hard-on, but damn, was she hot when she was bloodthirsty. I pulled at my tactical pants, making more room for my dick. Dex snickered from beside me. I hadn't been as discreet as I'd thought.

"I'll be watching the feeds for when you and Dex arrive…"

The way his head snapped to look at me was comical. Cupping his hands around his mouth, he whispered, "She's a wizard, Harry."

I rolled my eyes at him.

"Damn right, I'm a wizard. Now pay attention, this is important. I'll have to send the system into emergency power mode. It's the only way to override the biometric scanners. All the house lights will cut out, and the emergency lighting will trigger. Be aware that a fucking annoying alarm will also sound, but the chaos will probably help you out. The doors will still require a code to enter, but the scanner will be disabled. I'll change the code to four zeros when you arrive. Got it?" she asked.

"Fuck, you are amazing, Scar. I don't even know how I'll make this up to you, but I'm grateful for your help," I responded, a huge weight lifted off my shoulders since she agreed.

"We'll call this a trade of favors. When I need you in the future, remember this moment." She paused. "Besides… Ryan deserves to be happy and to get out from under that asshole's thumb."

I nodded in agreement, even though Scar couldn't see the movement. At least I didn't think she could. My finger hovered over the end call button when her voice rang out through the SUV once more.

"Oh, and one more thing…you better get her out of there, or I'll hunt you down. Got it…Special Agent McGregor?" she said, her tone deadly before it cut to a dial tone.

Even if she'd stayed on the line, I wouldn't have been able to come up with a response to that. Scar had managed to unravel an FBI-level deep cover record and fabricated ID in less than seventy-two hours. For twenty-four months, I had been Gunner, Skeletons of Society's sergeant at arms. My records showed stretches in county jails, job histories at local Skeletons establishments, and parents who lived in Scottsdale. Fuck, even my fake favorite color was supposed to come up—blue. The color Ryan had said didn't fit me because it didn't. My whole existence was fabricated, besides the reasoning behind my road name. Scout sniper in the Marines for eight years was a damn good reason for the road name Gunner.

"How the fuck did she find that out?" Dex asked as his hand raked through his hair. "None of the guys have suspected who you are, and they've been living with your ass for almost two years."

"Fuck. She had this whole-body scanner, but I thought my cover would be airtight enough not to matter…but I don't think that's what gave me away," I answered, walking through every moment of the meeting. Dex sat quietly, waiting for my brain to try to work out how this all happened.

I huffed. "I knew that dickwad recognized me," I mumbled. "Remember Caleb Callahan?"

Dex's brows wrinkled as he tried to recall the name before it dawned on him. "Holy shit. As in the Irish Mob, Caleb Callahan?" he asked.

"One and the same. He was at Scar's safe house. No clue why. I was hoping he didn't recognize me from my time in New York, but it seems I made an impression all those years ago."

I knew damn well I would have to keep my mouth shut about Scar. The FBI would love to get their hands on her, and when she refused—they would threaten her with a bottomless, dark hole. A new level of shock hit my system when I realized she'd known who I was when she chose to help me.

Snapping out of my shock, I threw the SUV into drive.

"She won't be the only one finding out I'm going off-plan. We gotta get a move on before this gets leaked and I get pulled." I looked over my shoulder at Dex. "If you want out, I get it. Your deal was to help me gather information to take down Mario. You didn't sign up for this other shit," I stated.

The grin on Dex's face was terrifying. "Gunner, I chose the outlaw biker life after we got out, remember? I live for this shit. Besides, me beating someone's ass to the brink of death is what got you into this whole situation to begin with. I've always lived for some vigilante justice," he stated, slamming a mag home, emphasizing his plan to see this through.

"Till Valhalla, brother," I stated, focusing back on the road.

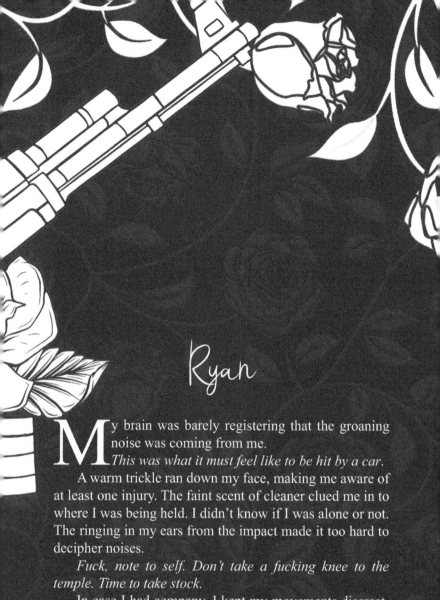

Ryan

My brain was barely registering that the groaning noise was coming from me.

This was what it must feel like to be hit by a car.

A warm trickle ran down my face, making me aware of at least one injury. The faint scent of cleaner clued me in to where I was being held. I didn't know if I was alone or not. The ringing in my ears from the impact made it too hard to decipher noises.

Fuck, note to self. Don't take a fucking knee to the temple. Time to take stock.

In case I had company, I kept my movements discreet. My hands were back behind my back; there was no wiggle room or knife hidden in my bra this time. But the silver lining was that my legs were left free, and they hadn't strung my arms up. They must have turned on the camera after I escaped my restraints. Why else repeat the same mistake? My eyes flew open at the sound of someone entering.

"Por qué mí Muñeca? Why would you anger me like this?" Mario asked.

His typically polished appearance was disheveled. It looked like he'd attempted to pull tufts of hair out at the roots. The top four buttons on his shirt were missing, and blood was splattered on the front. I swallowed a gasp when his eyes met mine—he looked crazed.

I didn't know what Mario would do to me. Would his fucked-up love for me be enough to spare my life? Or maybe it would be the reason he ended it.

"Fuck you, Mario. Anger you? You and Sergio are the ones who decided to go behind my back and plan against me." My voice shook. But not with fear—with pure rage.

It was their fault I was here, strapped to a chair, bleeding. How dare he speak to me as if I brought this upon myself?

A cruel laugh left Mario's lips. "Sergio? You think he was a part of this?" He moved closer, gently running his fingers along my face, smearing my blood. Staring at me like I was a prized possession. "Tell me, Muñeca, haven't you wondered why Sergio isn't answering when you call him?" He narrowed his eyes. "Always a good little pseudo daughter, weren't you?" he asked, his voice laced with venom.

His words gave me pause. I had wondered why Sergio wasn't answering. I assumed he was avoiding me. Sergio sanctioning the hit on the Skeletons after partnering with them was a part of the puzzle that never seemed to fit. My lack of an answer spurred Mario on, his sadistic grin growing.

"He was weak," he shouted, causing me to flinch slightly.

Fuck, he's unraveling.

It made him unpredictable. And I wasn't confident he wouldn't hurt me.

"He wanted to let you go, Muñeca. He said you deserved to be free of Los Muertos…of me." He spat as his fingers found the cut hidden in my hairline, pressing the fresh

314

wound. I hissed but refused to give him anything more.

"We couldn't have that now, could we? But now I see it; he wanted to take you from me." Mario nodded his head vigorously, answering his rhetorical question. He grasped a handful of hair at my crown with his free hand and wrenched my head so I was forced to look at him. He smiled at the discomfort he knew he was causing me. It was then that I noticed his pupils were blown, and he was twitching his nose.

"That's why he hired the Skeletons to begin with, even though I told him—I told him we were losing money not being in the skin game. But he didn't listen!" he roared.

"Where is he, Mario?" I asked, but I knew the answer.

Bloody fingers stroked my face in a caress before squeezing my jaw so tightly my teeth cut into my cheeks.

"He's gone, Muñeca. I'm the kingpin of Los Muertos. And you, my queen. As soon as I remind you of your place." As the words left his mouth, he pressed his lips to mine.

I yanked my head back in disgust. "Fuck you, Mario." I slammed my head into his.

He roared out in pain, blood pouring from his nose. I smiled, my teeth coated in blood.

"Eat a dick, Mario. I'm not your queen. I'm La Brujita, here to reap your soul for El Diablo."

He paced in front of me, looking like a caged animal. Swiping at the blood still dripping from his obviously broken nose. "What, do you think that man wants you?" Mario motioned up and down my body with his hand. "No, Muñeca. He doesn't have the decency to tell you the *truth*. You don't know him at all, and you think he cares for you?" A cruel laugh left his lips. "You're a distraction, a warm *cunt* to stick his dick into while biding his time. But don't worry. He'll be gone soon too."

I saw red at his words. Threatening me did nothing, but I wouldn't let him harm Gunner. I threw my body out of the chair, running at Mario with a battle cry. Our bodies connected, sending us sprawling to the floor. I used Mario's body to break the fall since my arms were still restrained behind my back. Rolling to my side, I tried to get to my feet before Mario could figure out how to pin me down.

Fuck, this was what caring for people got you. Fighting with your hands literally tied behind your back.

It was a good thing Mario's ass was high, and he'd never been in a fight in his life.

"He was telling the truth, Mario. I do yell out his name when he fucks me," I sneered, trying to keep him distracted while I figured out what the hell to do.

"You stupid bitch." He shook his head as he stood. "Which one of his names is it, you yell out?" he asked—a cold smirk on his face.

Before I could comprehend the shit coming out of Mario's mouth, an explosion sounded through the building, sending me careening to the side. My shoulder and hip slammed onto the concrete floor. The lights cut out, kicking on the emergency red lighting, and the door to the interrogation room was thrown open. Hope filled my body. Maybe Nikki got to Gunner, and they were here for me. But that hope was dashed when it was another member of Mario's assholes.

"Boss, there's major trouble. The building is under attack."

Shouts came from the hallway, and a body ran past the open door every few moments. Mario turned his back to me and seemed to be weighing his options as to what to do. Careful not to draw attention to myself, I worked on putting my legs through my shackled arm loop. My hands might still be zip-tied, but having them in front of my body would be an improvement.

But Mario looked over his shoulder before I could finish getting my arms in front. Rage flashed across his face. In two steps, he was at my side, his gun drawn. The tip of the barrel dug into my temple, causing my chest to heave. I wasn't scared of death. I'd always figured my life on this earth would be cut short because of my profession. But I was livid. Livid at the fact that I'd yet to kill Mario, livid that I would die on the floor, restrained, and livid that Mario was about to take my chance to look into a pair of soulful green eyes one more time.

"All you had to do was obey!" he screamed—the strings of his sanity unraveling.

My retort fell away when the sound of my name being called reached my ears. Mario's head snapped to the opening at the same time mine did. The guard poked his head into the hallway, assessing what was happening outside the room.

"That biker guy is coming, boss."

My heart skipped a beat at those words before plummeting into my stomach. My emotions were at war, not knowing if I was elated or terrified that Gunner was here. Mario's crazed eyes met mine, and panic set in at my gut.

"Well, Muñeca, what a perfect punishment for you. Knowing your lover is about to meet his demise while you are trapped in this room."

A guttural yell left my lips, but it was short-lived as Mario brought the butt of his gun down on my head, sending me sprawling back to the floor. Thank Santa Muerte the asshole didn't know how to knock someone out properly.

I scrambled to get back up and reach him before he got to Gunner. But the door shut as I reached it, and I heard Mario attempt to set the lock, but it never engaged. My teeth ripped on the end of the zip tie, pulling it tight enough to cut into the skin of my wrist. Breaking zip ties was a bitch, but the pain didn't register with the adrenaline coursing through me. Thrusting my elbows backward, the momentum and my body broke the plastic constraints.

"Nice job, bitch." A familiar voice sounded from overhead, causing me to scowl in confusion. "Now get your ass to the cargo bay. Your man needs some help, and I would hurry if you want to take care of Mario before the authorities do."

"Scar?" I asked.

"Yup. Your man called in a favor. Now get going," she

answered over the speakers.

I reached for the metal handle.

"Oh, and Ryan…don't be too hard on him when you find out the truth…"

Ryan

I didn't have time to ask what she was talking about. Sprinting down the abandoned hallway, I followed the sounds of men shouting. Their voices were muffled by gunfire. Good thing I knew the club like the back of my hand because it was hard to see through the foggy haze that hung in the air. I crouched at the end of the hallway, wanting to get a feel for everyone's position. In front of me lay one of Mario's men. The bullet hole directly between the eyes brought a smile to my face as I crept forward to inspect the handgun lying by his side.

"Dammit," I mumbled.

One round in the chamber and an empty magazine. My hands searched his still-warm body for more weapons since the ammunition supply was shit.

"Thank Santa Muerte you carried a knife too," I whispered, shoving the blade into my waistband as I poked my head around the crate. A flash-bang or smoke bomb must've been detonated because it was like trying to see through mud. Shouts rang out in Spanish from my left, giving me a good indication of where Mario's men were hunkering down. But it was a hunch. I didn't have time to sit around and contemplate my next move, so I took off toward the shouting. No one was expecting me, making me the perfect hunter. I switched out my gun for the blade, its weight bringing me comfort.

"*Mierda. Este gringo es como un segador*," they shouted.

I quirked an eyebrow at the two Los Muertos members crouched behind a shelving unit. A reaper. It seemed Gunner or whoever was making quite the impression. But they should've been paying more attention because they were about to be killed by an entirely different reaper.

Silently, I shot forward.

The sounds of choking filled the space. Over my victim's shoulder, I watched the next man's eyes widen in surprise and horror as he watched blood leak from his partner's throat.

"Adios, chico," I whispered as I dropped the dying man and lunged forward.

Taking advantage of his state of shock, I drove the blade into his carotid. His hands flew up to his throat, and he stared in horror at his life force coating his hands. His body slumped down. The sounds of him dying were drowned out by more gunshots and shouting. Crouching down, I reached forward and wiped off the blood covering both the blade and my hands.

"Thanks for the use of your shirt. Blood makes for a slippery knife. Hard to stab another asshole if it slips through my hand. Ya know? Oh, and death from a punctured carotid isn't as fast as they show in movies, huh? Tù compadre went into cardiac arrest from lack of blood to the brain, probably since I slit his throat...but you're taking longer. Want to know my guess as to why? I'm guessing because El Diablo wants you to suffer for the shit you've done to those women," I spat at him.

Even in his dying state, the man's eyes widened. I recognized the piece of shit the instant his eyes met mine. He was in the picture back at Scar's, and he deserved every torturous breath he took. I released the magazine from the gun he'd dropped when I stabbed him and checked how many rounds remained—empty. Same with his buddy.

A round pinged off the metal bar of the shelving unit I was crouched behind.

"Cinga tu madre," I swore under my breath.

The problem with staying stealthy is that I couldn't let Gunner and whoever else he brought with him know where I was. I went to move to another location when a yell sounded out in the cargo bay.

"If you don't want my men to stick a knife in that bitch's gut, I suggest you come out right now," Mario shouted.

The hair on the back of my neck stood up as I moved to see where Mario was positioned.

"Please don't take the bait, Gunner," I silently pleaded, hoping he wouldn't give himself up for me. Mario and two lackeys were pinned down behind a crate about fifteen feet in front of me. The crate had chunks blown off, and bodies littered the area—all with an instant-kill shot. The accuracy was impressive.

Indecision racked me as Gunner stepped out into the open, his arms raised in surrender, a handgun loosely held in his hand.

"All right, asshole. I'm here, and my gun is laid down. Call your lapdogs off her," Gunner stated, slowly lowering the gun and kicking it away.

"Your shirt," Mario called.

Gunner lifted it to show there were no more firearms tucked into his waistband. My eyes instantly bounced to the shadows behind Gunner, looking for where he had been staked out. Mario was too stupid and high to notice that the shots that had killed his men weren't from a handgun. Those were done with a rifle, sniper-style. And I was crossing all my fingers that Dex was back there, keeping Mario in his sights.

"What fucking arms dealer doesn't know weapons?" I scoffed.

There was still the problem of not knowing who, if anyone, was with Gunner. Did they have some plan in place that I would fuck up if I moved, or worse, didn't move? Crouching down farther, I mentally mapped out the quickest way to reach my target. I had no fucking clue how this would go down, but I would be damned if I tripped over one of these pieces of shit littering on the ground.

"Walk toward me, and don't think about trying to pull something stupid, or I'll have my Muñeca gutted," Mario called. Gunner's whole body tensed at the threat.

Mario shoved one of his men out from behind their cover, forcing him to go collect Gunner.

"Fuck you, Mario," Gunner spat as he approached.

Mario rammed his fist into his gut before sending another fist sailing into Gunner's jaw. A gasp escaped my lips before I could stop it, and I watched as the sinister grin appeared on Mario's face.

He knew I was no longer in the room he tried to lock me in. He was trying to draw me out. I needed to tell Gunner before he became a human punching bag because he thought I was strapped down with someone holding a blade to me just waiting for Mario's command.

Mario was an idiot. Had he so easily forgotten what I did to exact revenge for my parents? Being in love with Gunner made me deadlier, not weak. Making my decision, I centered myself, letting my mind clear before pulling the trigger. A yell rang out through the warehouse. The man standing behind the crate clutched his stomach and shouted out in pain and fear.

Gunner's head snapped up, registering that the shot hadn't come from the sniper's nest he'd left. I couldn't have shot Mario or the asshole holding Gunner. They were too close for me to make it safely and not hit him. But the message was received the moment I hit my mark. Hope flashed across Gunner's face at the realization that I wasn't being held hostage. But a scowl quickly replaced it. I was sure he was thinking the same thing I was. *How could we figure out a plan when we couldn't communicate with the other players?*

"Muñeca, that was not very nice. Is that what you want to do? Kill your fellow Muertos?" Mario called out as he searched the room.

I let the silence hang in the air, knowing Mario hated when he was left waiting. His agitation made him sloppy. But it also made him more reckless—I didn't have a lot of options.

"Answer me!" he screamed, pulling at his hair. I could see the crazed look in his eyes and how his chest rose and fell with his labored breathing.

"Don't you dare say shit, babe. Get out of here. Now," Gunner called. The next instant, his head snapped to the side as Mario backhanded him. Fresh blood spilled from my damaged lip as I bit down to hold in my reaction.

"What's the problem, Mario? Don't like that your plaything isn't cooperating anymore? She doesn't answer to men with smaller balls than her," Gunner taunted. His arms were being held behind his back. There was no doubt he could break the hold, but he was biding his time. There were too many variables. The most dangerous was Mario. Blood was dripping from a cut above Gunner's eye and he had a cocky smile plastered on his face. He looked deranged—in the sexiest way possible.

I've been around Dex and Nikki far too much. Who got turned on at a time like this?

My libido plummeted the moment Mario sent another first into Gunner's gut. The asshole behind him held him still while two more blows landed. Gunner righted himself before spitting blood all over Mario's face.

"It's like you want to prove my point. You have your cocksucker here holding me while you land some shitty blows. What's the problem, Mario? Afraid to get your ass handed to you in front of people? That narcissistic brain of yours wouldn't be able to handle it, huh? That's why you deal in women. Do you get hard over the power? And you thought Ryan would want you?"

The taunting tone of disbelief was thick in Gunner's voice, causing my grip to tighten around my knife. Mario had never stood for being insulted or belittled. His lackey was fidgeting, probably concerned that Mario's wrath would extend to him. Mario never did care who became collateral damage.

"Do you think she'll want you once she learns the truth, Gunner? Why don't you tell her?" Mario threw back.

Gunner's jaw ticked at his words. Scar's warning came rushing back, and I knew that I would hear something I didn't want to hear—another man lying in my life.

"Muñeca!" Mario called as he stepped away from Gunner and toward where I was hunkered down, arms stretched out wide in a goading fashion. "Did you know he was *using* you? That his attraction to you was never genuine? It was all a ploy to get to me." The look of victory was evident in Mario's eyes. As if, by proving another man didn't want to give me affection, I would come running back to his side, begging to be placed back up on my shelf.

A doll to collect.

The anger that rose inside me at his words was like a shot of adrenaline.

Mario looked over his shoulder at Gunner—gloating. "You thought I wouldn't know that you were asking about me? You and my father were plotting against me, weren't you?" He pulled his knife out and moved back to Gunner. "You were trying to turn my Muñeca against me, but she's mine. Tell her, Gunner. Tell her how you fucked her for information, how you turned her into a whore, like the ones she watches for me," he taunted, digging the edge of the blade into Gunner's throat and drawing a trickle of blood.

"Tell her who you are, Gunner. Tell her how no one will

ever care for her damaged soul."

But Gunner remained silent, his whole body taut with anger. But at what? Being caught in a lie? Mario snapped back around, moving once more toward where I lay in wait.

"You hear that Muñeca? You are damaged." His nostrils flared, and spittle flew from his mouth as he yelled at me. He attempted to thrust the proverbial dagger that were his words into my heart. "No one will ever care for a killer like you. You're destined to be my fucked-up marionette." A cruel laugh left Mario's lips. "You sure as fuck were never going to be loved by a federal agent," he called out.

My heart stopped. Blood running cold. Gunner's eyes found mine through the chaos, as if he could sense my panic. The look of pity was so evident that I didn't need him to speak. My heart didn't want to accept what was written on his face. But all the moments between us came rushing back—the hints he gave me from the start that I was too stupid to recognize.

"Ryan..." Gunner whispered, but his tone told me everything I needed to know.

When you're broken, you think of yourself as having some fucked-up version of invincibility. But Gunner showed me that broken pieces could be shattered. In that second, Gunner finished inflicting the damage that Mario started. I was numb. I couldn't hear or feel anything in the world anymore. I was ready to open up that door in the back of my mind, the one I shoved all of my emotional damage into, and crawl inside.

A humorless laugh fell from my lips.

"My savior was my next jailor," I muttered.

I'd known it wouldn't end well for Gunner and me, but I could never have prepared for this level of shredding of my soul. Dampness met the back of my hand as I swiped at my tears. I was angry at my inability to keep my emotions in check, could feel the bricks go back up around my damaged heart, entombing what little was left.

It had been less painful when I didn't know if Gunner

loved me or not. I could pretend that he did. Pretend that there was something redeemable about me, something worth loving about me.

I wanted Gunner.

I needed Gunner.

And Gunner was gone. Ironically, he was never even real.

That fantasy was destroyed, and the fucked-up part was that none of this changed how I felt about him. It didn't do a damn thing to change that I loved him, and I was about to sacrifice myself to save him. For a moment, I thought I was wrong about my worth.

"See, Muñeca, I'm the only one who will give you affection," Mario called out cockily.

He was right about one thing. I was a killer, and I didn't want or need his affection. My destiny was to have my hands drenched in the blood of guilty men. And Mario would be the next man I sent to El Diablo.

"Don't listen to him, Ryan. I can explain," Gunner pleaded. But I'd already tuned him out. I had to. There was no way I could function if I let him slip through my shield again.

Tilting my head up, I attempted to stop the tears from streaming down my face. It took all my willpower not to let out audible sobs. Now I understood why Nikki never let anyone close; this pain was worse than any physical injury. I forced myself to pull it together. To focus on the task at hand.

I was sure a therapist would tell me this disassociation was not healthy, but this was how I got shit done. And right now would be no different. Shoving my feelings away, I allowed the calm to overtake me. Part of me recognized I would probably never leave this cocoon of numbness—if I even survived.

I looked down at my blood-caked hands, clutching a blade I killed with.

Hands that had run over Gunner's body.

Did he cringe at the thought of the hands of a killer touching him? My eyes shut in shame at that thought. I worked harder at shutting everything out. I hoped he found love and that he would tell her she got to have him because of what I was about to do.

His voice cut through the noise in my mind, pulling my gaze back to him. I was powerless to resist seeking out the person whose comfort I craved, even if he was the one holding the knife that had carved out my heart.

"Babe, it wasn't all a lie. The man who stood before you was me, raw and uncut. You unlocked my cage, Ryan." Gunner's voice cracked with emotion. "I was a chained man living for nothing, and you came and changed that. Your soul isn't damaged, Ryan. You're strong enough to face what others won't, do things others aren't willing to do to save the lost. I see your soul, Ryan. I love you, all of you. Every fucking part," he yelled out.

His voice dripped in anguish, and the look in his eyes gave me pause. I thought he'd given me a look of pity, but maybe that wasn't the emotion his eyes had been showing. Or maybe I was latching on to any sign of hope. As if sensing the crossroads I was facing, Gunner continued on, a sense of urgency in his tone.

"I told you, babe, remember? I told you that I was keeping you. When all the shit hit the fan, when you fought me and questioned everything, I would fight for you. Remember? I told you how you own every piece of me, Ryan…"

It was as if the whole room was waiting on bated breath for my reaction.

"Babe, if we're doing some Cleopatra and Marc Antony shit, let me know, but you're not going anywhere without me." His voice grew louder—desperate. "I know you hear me, Ryan. I know you're trying to pack yourself up and shove that beautiful soul away, but don't shut me out, baby—"

Mario decided he'd had enough of Gunner's pleas and

thrust the blade he was holding into Gunner's thigh, causing Gunner to double over in pain while I cried out in shock.

Mario's crazed eyes searched for me.

"You think you can leave me because someone claims to *see* you? I made you. I made you into the monster you are!" he yelled out.

Another grunt of agony slipped from Gunner as Mario snatched the knife back out. Blood began seeping out of his injury. Fuck Mario for thinking that he could own me like some object, that he felt he could try to make me feel like everyone sought to use me the way he did.

Chaos erupted the moment my body collided with Mario. My hand met soft fabric as my blade slid into Mario's body like a hot knife through butter. Only the hilt was visible, the rest buried in Mario's chest. A shot rang out, and blood spray littered the air. The sound of Gunner's shouting let me know he was unharmed, and I focused on the warm body pinned under me. Mario's face was already turning ashen; his eyes were widened in shock, but the crazed look had yet to leave. His hips bucked under me to unseat me, the drugs in his system prolonging his demise. He deserved to die slowly, and I wished I had the time to make him pay. But him dying, knowing I would never be his, would haunt him for eternity.

"I gave you everything!" Spit hit my face as his yell echoed in the room, loud enough to drown out the commotion.

"You gave me nothing," I screamed back at him. "You kept me caged, dangling affection as a prize. But I never had your affection, Mario, did I? I was your obsession. But you made a grave miscalculation in thinking I was a meek creature. Now I'm going to rip your heart out like a trophy. I wish I'd known that I was letting a devil lead me away that day in the alley." I leaned closer to Mario's face, wanting him to see the hatred for him in my eyes. "I should've made you my second kill that day. Done El Diablo the favor of collecting you early. Say hello to him for me, asshole," I said through clenched teeth.

Blood spilled from his mouth when he opened it to speak, an evil glint in his eye.

"I'll see you there soon, Muñeca," he whispered as I was hit with the familiar feeling of skin being punctured. I looked down to find a knife protruding from my abdomen. A yell sounded from behind me, but my vision started to blur, the last of my adrenaline leaking from my body. Before I could hit the floor, warm arms surrounded me.

"Damn it, Ryan. I was kidding when I asked if you were pulling some Cleopatra shit. You better not die on me."

Suck a dick, Gunner.

"Words, babe. I want your words."

I thought my mouth was opening and closing, and I'd said that aloud.

"I'm pretty positive you're verbally castrating me in that pretty little head of yours. I want to hear it, babe." The panic in his voice had a vise grip on my soul. "Give me something, and I need you to open your eyes. Damn it, Ryan," he rushed out.

I hadn't realized my eyes were closed. I tried to peel my lids back open, but they felt heavy and refused to cooperate. Rough fingertips brushed blood-matted hair away from my face, and the sounds rushing past clued me in that we were moving.

My throat felt cracked and raw while my lips were bruised. The toll of what my body had gone through was catching up, and the world went black.

Ryan

"**M**s. Hernandez, if you touch those IVs one more time, I'll whack you upside the head."

I rolled my eyes at the charge nurse but didn't rip out the plastic tubes like I wanted. She *would* hit me. I'd learned the hard way when I first woke up.

"Yeah, yeah, yeah. I won't touch them…but only if you smuggle me an extra pudding," I demanded, crossing my arms over my chest. Her hands landed on her hips, and she raised an eyebrow. Her salt-and-pepper bun moved back and forth as she shook her head. This must've been the mothering look people talked about.

"Please," I tacked on, adding a sugary sweet smile that wasn't anything like what I felt.

She gave a curt nod before leaving the room, and I was alone—again.

Two days.

That's how long I'd been in this stark room with no clue

what the fuck was going on. No Dex. No Nikki. *No Gunner.*
I swiped at the tears streaming down my face. Every time
I thought of him, those fuckers showed up. It pissed me off
that my body reacted that way. I was angry he'd lied to me,
angry I'd trusted him. And I was angrier that I still missed
him, that when I'd felt his arms around me before the world
went black, I'd bothered to hope he would be here when my
eyes opened.

But he wasn't.

Mario's words came rushing back. *Tell her, Gunner. Tell
her how you fucked her for information.*

My thoughts were so jumbled. How had I not known?
But then again, how would I have known?

"The man cut off a fucking finger for me. What kind of
agent does that?" I yelled out, my hands coming up to tangle
in my hair. But there were also clues from the beginning.
Clues from Gunner himself.

Legally acceptable? You think I'm a cop or something?

A humorless laugh fell from my lips. "Damn, you even
asked me outright, didn't you?"

I turned to my side and fell asleep, hoping my dreams
wouldn't involve a man with piercing green eyes.

A faint knock came from the door. But I didn't bother
acknowledging it. I just stayed curled on my side, staring at
the wall. Like I had been for hours.

Soft footsteps mixed with the beeping of machines, and
I felt the slight dip of the mattress behind me. Nikki nestled
herself against my back and wrapped her arm around me.

I stopped crying hours ago, like my body couldn't keep
up with the quantity of tears needed.

"Babe, we've got shit to talk about. I need you to
snap out of it. You've been like this for two days," Nikki
whispered into my hair. My brows furrowed. Why had I

thought I'd been alone?

In the next moment, Nikki's heat disappeared, and I was suddenly staring at a pair of blue eyes.

"You don't remember me being here because they kicked me out every time you woke up. I passed out the first time they cleaned your wound...so it got me banned from the room. And you've been catatonic the rest of the time." Her fingers brushed away a stray hair on my face.

A sigh left her lips. "Listen, from one broken bitch to another. It's time to heal. And while we've never gotten into it fully, you know I know what I'm talking about when it comes to this shit. You pulled me out of the dark, and now I'm returning the favor. And let me tell you, you were a bitch. So you're lucky I'm much nicer," she said, a playful smile on her lips.

I smirked at her words. She was right. I was a major bitch when I found Nikki. I knew she was a diamond in the rough, and I couldn't let her soul fade away. But I was all jagged edges, so I didn't know any other way to handle her than to drag her ass out. This was a taste of my own medicine.

Nikki stood up and yanked the blanket off my body before standing there with her hands on her hips and determination in her eyes.

"No more of this. I'll pull that shitty card and tell you Gunner would not want this for you. And you are too much of a bad bitch for this."

The mention of his name was a punch to the gut. "Gunner wouldn't fucking care what happens to me," I whispered.

She kneeled back down. "You don't know what you're talking about. That's what I'm trying to say. There's a lot of shit you need to be filled in on, but you have to be willing to listen. Believe me when I tell you, Gunner is one of the good ones. He's been trying to get in, but the suits won't let him. They had to restrain him when he knocked out a guy guarding your door," she whispered. My heart clenched at her words, but I didn't show her a reaction.

Her finger hooked under my chin, bringing my eyes to hers. "He's a man, Ryan. Of course, he's going to fuck up. It's in their DNA. But him not telling you the truth wasn't entirely his call," she stated.

I yanked my face away. I knew there was logic to what she said. I had kept secrets from him too. Hell, Nikki had kept secrets from me. I'd always felt other people's shit was their own. They didn't owe me explanations. But listening would mean opening myself up again, and I was shattered. Who would even want that?

"This is a clean break from me, Nikki. He can walk away. No need to explain to the broken girl."

Nikki forced my eyes to her once more. "Broken things can heal. And we need you, Ryan. Lotería needs you, and all the women you have saved? They need you. I need you. And that man…that man needs you. Believe me. I punched the fucker for you, broke my damn finger doing it." She lifted a bandaged hand I'd somehow missed. "Listen to him, okay? He's hopelessly in love with your crazy ass."

I gave a curt nod, unsure that I could form words.

Her lips brushed the top of my head. "I'll send him in," she whispered before leaving the room. I heard the door open, and I didn't have to look to know it was him—his presence like a warm blanket.

"Ryan…" he called out, his voice laced with emotion.

I wanted so badly to not look at him, to ignore him. But I couldn't. When I turned, I faced the man who had haunted my every moment for forty-eight hours. I couldn't help the way the corners of my mouth pulled up at the sight of his black eye.

"Nikki really did hit you," I whispered.

A sheepish grin appeared on his face, and Gunner was at my side the next instant. His hands cupped my face, pressing our foreheads together. His scent enveloped me, drawing out more tears, and I felt his thumbs swipe them away.

"I tried so fucking hard to stay away from you, but you

were made for me. The other half of my soul," he whispered into my hair. "And I swear on my life, as soon as I knew that, I wanted to tell you, Ryan. I couldn't figure out how without risking you."

A sob caught in my throat.

"Sweetheart," he said as I pulled my face from his hands, shoving my finger in his chest.

"No, I want answers, Gunner. Fuck, I don't even know your name," I yelled. It hurt. It hurt so fucking bad when I looked at his face. The man I loved had never been never mine.

"Greyson McGregor. But I really did earn Gunner. That name wasn't a lie," he answered.

A humorless laugh left my lips—his tattoo, another clue.

McGregor. The name of someone I once knew. From an old life.

I shut my eyes, trying to block out the pain—the loss. The love I still had for him. The bed dipped, and muscled arms surrounded me. If I were stronger, I would push him away—tell him to go fuck himself. But I wasn't. So I curled into him. Burying my face in his chest, pretending I could stay there forever.

"Baby, you can stay here forever. I'm not going anywhere. You're mine, you hear me? I told you that. Remember, I told you I was keeping you," he whispered, his calloused hand smoothing my hair as I sobbed into his shirt.

"You can't stay when you were never really here," I cried.

"It was always real with you, Ryan. I promise I'm here. I promise I love you, and I'm staying with you forever," he pleaded. "Will you let me stay, Ryan? Will you let me love you, Brujita?"

Santa Muerte, I wanted to say no. I couldn't be hurt if I didn't let him in, but he was already there. He'd already carved out my heart and held it in his hands.

My lips clamped shut, but I nodded my head because

I loved him, regardless of all the shit that had happened. I loved him.

"Words, Ryan. I need your words," he whispered, his voice thick with vulnerability. His finger gently raised my chin so our eyes met.

"Yes, Gunner. I'll let you love me because I can't help but fucking love you too," I whispered against his lips.

Epilogue

GUNNER

A week later
I hated that we had to be here, but it was a necessary evil if we wanted to move forward. My gaze drifted over to Ryan, who was lounged in her chair, looking entirely at ease—powerful. Fuckable.

I adjusted the crotch of my pants, catching her eye. A smirk spread across her face as she winked at me.

Tease.

But our attention was drawn to the door as someone finally walked in to meet with us. Fucking government time worked slower.

"Agent McGregor." I received a curt nod before his focus drifted to Ryan. "Ms. Hernandez, I'm disappointed you're not in cuffs considering who you are and your record," Stewart said, leering.

My chair crashed behind me as I stood up, shoving my finger in Stewart's face. "Don't you fucking think about it, Stewart, and keep your eyes off my girl. Read the fucking orders again. This assignment was highly classified, and a green fucking light was given to me," I seethed. "*Agent McGregor is free to take any actions necessary to obtain or dispose of Mario Jimenez,*" I recited back from memory, watching as Agent Stewart's jaw ticked. The asshole and I had never gotten along. He was pissed his cock sucking hadn't gotten him farther up the ladder at the FBI.

"Babe." Ryan's sensual voice cut through the haze of anger as her fingers curled around my bicep. I was supposed to keep my cool during this meeting.

"Yeah, *babe*, listen to your bitch and settle down," Stewart sneered, a cocky grin slapped on his face.

"If it's small, just say that, Stewart," Ryan responded, crossing a tanned leg over her knee. The movement drew his attention. And I balled my fists to avoid tearing his eyes out of his head.

"If you read my record, you know what I do, Stewart. I break bitch-ass men like you in minutes." She inspected her nails, utterly unfazed by Stewart trying to intimidate her. Her eyes finally met his. "So before you try me, really think about if you want to play this game," she said coolly.

Stewart's face turned beet red, looking like he was ready to have a conniption. But the door to the interrogation room opened, and steely gray eyes met mine.

Head of the snake had arrived.

"Agent Stewart, please leave. Go do something you were actually asked to do." The new man called out, not bothering to look at Stewart as he slinked out.

"It seems we are at a crossroads here," he stated as he sat in the chair across from us. "Ms. Hernandez, I trust that Agent McGregor has filled you in on the nature of his assignment," he said, barely masking his condescending tone. He didn't feel she was worth his time.

The corner of her mouth tipped up. "Oh, Gunner

filled me all right," she replied. Her innuendo caused the newcomer to clear his throat and me to smirk.

She wasn't wrong. After we left the hospital, I filled her. Again and again. And then she verbally tore me a new one, demanding I tell her everything.

Which I did.

I told her how Dex and I were childhood friends and served two tours together—scout snipers. Dex was my brother through spilled blood. My spotter. But when we got out, life took us in two different directions. He didn't like all the red tape, said it slowed down justice. So he joined the Skeletons of Society MC. Asked me to join with him. But I was naive and thought I could somehow change the system, so I went the route of the FBI, and I became a rising star. Doing long stints undercover.

Ryan's voice pulled me back to the present.

"Twenty-four months ago, Dex used his one phone call on Gunner. Excuse me, Agent McGregor." She glared at me. I would be groveling for the rest of my life. A punishment I would happily accept as long as I got to grovel between her thighs. "He'd beaten a man within an inch of his life for trafficking his little sister. And he called Gunner because you assholes wanted to throw him in jail for it," she seethed.

"Ms. Hernandez, citizens can't go around taking justice into their own hands. And it wasn't the FBI who wanted to send him to jail," he said, speaking to her as if she were dense.

She quirked an eyebrow but didn't comment, continuing with the rundown of what I'd told her. "Gunner pulled strings for his brother, getting him a deal. No jail time *if* the Skeletons agreed to take in Gunner as an undercover agent. The only people who knew about it were Dex and Pres. His assignment was to gather enough evidence to prove Mario Jimenez was involved in the skin trade. Gunner got the green light to use any means necessary. Disposal was sanctioned if there was no alternative. Have I gotten it correct so far?" she asked.

His eyes cut to mine. He hadn't expected me to have shared everything with her. It was against protocol, and up until recently, I was the poster boy for protocol. He thought he was coming in here to nail Ryan to the wall with my help.

I draped my arm across the back of Ryan's chair, twisting a lock of her hair around my finger. "Is there a problem, sir?" I asked, unable to keep the smartass tone out of my voice.

Now that Mario and Sergio weren't around, the FBI wanted someone to parade around as the bad guy—or girl— for their media tour. The assholes were always looking for the pat on the back and the funding. But none of them looked out for the women who were trafficked.

Ryan had done more for the women than the FBI ever did. Or ever would.

"Yes…that seems to be correct so far," he answered tentatively.

I smirked, knowing the tables had turned on him, and he was trying to think on his feet of what move to make next. But Ryan didn't give him a chance.

"See, here's the problem, Ken. Can I call you Ken?" she asked.

His eyes widened at the use of his name. He hadn't introduced himself on purpose.

"It seems the plan was to convict Mario, or whoever, really. Because I'm guessing that file you're clutching has my name listed as the convicted trafficker. Because it was never about the women or the trafficker, was it? It was about keeping the heat off the Circle, huh? Mario was going to be the scapegoat," she stated.

The color drained from his face.

My hand wrapped around the phone in my pocket, pulling it out and sliding it across the table so he could view what was on the screen. The moment his eyes locked on the contents, he turned as white as a ghost.

"Ken, you're going to hand the file to my beautiful girl here, and after this meeting, you're going to delete all traces of it. And we will know if you don't." His eyes popped up to mine, fear clearly visible. "Ryan is free and clear of any wrongdoing regarding Mario Jimenez's death or anything with Los Muertos. You're going to make it so she's a saint on paper," I finished.

"Where did you get this?" he asked, clutching the phone.

Ryan's fingers laced through mine, giving my hand a gentle squeeze.

"Unlike you, I don't have shit resources and intelligence," she answered. "Oh, and Ken, Scar said to stop interfering. The Circle will be handled, and you should keep your grimy fingers out of it." Ryan took the file from his shaking hand.

"Or I'll personally chop them off," I added, pulling out my gun and badge and slamming them on the table.

"Here's my formal resignation. I've decided to go into the club business," I said, a smirk plastered on my face. Ryan's eyes locked on to mine, a sly smile on hers.

"Welcome to the toxic paradise."

AUTHORS NOTE

Okay, first of all. Thank you from the bottom of my heart for taking a chance on my debut book. Just writing that sentence feels surreal. It would mean THE WORLD to me if you left a review. It helps us authors tremendously. Like, seriously, so helpful.

Second, I know. I hit you with a bunch of shit there at the end. *Gunner was an FBI agent?* Who is The Circle? Who are the three assholes with Scar? Nikki is married to a Russian Mobster? Will Dex get laid with a luchador mask?* And then I gave you an epilogue that happens just two weeks later. Here's the thing…I am totally not sorry about it. These characters are driving the boat in this whole story. And Ryan and Gunner decided they were done for now, but we will see them again—probably soon.

I need to give the biggest shout-out to my Alpha/Beta readers, Ashleigh, Jenni, and Jordie. You guys were troopers and saw the diamond in the rough before Beth got her hands on it and fixed *thousands* of commas.

Thank you to all the author friends who helped me! But especially to Serenity Fox. You legitimately were my first author friend and now closest. It was a match made in heaven from the start, and I can't wait to frolic at the Renaissance Faire.

And thank you to all the Discord girls. Sincerely the best bunch of people ever! All of you!

After this, there's a teaser for the next book. I think you are going to love Scar. Want to see a list of some of my favorite hidden hints?
http://subscribepage.io/bN1vzk

OKAY, THE NEXT PAGE IS THE TEASER. PROMISE!

But here is where you can find me!
And, again, if you would be so kind as to leave me a
review. It would mean the world to me! The former
overachieving child in me lives to know how I did.
Xoxo
Marie

@m.maravillabooks on Instagram
https://marie-maravilla.square.site for my website

P.S. If you sign up for my newsletter, which I will
warn you is chaotic, you will get spicy goodies.
AND I won't blow up your inbox—mainly because
I don't have the time management skills to send
you more than like two emails a month. Haha.

SYNDICATE OF SINS

The problem with caging a predator, someday, they may get out...

Scarletta

Bastard, daughter of a traitor.
To the Italian Don of New York, I'm nothing more than a tool to be wielded. My obedience was the price I had to pay for the sins of my father. But Dominick Romano should have worked on gaining my loyalty because the chains he shackled me with have been undone.

The Four Families have always run New York.
Italian Mafia, Irish Mob, Russian Bratva, and the Jirocho Yakuza Clan. An alliance cloaked in proclamations of peace while they hold knives to one another's backs. But a new player has emerged, The Syndicate. Three men born of the same blood as those whose kingdoms they've come to conquer.

They think they can use me the same way my uncle did, but they're in for a rude awakening when they realize I'm not a damsel in distress. There's been a blade in my hand this whole time, and I've been waiting to land the blow that starts the bloodbath.

I will not bow at their feet.
But soon, all of New York, and those who think they can rule it, will kneel at mine.

These three included...

Made in the USA
Monee, IL
08 October 2023

44195553R00197

SO THE STREETS TAINT ANOTHER SOUL...

Ryan

TO SURVIVE IN THE LOS MUERTOS CARTEL, YOU HAVE TO STAY USEFUL,
ESPECIALLY WHEN YOU'RE A WOMAN. SO I MADE SURE I COULDN'T BE REPLACED.
NOW MY NAME IS WHISPERED ABOUT IN THE SHADOWS—LA BRUJITA DE LOS MUERTOS.
TOO BAD I FORGOT THAT LIES AND DECEIT ARE THE LIFEBLOOD OF THIS TOXIC PARADISE.
I SHOULD HAVE SEEN THE BETRAYAL COMING.

MY HANDS WERE ALWAYS DESTINED TO BE DRENCHED IN THE BLOOD OF GUILTY MEN.

Gunner

SOMETIMES IT TAKES SOMEONE WILLING TO WALK IN THE DARK TO ALLOW
OTHERS TO LIVE IN THE LIGHT. SHE IS A BEAUTIFUL SAVAGE.
ALL THE THINGS I AM NOT SUPPOSED TO HAVE AND MAYBE NEVER WILL.

MEETING HER CHANGED ALL OF MY PLANS. ALTERED THE VERY FABRIC OF MY FUTURE.

ISBN 9798817225709

90000

9 798817 225709